Diane Nielsen was born and raised in the Nebraska panhandle. She has been entertaining family and others with her creative stories since the age of nine.

Besides her passion for writing, Diane loves spending time with her two sons, her family, rock hunting and the Nebraska Cornhuskers.

"Dark Secrets" is Diane's third published book in The Guardian Series. The author plans for five books total in The Guardian Series. She has already begun on Book #4, yet untitled.

Author's Credits:

Book #1 in The Guardian Series "Wish Me Dead"

Book #2 in The Guardian Series "Dark Whispers"

And Now: Book #3 in The Guardian Series "Dark Secrets"

Dark Secrets

★ Book Three in The Guardian Series ★

DIANE NIELSEN

Order this book online at www.trafford.com
or email orders@trafford.com

Most Trafford titles are also available at major online book retailers.

Printed in the United States of America.

ISBN: 978-1-4907-3566-5 (sc)
ISBN: 978-1-4907-3567-2 (e)

Trafford rev. 05/13/2014

 www.trafford.com

North America & international
toll-free: 1 888 232 4444 (USA & Canada)
fax: 812 355 4082

This book is dedicated to Dylan, Kendal, Jeannicca, Jaxon and Angel. Never forget I love you!

And to my good friends Chuck Wood and Julie Petty. Your friendships are appreciated more than you can imagine!

nk black skies were being ripped apart by bolts of lightning that lit up the heavens, turning the under bellies of the heavy rain clouds into billows of light. Daylight was no brighter than the electric blue that sizzled and snapped, as if the Gods were fighting a mighty battle, blades striking and war cries bellowing.

Saul, an Immortal Guardian of mankind, walked unseen through the streets that should have been deserted. But instead there were hordes of humanity grouped together, huddling in angry masses.

It was hot and the rain gave no relief. Instead it made the air heavy and hard to breathe. The summer heat of late had been almost unbearable to the humans, making their skin itch, as if it were too tight for their bodies. Tempers were short and ugly as everyone tried to cope and failed.

Saul often walked among those he guided, helping them to fulfill the destinies that had been written for them at birth. But tonight something was different. For some time now he'd had an uneasy feeling, an itch between his shoulder blades, that warned of danger and evil. As he walked the pavement, he sensed that evil had been this way not that long ago, leaving in its wake death and despair in abundance.

The Dark, as it was known among the Immortals, walked among the humans much the same as the Guardians did. Its purpose, however, was to find a mind, body and a will that it could control and turn from the path chosen for it.

Saul and the other Immortals did not go looking for the Dark, but did battle for the souls it had picked when their paths crossed. Sometimes the Guardians won, leading the way back to the destiny as written and a good life. But sometimes the Dark won. When it did, lives were taken and ruined, never to be redeemed.

Most times the Dark caused only mischief and could be sent back to the shadows from whence it came. But once in a great while, powerful bringers of the Dark grabbed hold of a soul and the damage was immense. Proof being the serial killers rotting in jail, or leaders of men and nations that history had named evil incarnate.

Saul could not ignore the feelings building inside him, as they warned and urged him to take action. He wondered why the Guardian of the soul that the Dark had chosen had not defeated it or, at the very least, sent out an alarm of danger coming.

Saul's hunt for a glimmer of the identity of the Dark drew him to stand below a window on the third floor of an apartment building, its light glowing weakly through the rain and heat. He stood below and looked up.

A man, wearing nothing but a pair of boxer shorts, stood on a stingy balcony, leaning his arms on the railing. He was in shadow, as the light was to his back. Saul noticed that the rain didn't bother him in the least as it pelted his body and ran in streams from his long, black hair. The flashes of light from the sky gave Saul a glimpse of a man of above average height with muscles tight from use. His face, however, remained in shadow.

Saul did not feel the Dark in this man, but rather great strength and a will of iron. Saul found goodness within the soul of this man and decided, on the spot, that this would be the human he would guide and use to find and defeat the Dark.

As Saul watched, the man straightened and slowly moved back, standing just inside the apartment, away from the window. The light went out. But Saul knew the human was still looking out, trying to see why he had the feeling of being watched. This human had good instincts and Saul would use everything and anyone he could to bring about order as it was meant to be.

Saul began to fade, satisfied for now having found his weapon to begin the battle. He knew, as he shimmered away, that the Dark was not going to be easily defeated this time. He would pit his mighty strength against the Dark and, hopefully, be victorious. Immortal and human would stand shoulder to shoulder to fight this battle. But only one side would come out alive. Which one remained to be seen!

Chapter 1

Jaxon Riley stood on the balcony of his rented apartment, letting the rain wash over his hot skin. He watched the forks of light fry the night sky and waited for the people on the street below him to run for cover. But no one moved inside. Instead they moved further into the street, clogging the avenue. Even being on the third floor, he could hear the angry, confused mutterings of the crowd below.

From what he could gather, two of the neighborhood boys, usually best of friends, had been hanging with a stranger for the last couple of weeks and now one of them was dead. No one seemed to know who the stranger was, only that he hooked up with the boys somewhere out of the neighborhood. Both mothers were a mess, saying how it was the stranger's fault. That since he'd shown up, the boys had been acting odd and now one was gone. Gone for good!

The police had found the boy cut to ribbons, his buddy standing over him. It was unclear if one had done in the other, but it didn't seem that way to Jaxon. No weapon was found. The boy left alive was in a state of shock, in the hospital, and under police protection, of course.

Jaxon had connections with the neighborhood police, having spent his childhood hanging out at the police station. When he graduated from high school he passed up college to join the Marines, eventually being chosen and trained for Special Forces. And he was good. In fact he had been one of the best. He was cold and deadly when it came to missions, never failing, never flinching or balking at his assignments. His black Irish ancestry had earned him the nickname "The Laird", and his unit was "The Clan". When a mission with top secret value came across the desk of whoever was in charge, the choice was always, "Bring in The Laird! Get The Clan on it, now!"

He led his unit in and brought them out, never losing one, never leaving anyone behind. And they had been in some real hell holes. Odds were always against them, but his men trusted him to keep them alive and he had. They protected his back and gave him their loyalty. They stayed close at home, but were even closer on a mission.

The Clan never talked about what they did, except to each other. They never fell apart under pressure, and there were no weak links amongst them. They were the envy of the Special Forces. To be chosen as a member was an honor not taken lightly.

Jaxon spent thirteen years in the unit and would have still been there now if he hadn't gotten injured himself, saving one of his men on their last mission.

They had been sent into the Middle East to extract a diplomat who had been grabbed by the other side and was being used as a bargaining chip to release some of their own who had been captured in a raid. The exchange was unacceptable, so The Clan had gone in and gotten him out.

Jaxon had been bringing up the rear, covering his men, when he had been shot by a pimply faced kid. Seconds before the kid would have shot one of his guys in the back, Jaxon had jumped in the middle and took the bullet instead. Rather than the bullet bringing him down, the injury had just pissed him off. He had eliminated the threat with no qualms and no regrets, ending the young man's life, leaving him in an ever-widening pool of his own blood.

By the time his team had gotten back to safety, Jaxon had lost a lot of blood and had spent a couple of weeks in a military hospital recuperating. The day he was to be released, some big wigs, with enough brass on their chests to choke a horse, came in and told him he was to be retired with full pension. They had given him a medal, shook his hand, and walked out, leaving Jaxon at loose ends as to what to do next.

He really was not upset at being retired. He had seen and done things in his time that had left him hollow-eyed and cold as ice. His feelings had been tramped down until he was happiest when he was alone. If he did not get close to anyone, no one could use them to get to him, to hurt him. People were unnecessary distractions.

When he left the service he had gone home. Back to the only place he had ever called home, Denver, Colorado. He had no family left to welcome him, no friends from school left that he had stayed in touch with. No one.

So he had arrived at DIA, picked up a local paper and found a cheap, furnished apartment to live in, and began trying to decide what to do with the rest of his life.

Shortly after word had gotten around the neighborhood that he was back in town to stay, he'd gotten a visit from the Chief of Police, Donny Mack, one of the officers Jaxon had hung out with when he was a kid before he went into the service.

Donny had invited Jaxon out for lunch. They went to a neighborhood grill and ordered up cheeseburgers and a beer each. After they had downed a couple of beers the Chief had broached the possibility of Jaxon joining the SWAT team.

"I am pretty certain the team could use your talents Jaxon. You certainly would be able to enhance the unit."

"I'll think about it." Jaxon had told him. And he had. But he had a feeling in his gut that he was meant for something else.

Jaxon had his pension and really didn't need to work if he didn't want to. But he just couldn't see himself just sitting around doing nothing. He was already getting restless. So far he had not been able to get a grip on the feelings causing his restlessness. The clues, it seemed, were just out of his reach. But tonight would change all that.

Jaxon knew that the neighborhood killing had something to do with his future. He was going to be called into action over this. He just didn't know who would do the calling. He knew the Police would investigate, but he had a feeling that he would be more successful than they would.

Jaxon was leaning on his balcony, or at least what the manager had said was a balcony, trying to hear what was being said on the street. The rain did little to interfere with his focus, and did nothing to relieve the heat that had blanketed the city for the last two weeks. He'd been in hotter spots than this many times so the heat was a minor irritation that bothered him very little. He just let the sweat run down his body and kept on going.

Tonight he had come out to stand in the rain and listen, but that was not all he found outside. He felt eyes on him. Eyes that looked only at him. His instincts had been honed to razor sharp perfection in Special Forces, saving his life many times. He listened when they spoke, and they were screaming right now, telling him that something was not right tonight.

Jaxon remained where he was, leaning on the rail with what seemed like nonchalance, just enjoying the rain. But in fact his eyes, which were in shadow, were scanning the crowd and the area, looking for anything out of the ordinary. He kept his eyes moving but he could see nothing that would set up an alarm. After a few minutes he pushed himself upright and faded back into his apartment, reaching over and shutting off the light. He stood in the shadows, watching for that tell-tale movement that would show him where his enemy was hiding.

As he watched, he saw a slight shifting in the night air. *'That couldn't be,'* he thought. *'Things like that just don't happen. Maybe it was the heat rising up in the air.'* But Jaxon knew that wasn't it. Something had been there, watching him. *'Yeah,'* he thought, *'something, not someone.'*

The feeling of being watched was gone, but the feeling that he was needed was not. It was growing stronger by the second. Jaxon cocked his head to one side and listened. He could almost swear he could hear a voice speaking to him, but the words were just out of his reach.

Shaking his head, he stripped off his wet boxers, went to his bed and lay down on top of the covers. He didn't towel off, preferring to let the rain on his skin dry and cool him as it did. He folded his arms behind his head and willed his eyes closed. Tomorrow was a good time to start nosing around. Tonight he wanted to get some sleep.

One last thought swirled through his brain as he slowed his breathing and began to go under. It seemed death had followed him home, but this time he had not caused it. This time. This time he would be the hunter.

The hunter of what was hiding in the dark.

Chapter 2

The sounds of the city had Jaxon jerking from sleep. The results of having been trained to sleep light and come awake ready to defend his Unit and his life.

By the time the sun was starting to turn the eastern sky purple, Jaxon had given up trying to get some good sleep and swung his long, muscular legs over the side of the bed. He felt a dull ache behind his tired eyes. The grit of the futile night that had gathered in the corners of his bloodshot eyes, felt like shards of glass as he rubbed his fingers across them, urging them to open.

With a groan, Jaxon hoisted his 6 foot 5 inch frame off the mattress and stretched his arms over his head, bending and twisting until he was satisfied that the kinks of his restless night had been worked out. He walked naked across the bedroom, stopping to grab a light tank top with baggy arm holes, boxers and a pair of basketball shorts from the dresser, before heading into the bathroom to shower for the day.

'Not that a shower would do any good,' he thought. The heat would have him dripping by noon. But despite that,

Jaxon had an appreciation for being clean, having spent so much time in places where a clean body was the least of his worries and a hot shower was a luxury.

Even though the day was to be in the high 90's, Jaxon turned the water to hot and stepped in to let it beat down on his neck and shoulders. He braced his hands on the shower wall and bowed his head, thoroughly enjoying the water as it sluiced down his body. He happily let it finish the job of loosening his muscles and erasing the ache in his head.

The water had begun to cool before he lathered his long, black hair and scrubbed his body clean with a bar of soft soap, guaranteed to make his skin as soft as a babies butt. Jaxon thought it smelled a little girlie, but he didn't care. It did the job and, though he would never admit it to anyone, his skin did feel softer, not dry and cracked from the heat. He rinsed off with the lukewarm water and stepped out, grabbing a big, new, fluffy towel which he barely swiped over his skin, as usual, preferring to air dry.

Jaxon stood in front of the mirror, dried his hair and hung the towel on a bar to be reused tomorrow. Why get a new towel every day, after all he was clean when he dried off, right?

Jaxon combed his black hair back from his face and, not waiting for it to fully dry, gathered it into a thick, glossy ponytail slightly above the nape of his neck. Looking into the mirror, he did not notice how the style threw his cheekbones into prominence, or accentuated his mouth, and drew attention to his eyes that were so dark they appeared black with a fringe of thick, long lashes shading them. The reflection looking back at him was still and hard, showing no emotion, and appeared cold to those who did not know him.

His men had looked past the normal facial expressions to his eyes that told all. When he was relaxing with them, they crinkled at the corners and held a twinkle in their dark depths. But when he was angry, serious, or on a mission, they were black and dead as snake eyes. Lifeless eyes that gave a personal invitation to the pits of hell and then showed his enemies the way.

Jaxon gave one swipe of his hand over his cheeks and chin, deciding that the whiskers could wait one more day before he scraped them off. He did not notice, and would not have cared, that the dark stubble added the finishing touch to his obvious unapproachable air.

He pulled on his clothes, not bothering to look at his body before he did. He had wide shoulders, a lean waist, and arms and legs that had rock hard muscles rippling under tan skin. He had only to look in the general direction of a woman and she fell under his spell. His for the taking. If he wanted. But he had no desire to have a permanent relationship, choosing instead to steer clear of the women who had the look of husband hunters on their faces.

Sitting on the edge of the bed, he pulled on socks and running shoes before going to the kitchen to grab an energy drink from the fridge. He tipped the bottle and half of the contents slid down his throat before he recapped it. Carrying it with two fingers, he went to the door and walked outside. He thought he might spend the day walking around the neighborhood, listening to the gossip, and maybe going for a run. There was a park with a trail nearby where he could run laps, before the day started to blister with heat.

As Jaxon made his way across the street, he noticed that there were already clumps of people sitting on doorsteps and hanging on the corners. But no one approached him, called out to him, or bothered him. Not even the punks leaning against buildings that liked to harass pedestrians, or the drug dealers that stood in the shadows just inside a doorway. He looked tough. He looked confident. And, let's face it, he looked the way every want-to-be macho guy wanted to look-like he could open a can of whoop-ass without breaking a sweat. Jaxon did not work at portraying this image. It was just the way he was.

He made his way to the park and stashed his drink up high in a tree before taking off at a lope, racking up five miles before he stopped for a breather. Sweat ran from his body, not just from the exercise, but from the heat that was already in the high eighties. And it was just barely ten a.m. in the morning!

Jaxon made his way back to the tree where he had left his drink, only to find it was not there. He scanned the area but had no luck in finding it.

"It's not there," came a frail sounding voice from behind him.

He turned and saw a little, old lady sitting on a bench in the shade. Her face was a map of wrinkles and lines that spoke of a life well lived. She held onto a cane between her knees and gestured with it to the tree as she spoke.

"Some snot-nosed kids came by and saw it. Probably thought it was booze. So they crawled up, got it down, and took off running with it. Down that way," she said, again pointing with her cane to the left.

"I'm Carry," she said in a no nonsense voice. "I live in the neighborhood just over there," she stated, nodding her head across the street. "Who are you? I don't remember seeing you here before. You aren't one of those no-good crack dealers are you?" she asked in a demanding voice of disapproval.

Jaxon made his way to the bench and took a seat beside her, leaning his elbows on his knees as he looked at her. "My name is Jaxon," he said, "and no ma'am, I am not a crack dealer. I just moved into an apartment over there about two weeks ago," he said, gesturing to the apartment building he now called home. He held out a hand and watched as Carry's still bright blue eyes sized him up before she took his hand and shook it with surprising strength.

"You that Marine that just came in?" she asked.

"Yes ma'am" he said slightly smiling, as he found himself liking the old girl.

Despite her age, her eyes were shrewd and showed intelligence. Jaxon figured that not much happened around here that she didn't know about. And the way she waved her cane around, he also figured that more than one head or butt had felt her displeasure.

"You got a job?" she asked, not mincing words when she wanted information.

"Not yet," he answered, a twinkle beginning to show in his dark eyes.

"You planning on living off people like me that pays for welfare?" she demanded, a hard glint in her eyes and sharp tone in her voice.

"No," he replied leaning back against the bench. "I have a pension that gets me by just fine."

She nodded her head and thumped her cane once in approval. She swiveled on the bench to face Jaxon more fully. She gave him the once over, looking him up and down, before a knowing smile made her face appear even more wrinkled than it was.

"You're going to have all the young ladies in a twitter, you are." she said. "Good for you. Shake up some of these 'I'm all that and a bag of chips' peacocks around here."

Jaxon smiled and then let out with a heart-felt laugh at the straight-forward talking woman at his side. There was just something about her he sincerely liked.

"You ought to do that more often," she said, gesturing at his head with the cane. "With that smile of yours, if I was fifty years younger, I'd chase you around till I caught you and made you my honey."

"Well, Carry," Jaxon said, rising to his substantial height, "how would you like to accompany me to the drugstore on the next block and have a cool drink with me?"

Carry scooted her skinny behind to the edge of the bench and, with a helping hand from Jaxon, stood up and grabbed on to his arm like a young lady going on a date.

"Let's go," she said, "but not too fast."

Jaxon followed orders and kept the pace slow as they made their way to get that drink. He liked her, he decided, as he looked down at her bent frame just reaching past his waist. He was going to enjoy his afternoon with her and when it was over he had no doubt that he was going to have all the information he needed, plus some, to get started on finding out the who and why of the recent murder.

It wouldn't be the first time he had hunted a murderer, he thought to himself. He was no stranger to their kind. But it would be the first time that this one had him on his trail. And he knew that HIS face was going to be the last thing this one ever saw.

Chapter 3

By the time Jaxon escorted Carry home it was almost dark. The worst of the heat had passed and people were beginning to come out to sit on their stoops, trying to catch a faint breeze to relieve the blanket of heat that smothered the city.

He left her standing by her door. "I promise to stop by in a few days to visit and catch up." he assured her as he stepped back down off her stoop.

Carry had held her head up high as she entered her house. She knew that her neighbors were watching. She was going to be the envy of her friends for months to come. Good looking young man bringing her home. "Yes sir, I'm going to make the tongues wag." she said with a smile of satisfaction on her face.

For Jaxon's part, he had enjoyed the afternoon he had spent with his newest friend and informant. He sprang for lunch and hadn't had to say much, as she'd talked non-stop for hours. A few well-placed questions had directed the conversation where he wanted it to go, and he was mulling things over in his mind as he walked back to his apartment.

Jaxon paid little attention to the heads that turned or the whispers behind hands that his presence caused as he passed by his neighbors. His senses detected no danger as he wandered, so he walked with ease up and down the blocks until the harsh sunlight had completely faded and stars came out to shed cool light on the city.

He had a lot of pent-up energy wanting to be released, so he took one more run through the park before heading home. The thought of being stopped and mugged as he made his laps never entered his mind as a possibility. Any thug who was stupid enough to take him on would find out what a big mistake they had made within seconds of the encounter. They would be picking themselves up off their asses before they knew what had hit them.

Jaxon ran until he felt himself settle, and then he ran some more, making sure he was tired enough to get a good nights sleep.

He made his way back to his building and climbed the three flights of stairs, not making a sound as he took each step. Old habits were hard to break. Pulling his keys out of his pocket, Jaxon opened the door that he had oiled the first day he had moved in. Walking in, he closed it and locked it behind him. He went to the balcony doors and opened them to let in the slightly cooler night, trying to freshen up the air that had been trapped inside all day.

Feeling satisfied that all was as it should be, Jaxon emptied his pockets on to the dresser, stripped off his clothes, and grabbed a clean pair of boxers. He made his way into the bathroom for a cool shower to wash away the heat of the day and clear his mind.

Turning the water on cool, he stepped in, letting out a sigh of contentment as the cool spray refreshed him. It felt so good, he even thought about plugging the tub and sitting in a cool bath for awhile. But, with one quick look at the size of the tub, he knew his knees would either be under his chin or his legs would be stretched up the wall. Neither option being his idea of comfortable. So he just stayed standing under the shower's spray. Heaven, he decided, was taking a bath whenever you wanted.

Rousing himself from a half doze, Jaxon finished washing and, once again, only swiped at the water on his skin with the towel, before donning his boxers and going out into the living room.

He had only taken one step before he froze, all his senses coming alive. Someone was in his house. He could feel their presence. He didn't waste time on stupid thoughts, like how did they get in or why hadn't he heard them entering. Instead he reverted back to his training, moving into a crouch as he backed into the shadows, remaining perfectly still, letting the intruder make the first move.

Jaxon stayed that way, silent and patient, until he was sure there was no one in the living room, before he slowly moved further into the room. He was careful to place one foot down gently before moving the other, making no sound. Continuing this way, he made his way around to the kitchen. Using the windows to his balcony, he looked around the kitchen without having to actually go into it, saving time as he made his way toward the only room left in his apartment, the bedroom.

It was dark in the bedroom, the only light coming from the street light through the curtains. But it was enough for Jaxon to see into the corners and figure out that no one was there. He crept to the closet and, bunching his muscles, flung open the doors, while at the same time diving and rolling to the side, coming to his feet in an attack stance to face his enemy. But no one jumped out, and no one could be seen lurking there.

Jaxon did not relax his guard though. He could still feel someone nearby. But where? He made one stop by his bed to grab a gun he kept in his nightstand before, once again, moving in silence back through the door to the living room.

Holding the gun down at his side, he stopped and let his eyes move, in one long sweep over the room, before he lifted it and growled with pure menace, "Come on out you son of a bitch! You picked the wrong place to break into!"

One second the room had been dark and empty. The next a light had appeared in the center of the room, almost blinding Jaxon with its intensity. When Jaxon's eyes adjusted, he made out the figure of a man standing in the center of the glow.

He wore a long, flowing, white robe. His hair was dark and hung down to his shoulders. Jaxon pretty much doubted his sanity, as he noticed the man had no feet and seemed to be floating above the floor. Jaxon focused on the face, noticing the beauty there, the dark eyes that looked back at him with calm curiosity, and the mouth where a half smile played at the corners.

Not lowering his gun, Jaxon made a half turn to present a smaller target, before finding his voice and asking "What the hell are you?"

The vision smiled more fully, before opening its hands in supplication and replying in a deep rich voice, "Hello, Jaxon. My name is Saul, and we have business."

Chapter 4

Jaxon did not relax his guard as he faced the vision in his home. His hand, that held the gun pointing dead center at Saul's chest, did not waiver, even though his mind was going a mile a minute trying to come to terms with what he was seeing. He had always checked out clean for chemical and bio-contaminations but that was the only explanation he could come up with for seeing what he was looking at. *'Hallucinations? Maybe. But why?'* Jaxon wanted answers, and he was not a patient man when it came to getting the answers he needed.

"How did you get in here?" he demanded, his voice low and serious.

"I simply appeared," Saul answered, calmly and straight forward.

Jaxon narrowed his eyes as he thought this thing was being smart with him. "What are you?" Jaxon demanded.

"For lack of a better explanation that you can understand, I am a Guardian of humans, entrusted with guiding them along the path that destiny has written for them." Saul replied calmly.

"Sure you are," Jaxon growled, not being able to process this information, not believing what he heard. "One more time," he said, with deadly intent, "How did you get in here?"

Saul rolled his eyes and gave a sigh. He hated to perform what he thought of as parlor tricks to convince humans he appeared before that he was telling them the truth, but he saw no other way to speed this part along. In the blink of an eye he disappeared, taking the light with him, and leaving Jaxon almost blind in the dark.

Jaxon swung his head around, trying to figure out what had just happened. Still leading with his gun, Jaxon made a full circle, looking for his target. But he found nothing. Stopping at his starting point, Jaxon lowered his gun and took one step farther into the living room.

One second the room was in shadow and the next it was again flooded with light. Saul, having appeared again, was standing right beside the human.

Jaxon had been trained too well to jump in surprise, but without thinking he swung around to face Saul.

"Lower your weapon, Jaxon," Saul said in a reasonable tone of voice. "You can't hurt me. I am Immortal and not of this world, so your means of protection will do you no good."

Jaxon hesitated, but in the end had to comply as he believed he had no choice.

"Sit down," Saul said, as he gestured towards the second-hand couch that had come with the apartment.

Jaxon moved on slightly watery legs, his head still swimming, until he could lower himself to the edge of the sofa and sit down. Looking at the Guardian, as he floated to a stop before him, Jaxon decided to go along with this, whatever it was, for the time being.

"Okay Saul, did you say? What now?" Jaxon asked, still with a sound of disbelief in his voice.

Saul sighed to himself, for he knew that Jaxon was not convinced, but he would be by the time he was finished this night.

"As I said before, I am a Guardian of humans, and I have chosen you to aide me in a situation of grave importance." Saul could read the disbelief in Jaxon's eyes, so he again started at the beginning.

"I am Immortal," he said with patience. "I have been in existence since before the beginning of time. My sole purpose is to assist humans under my guidance in fulfilling the path destiny and the Fates have written for them at their birth. Sometimes Dark forces come into play and must be defeated to save human lives that are not supposed to die by another's hand. You already have had a brush with this force."

"The dead boy?" Jaxon asked.

"Exactly," Saul said, glad that Jaxon had a fast mind. "This thing we Guardians call the Dark, has taken the body, soul, and mind of a human to do its work for evil. It will be your job to protect the next victim and, in doing so, break the chain, find the killer, and restore order to the universe."

"You're not expecting much, are you?" Jaxon asked, scorn in his voice.

"I know you," Saul replied, trying for patience. "I would not ask more of you than you are able to deliver. You are a protector," he continued. "This mission, if you want to think of it as that, is something you are good at, have been good at, and will always be good at. Your attention to detail and your deep down goodness will allow you to succeed, I think." Saul finished, searching the human for a hint of understanding.

"Thanks for the vote of confidence," Jaxon shot back.

"This task, though sounding simple, will be to find the next victim and keep them alive, while hunting for a possessed killer. It will take all of the skills you have learned and perfected so far," the Immortal told Jaxon.

"You must be out of your mind," Jaxon said, rising to his feet, still trying to figure out what was going on.

Saul had had enough of the doubts. He rose another foot in the air, then began to radiate light so bright that Jaxon thought he was going to get a sun burn.

Jaxon lifted one of his hands to shield his eyes, but could not block out the next shock that came at him out of the blue.

Hovering before Jaxon, Saul unfurled his massive opal-colored wings to their full length, spanning the whole living room from wall to wall.

"I've had enough of your doubts!" Saul said, his voice booming until the walls shuddered and the floors quaked. "You have been chosen for this mission, and you WILL succeed or the fabric of the universe will be thrown into irreparable chaos. The Dark MUST be defeated, or more innocent lives will be lost. Do you have any doubts that you will be able to do as I have asked?"

It finally sank into Jaxon's head that this was real! This was happening, and that this was probably the reason he had been feeling restless lately. All this was coming his way like a runaway freight train and he was the one that had to stop it.

"You are the chosen one," Saul said, his voice lowering only slightly as he looked down at the dark head below him. He sensed Jaxon's acceptance and came back to the floor to be on the same level as his charge. "I will help you in every way that I can, but the bulk of the work will be yours. I have faith in you, as you must have in yourself. Do you believe?"

Jaxon met the Guardian's eyes head on and said, "Let's suppose for the time being that I believe what you have said. Just exactly what am I supposed to do? How do I do it? And," Jaxon paused for a slight second, "where do I even start?"

Saul relaxed as he knew he had Jaxon's full attention at last. "Before I leave you this night, I will give you a name. It will be the name of the next victim you need to protect. In doing so, you will, as I have stated, break the chain of events and be able to identify and defeat the Dark one. More innocents do not have to die if you succeed in your task."

"Meaning if I don't succeed, I will be responsible for lives being lost?" Jaxon asked, looking at Saul with a slightly sinister sneer on his lips. "You know that is not acceptable to me, don't you?"

Saul gave him back look for look, as he gave a slight nod of his head. "As I said, I know a lot about you. The situation is desperate. I will use whatever means are necessary to achieve what I want."

"Great," Jaxon mumbled, "No pressure here."

Saul let a small smile flirt around the corners of his mouth, as his expression softened. He clasped his arms behind his back. "I have all the faith in the world in you. You will do what needs to be done, and all will be well."

Jaxon finally nodded his head as he stood up straight and tall. "Okay," he said, "I'll do what I can to help you. I will give you the same pledge that I gave to my men. I will succeed or die trying."

Saul's face sobered and his dark eyes became stormy, as he looked into the future at the chaos that would occur if Jaxon failed. Jaxon had to strain to hear what Saul whispered, and even then he did not want to believe what he heard. The Guardian's whispered words sent a freezing chill down his spine, and he finally felt the full effect should he fall short.

Saul's whispers echoed in Jaxon's soul, "You'll die, and so will everyone else."

Chapter 5

Saul folded his wings and dimmed the bright light around him, before gesturing for Jaxon to again sit down and be comfortable. Rather than complying, Jaxon went into the kitchen and grabbed a cold beer. He looked back over his shoulder and held it up in an invitation for the Guardian to join him. Saul smiled in amusement, before shaking his dark head to decline the offer.

"I do not drink or eat," Saul said, "I have no need for such human requirements."

Shrugging his shoulders in defiance, Jaxon twisted off the cap and took a long, cooling drink before shutting the fridge and walking, with nonchalance, back to the couch and sitting down.

"I'd tell you to start at the beginning, but I have a feeling that would take too much time," Jaxon said as he set the beer down and sat back, stretching his arm along the back of the couch. "So Saul, let's just start with the recent events and what they have to do with me."

Saul came to rest before the only other chair in the room and sat down, preparing to impart all he could to his human.

"A powerful bringer of the Dark has emerged into this world and has taken over a weak soul to do its bidding. It has given this person greater powers than any mortal should have. Powers to find its prey and to kill without remorse. Hunting and killing will be its only purpose. It's only pleasure."

"You said you would give me the name of the next victim, correct?" asked Jaxon.

Saul nodded his head and waited for the next question he knew was coming.

"Why can't you just tell me the name of the murderer and be done with it? Wouldn't that be the fastest and the easiest way to handle the situation? Then you wouldn't need my or anyone else's help." Jaxon confronted Saul with the question he knew was coming.

A slight frown marred the Immortal's brow, as he sat forward in the chair. "I'm sorry to say that it does not work that way. The Dark is able to shield itself from the Guardians, becoming known to us only as its evil is brought to light, as the soul it has taken begins to stray from its path. Most times we are able to drive it out of the human and return it to the shadows where it came from. But when the Dark one is powerful and strong, then we must enlist humans to aid us in finding it. And Ultimately defeating it."

"I still don't get it," Jaxon said, moving to sit on the edge of the couch as his intensity grew. "Why didn't the Guardian of the possessed one, if that's the right word, already take care of the problem, instead of letting it get this far?"

Saul's frown deepened, as the question floating in his mind was brought to light. "In the past, the only way for the Dark to take a body and soul to accomplish this level of destruction, is for it to defeat the Guardian who was watching over it."

"What do you mean by defeat?" Jaxon asked, deep furrows on his brow.

"Kill it," Saul bluntly stated.

"Didn't you just tell me you were Immortal? How can someone or something that is immortal die?" Jaxon asked Saul, disbelief in his voice.

Saul looked at Jaxon from across the room. Jaxon could see the darkening of the Guardian's eyes, the flashes of rage that streaked across the dark irises, as he ground out his answer in a voice deep and roughened with anger.

"Only another Immortal can destroy a Guardian or the Dark. It takes great power and great hate to end our existence. The battle is fierce. The outcome can tip the balance of the powers, as it has in this case. I do not like to think it has gone that far, but I cannot ignore the deaths that have taken place up to now. So the fact must be faced. An Immortal has been eliminated."

"What do you mean deaths?" Jaxon asked, jumping on the new information just released.

As he waited for Saul to answer, Jaxon picked up another clue into the being sitting in his living room. They were capable of more than just good. The anger rolling off Saul made the air in the room electric, and it smelled hot, as if an appliance was over heating. Evidently these Immortal Guardians were able to feel strongly. Jaxon had a feeling that whatever was on the receiving end of his wrath, would feel the lash of his powers to the bone. *'A good ally to have in his corner,'* he thought.

"There have been three other killings besides the one that has affected this neighborhood," Saul finally said. Reining in his anger had taken an effort on his part, and he fought for control of his Immortal rage.

"Tell me about them," Jaxon gently demanded as he coaxed information from Saul. He was not going to go into this without having every scrap of information he could get.

"There have been two females and one male, besides the young boy that was taken here. Each possessed a power, if you want to call it that, that would have played a part in shaping the future around them." Saul answered more calmly now.

"Powers?" asked Jaxon, his doubt evident in his tone of voice.

A ghost of a smile touched Saul's lips, as he knew what Jaxon was thinking. "No," he said, "they were not powers like in comic books, but were more like the powers of compassion and goodness. They all would have made an impact on the lives that they touched, causing a ripple to go out and grow from its center. If you haven't noticed, this world is in desperate need of all the goodness it can get."

Jaxon looked at Saul, with eyes flat and cold as ice. "You're preaching to the choir," he said matter-of-factly. "But I will not defend what I have done to bring about peace to the world. I have no feelings of guilt. I do feel regret that the actions I have had to take were necessary. If I had everything to do over again, I would change nothing. I would still take the lives that I did, without a second thought, and feel fine with the decision. If you're trying to guilt me into helping you, don't bother. I'll make my decision on the facts you have to tell me and if I say I'll help, then nothing will make me go back on my word. If I decline, then the same goes, nothing will make me change my mind."

Saul looked Jaxon dead in the eye. His stare filled with the Guardian's power boring into the human. "I can make you help me," he said, simply stating a fact.

Jaxon did not blink. He refused to break eye contact with the Guardian, even though he felt Saul's control creeping through his mind, giving him a taste of what the Guardian could do, if he wanted or needed to.

"Try it!" Jaxon spit out, "See how far it gets you. I'll fight you with everything I have. I'm not your puppet!"

Saul let up and sat back in the chair. "I believe you would," he said, with respect. "You have already agreed to help me, but I will tell you the rest and see if your decision still stands. The next victim in line is a female. This one, unlike the other victims before her, has unusual powers. She has the power to see evil in a person's soul. She can tell if a person is good or bad after talking to them for only a short time. She is able to see evil in its true form, as it transforms the face of the human it inhabits. This ability has allowed her to be of help to law enforcement, anonymously of course, in finding criminals and bringing them to justice. She is able to direct people in their choices in mates. Very few people know of her skills. She guards them well, as do the chosen few she has helped. I am asking you to find this woman and protect her. Why? Because the Dark and its human will come at her with everything they have. Her death could insure the success of the plan the Dark has designed."

Saul stopped talking and gave Jaxon time to digest the information given to him. Letting him decide if he would indeed aid the Guardian or not.

Jaxon's mind raced as he took in the details Saul had given him. It didn't sound so hard, find the woman, keep her safe, and wait until the bad guy made his move. Take him out. Job done. Move on. Too easy.

"Let's stop dancing around," Jaxon said. "What's the catch?" he asked, looking at Saul, feeling sure that he was right in his assumption that there was more.

Saul again nodded his head, pleased that the human had such a quick mind, showing him that his choice of a warrior was a good one.

"If you fail, you both die. Your souls will be no more. There will be no coming back. Do you still offer your aid?" Saul asked, once again rising to float above the floor.

Jaxon had always liked a challenge, and had never shrunk from one. Looking at Saul, Jaxon let a little of his deadliness seep out and enter his black eyes. Nodding his head and holding out his hand for the Guardian to shake and seal the deal, Jaxon cocked an eyebrow and said quiet and deadly, "I'm your man. Now give me a name."

Chapter 6

Jaxon woke up the next morning feeling a lot better than he had a right to, considering he had spent most of last night talking to an Immortal Guardian about murder. The four already committed and those to come, that is. Jaxon still had doubts, but they were small and not really doubts, unless you considered the one where he doubted his sanity. It wasn't every day or everyone that could say they were visited by an Immortal, and given the task of saving lives and righting the wrongs evil had committed.

It had been late into the evening before Saul had stopped questioning and testing Jaxon, finally confiding in him the name of the person he would be responsible for, Hannah Rose Priest. Saul had been no help when Jaxon asked for an address, but had told him that she was a shop owner. A Mystic shop owner.

Jaxon had rolled his eyes and groaned under his breath, thinking that he was going to have to deal with, and probably have to spend time with, a kook that wore a ton of scarves, had frizzy red hair, and claimed to be in touch with the dead. Great! Saul would not have to worry about the Dark getting to her if she was what Jaxon pictured her to be in his mind. He might just do the deed himself.

Saul smiled, having read Jaxon's mind, and with a touch of humor in his voice said, "Jaxon, try to restrain yourself from doing Hannah in."

Jaxon had cocked one eyebrow and felt a small pinch of anger that his thoughts could be so easily read by the Immortal. "Are you going to be doing that a lot?" he asked, his annoyance leaking through.

"Doing what?" Saul asked, a bit of playful innocence in his voice.

"Messing around in my head," Jaxon replied.

"Oh that," Saul said, with no hint of remorse in his voice and body language. "I guess you could call it an occupational hazard. In human terms that is."

"Whatever terms you want to use, I don't like it and would appreciate it if you would not do it again," Jaxon said, his tone leaving no doubt that he would not be so understanding should there ever be a next time.

Saul nodded his head. Looking his warrior straight in the eye, dark eyes to dark eyes, he said "I can give you my word that unless it is necessary to do so, I will not trespass unless asked."

Jaxon met the Immortal's look head on and did not flinch as he considered Saul's answer. Then he too nodded his head and let the topic go.

Jaxon had visited his fridge a couple more times throughout the evening but he laid off the beer, instead opting for cans of pop and a few munchies to keep him awake and his mind clear. By the time Saul had risen from the chair, again floating a foot off the floor, the dark of night was beginning to draw back and make room for the coming of a new day.

"I'll try to stay close in case you call," Saul said to Jaxon. "I do have other charges and must assist them if needed, but I will come if you call."

Jaxon stood and faced the Guardian, his hands finding their way into his pockets, his legs slightly spread, and his shoulders straight.

"I'll gather some information tomorrow and see if I can't find this Hannah Priest. I'll just have to play it by ear and trust my gut until this Dark makes a move. Then we can get down to the business of sending its Dark ass back to where it came from."

"That will be my job," Saul interjected. "As I said before, it takes an Immortal to defeat another Immortal."

"Fine by me," Jaxon said, letting a yawn that cracked his jaws tell Saul he had had enough for one night.

As Saul began to fade from the third floor apartment, he left Jaxon with one last bit of advice. "I will help all I can, but the brunt of the work will fall on your shoulders. I am counting on them being wide enough to carry this burden. Remember, be on your guard at all times, and protect Hannah. You may very well be mankind's one and only defense against what the future could be."

One second Saul was there and the next he was gone, taking the bright light with him, leaving Jaxon alone but not totally in the dark. '*No pressure here,*' he thought. First he needed a few hours of shut-eye, and then he would begin to unravel the mystery of Hannah Priest.

Moving into the bedroom, he dropped his clothes beside the bed and climbed on top of the sheets, filing the night away until he woke up.

A few hours later Jaxon swam up from the dark folds of sleep that had, for too short a time, taken him captive, letting his over-loaded mind have a break. Getting up and moving into the bathroom, he took a quick shower, in a hurry to get down to the business of finding this mysterious mystic. He allowed himself enough time to drag a razor over his face and wipe the stray traces of foamy soap from his skin before turning away from the mirror without a second glance.

Jaxon was not planning on going out for awhile, so a shirt was not necessary. He drug a pair of worn and comfortable cut off shorts out of his dresser and pulled them up over his lean hips. Making his way to the kitchen, he took time for a quick breakfast, consisting of a bottle of water and a day old doughnut, before dragging out the thick Denver area phone book and dropping it on the kitchen table.

He ran his finger down the list of P's, searching for the mystic's last name, but came up empty. Searching for a mystic shop in the yellow pages that might have her name in it, again came up with nothing. It finally took Jaxon opening up his laptop to find the needed information he sought.

It appeared she had a shop located in the suburban town of Golden. Away from the busy hustle of downtown Denver. *'Why would she want to be way out on the west edge of the city?'* he wondered. She would probably have more customers if she was where the people were. Even the "Republic of Boulder" would be an improvement, as they had a lot of white witches living there and everyone was just strange enough to buy into the idea of magic, or whatever you called it.

Jaxon spent a good hour searching and reading all the information he could dig up on the shop owned by one Hannah Priest, called The Inner Self. *'Weird name for a business,'* Jaxon thought. The ad didn't say what kind of services were offered, or even give any clues as to what kind of business it was. Unless someone knew what to look for, and who to look for, they would never think to look under the name of The Inner Self. *'Why was that?'* he wondered. *'Did she have something to hide?'*

Jotting down the location and the phone number of the shop, Jaxon shut down his computer and sat back in his chair. Tapping the eraser of his pencil against his chin, he took his time in deciding a plan of action.

First he was going to have to go and check out the area and the building itself to see how much of a problem it was going to be to provide protection while she was at work. After working out that problem, he would have plenty of time to meet the woman face to face, and decide what to tell her and where to go from there.

Dressing in a t-shirt and shorts, Jaxon grabbed a pair of dark sunglasses with mirrored lenses, before leaving his apartment and heading out to his car. Jaxon started the car, adjusted the mirrors, and slowly pulled into the early morning traffic. Settling down into the comfortable seat, Jaxon turned on the radio for noise, and pointed the car's nose west.

'Ready or not,' he thought, *'Twilight zone here we come.'*

Chapter 7

Jaxon hated rush hour traffic and had timed his drive to only catch the tail end of it. He figured the shop would probably open around nine or ten and planned to give himself all the time he needed to take a look around outside, from every angle, to get the lay of the land.

That was the first order of business. If it took all day, that was fine with him. He wanted to know how busy the streets got, what kind of people were in the area, and what kind of people entered the store, before he himself ventured inside. Outside first, inside last.

Feeling good about his plan, he gave his attention to the traffic and signs. Within the next half hour, he found himself squeezing into a parking place across the street from The Inner Self. He shut off the motor and listened to the hum of cars speeding by, as people made their way to and from appointments or destinations.

Not a lot of people he observed, but then again it was early. The neighborhood was nice, with clean little store fronts decorated with wares to catch the eyes of those who went by. "Come on in," they invited, "Spend your money here. We have something that you just can't live without. Even if you don't know it."

Shop owners came out from their buildings, sweeping the sidewalk and even the streets directly in front of their businesses, removing the trash and cigarette butts that pedestrians had dropped in the gutters, not caring where they ended up. Flowers were freshened and windows washed until they sparkled in the morning sun, all in the effort to make their shops the most inviting.

Jaxon waited and watched the activity, hoping to get a glimpse of Hannah as she followed suit with the front of her store. But she never came out. His wait was not unproductive though. He gathered information, memorized faces of owners and workers, and found out opening times for each place, as signs were turned around and doors opened for the business day.

It did not take long for the heat of the day to make sitting in his car most uncomfortable. He rolled down every window, trying to catch even the slightest breath of a breeze, as he waited for the foot traffic to pick up enough to let him blend in as he walked.

Finally, leaving the windows cracked, he got out of his car and walked the streets, his eyes moving behind the mirrored lenses, filing information. He strolled around the block, noting back entrances, second and third floor windows, and dumpsters that could be pushed and pulled into position to gain access to the upper floors of Hannah's building, and the ones on either side of it.

He made mental notes of the bad, as well as the good. From what he could see, the bad far out-weighed the good when it came to defense and protection. He was definitely going to have to work some long hours to find a solution to protecting Hannah.

It was well past noon before Jaxon was satisfied that he had the lay of the land down and memorized. The street was as hot as an oven and the air barely moved, making being outside on the pavement another incentive to go into the cool stores and browse.

Jaxon did not want to miss the opening of The Inner Self for business, but if he kept walking around, he was going to attract the kind of attention he was trying to avoid.

With his shirt sticking to his torso, he finally decided no more could be done from the outside. Earlier he had discovered a small coffee shop tucked into a small space across the street and down a few doors, so he gave in and went inside to cool off and get something to relieve his dry throat.

Pulling the door open, he was greeted by a puff of cool air and the smell of fresh baked treats. His stomach growled, reminding him he had not eaten anything since early this morning.

The interior of the shop was dark compared to the blazing sun outside. Jaxon took a moment to raise the dark glasses to the top of his head and let his eyes adjust. When he could see again, he liked what he saw. A small cozy area with a few small tables arranged to let the occupants look out the front windows. Shelves lined with assorted bags of coffee, mugs, books, and what-nots covered one whole wall and the other was taken up by a counter where you could order and choose a tasty treat from inside a large glass display case.

At the moment no one was behind the counter, so Jaxon took his time looking over the sweets and making his choice from the hand-written drink list hanging up on the wall.

By the time a girl appeared from the back room, he had made his choice and had gone back to looking at the interior of the shop. As he sensed movement behind him, he swung around to face the intruder. '*No*,' he thought, '*intruder was wrong. It was just a girl. Stranger for sure, but just a girl.*'

It only took him a second to take in everything about her, but her inspection took longer, as she studied the man at her counter with eyes that widened at first and then narrowed with appreciation. Her steps faltered and she stopped, her eyes moving up and down his body before she went to stand behind the counter.

"Hi," she said, with a purr in her voice. "My name is Kim. Welcome to My Place. Well it's not my place," she said flapping her hand as she spoke. "The name of the store is My Place. Have you decided what you want?"

For the first time in a long time she wished her hair was not the ebony with bright pink tips that she had dyed it, and that her eyes were not so thickly lined in black. Maybe she would even look okay with her lips a more natural color, rather than the blood-red she had just reapplied in the back room. Instantly, a thought crossed her mind. '*What would it be like to have this gorgeous man reply with only one word to her question. You.*'

She would have thrown off her little apron and vaulted over the counter, landing in his arms. He would carry her out the door and away to live out her every fantasy. He looked like he could do it, too, Kim thought as she licked her lips.

His shirt was clinging to his body from the sweat that he had worked up out on the street, and she noticed a small trickle of the same making its way down his tanned jaw, just in front of his ear. She wanted to reach out like they did on TV and catch the single drop on her finger tip, placing it on her tongue in such a way that he would know what she wanted, and would be happy to give it to her. All afternoon.

Jaxon watched her eyelids droop over her eyes and the dreamy expression that covered her face for just a second, and knew what she was thinking as if he was reading a book. When her eyes finally came back to his face, he let one dark eyebrow cock upwards and gave her a smile that had her heart jumping like a drop of water in a hot skillet.

'*Holy crap!*' she thought, as she swallowed to try and dry up her mouth before she started to drool. Thick, long, dark hair, dark mysterious eyes, a killer body rippling with muscles, and a smile that was pure sex, all had her mesmerized and under his spell.

Not that he wanted her there. On Jaxon's part, he noticed a young girl, late teens to early twenties, shocking hair, too much make up, trying to be all grown up. He would wager she was probably still living at home with her parents.

As if on cue, a middle aged woman with short, blonde hair came through the same back door and walked up to stand by Kim.

"Hey honey," she said "I'm back. Thanks for helping. I'll get it from here." She gave the punk hair do a quick stroke before turning to wait on her customer. '*This was mom,*' Jaxon surmised. He was correct, too.

"What can I get you?" she asked with a quick flash of appreciation in her eyes. Hey, she wasn't dead, right?

Jaxon ordered a strawberry blast and a gooey cinnamon roll to go with it. Strange combination, but he couldn't help himself now that he was back in the states and able to get the things he had gone without for so long. The drink was to cool off, but the roll was for pure indulgence.

Jaxon paid for his order and went to sit by the window so he could keep an eye on the store down the street. He heard the giggling behind him as he walked away, and just smiled to himself as he kept going.

The first bite of the roll melted in his mouth and had him slumping in his chair in pure pleasure. He tried not to wolf it down, but finished it off down to the last gooey crumb in no time at all. He took a drink and sighed in satisfaction. Life was good.

In the midst of his bliss, his eye caught a movement at the door to the shop that held his interest. He watched as a woman in a dark business suit tried the door, and walked in as it opened. The door closed behind her.

'*Shit*,' he cursed to himself. '*When had Hannah opened the store?*'

Finishing his drink, with a speed that had him fighting a brain freeze, Jaxon took his empty containers to the waste can and exited the cool store. The merciless heat hit him like a wall as he stood on the sidewalk. He pulled his sunglasses from the top of his head, covering his eyes, which were zeroed in on the doorway across the street. Jaxon made his way to the corner and crossed the street.

'*It was time*,' he thought, as he stopped in front of the glass door. Time to put his skills to work and see if he could save a life. Hannah Priest's life. And maybe his own.

Chapter 8

Jaxon did not hesitate when he reached the store, pushing the glass door open with one strong hand. It gave with ease and he stepped inside, letting it slide shut behind him without a sound. The interior was cool and smelled like spices, or was it incense, or maybe it was candles. *'Whatever it was,'* Jaxon thought, *'it smelled deep and dark. It smelled like power.'*

He didn't like it. It made his muscles bunch and his hands clench, as if anticipating trouble. And he was. Danger was here. He could smell it. His eyes moved around the inside of the store looking for the source, but he found nothing on the surface.

The walls held shelves of candles, crystals, books, charms, and small bottles of unknown liquids. The middle of the store's floor was open and free, with only a couple of racks with loose-flowing clothing hanging on hangers, and a glass case with amulets and other pieces of jewelry inside. On the back wall were shelves of rocks with descriptions in front of each type, explaining their powers in detail.

Jaxon also took notice of what he assumed was a back room, of which the entrance was covered with a deep, rich, midnight blue curtain. Within its folds were unfamiliar symbols that shimmered and glowed.

Even though Jaxon had seen only one person enter the store, there were three people inside. One older female, possibly in her late sixties, was sitting behind the counter on a stool. A female in a blue business suit was browsing the store, while another woman, with rich brown hair, was standing with her back to Jaxon. He couldn't tell much about that one, except she was wearing comfortable old jeans, almost worn through on the butt, and a dark tee-shirt that was tucked into the waist of those faded jeans. When she reached for a candle on the shelf, he noticed she had a ring on each pointer finger and one on her right thumb. From the quick glimpse he caught, her hands looked young. He figured her to be another customer. Or maybe not.

As Jaxon stood and looked at her, the hair on his arms and neck started to rise. His sense of danger kicked into over drive, and without thinking he moved to put himself between the female behind the counter, who he assumed was Hannah, and the young female that his senses zeroed in on as the threat.

He picked up items and tried to appear to be interested in what he held, without appearing to hover as he waited. He felt that if a move was going to be made, it would be when items were brought to the counter to be paid for. He needed to stay in the area to pull Hannah to safety, or to protect her with his body if needed. He would be her shield against any attempt on her life. He had promised.

He managed to appear to be engrossed in the charm he held in his hands. But if anyone had asked him about it, he wouldn't even have been able to give the color of the stone that held a place of honor in its center, let alone anything else about it. He hung it back up and took down another that brought him one step closer to the cash register and the woman who manned it.

He stalled as the woman in the business suit brought her items to the counter, and appeared not to notice as she gave him a long, appreciative look. She fluffed her hair and tossed it over her shoulder in an attempt to draw his attention to her. Her hand slipped down to the buttons of her jacket, as if she were going to undo a few. She hesitated as the stranger's cold, black eyes pinned her for just a second before dismissing her and moving back to the jewelry in his hand.

The woman's hand had frozen in mid air and the smile of seduction had left her face. She was scared. Those dark eyes had held no warmth. What she saw in their depths were menace and death. The man was the best thing she had ever seen, but the restrained violence was more than she was willing to attempt to take on. Grabbing her bag she clutched it to her chest and backed up a few steps, before whirling and exiting the store as fast as her stilettos allowed.

After the first glance, Jaxon had dismissed her as no threat, nothing to worry about. He had seen the way she had looked at him, and was no stranger to the spark that had come into her eyes. But he was not interested and, with a single glance, had let her know.

With her gone, that left the woman behind the counter and the one still strolling through the store.

Jaxon liked those odds better. The least amount of witnesses there were if something went down, the better.

He continued to pick up merchandise and put it back, always staying in the area closest to his target. The young female seemed in no hurry to buy anything, and it took all of Jaxon's patience to not confront the woman and get everything out in the open. But he clamped down hard on his impatience and waited. He loitered long enough that he began receiving questioning looks from the woman behind the counter. He just nodded his head at her and kept his attention focused on the other occupant.

When his patience was at its breaking point, the young woman turned and approached the counter. Jaxon kept whatever he had in his hand at the time and moved to stand behind her, appearing to be next in line. His muscles tensed and his attention was totally on the form in front of him. One off move and he would grab her. She would have to be held until Saul could get there to kill the Dark, but Jaxon thought he could manage until then, as the woman looked to be more of a girl than woman at closer range.

Standing, she only came to the bottom of his chin and her frame was slight and trim. She had muscles on her though, as she reached a hand back and tucked something into her back pocket. The short sleeves on the shirt pulled tight and he saw the slight rippling of the underlying muscles as she moved. If the circumstances had been different, Jaxon might have been attracted to the tight compact body so close to his. But things weren't different, and he had a promise to keep.

He readied himself and was about to move, when he heard a voice, filled with smoke and velvet whisper lowly to the woman behind the counter.

"Go ahead and take your break Regina. I'll watch the register and things until you get back. Take your time." she said.

Jaxon stood quietly where he was, trying to digest this latest bit of information. It seemed that the woman behind the counter was not Hannah Priest, but an employee. Though his mind was going a mile a minute, Jaxon still caught the brief look the older woman, Regina, gave him. It spoke volumes, saying that she thought he was strange, and did not feel good about leaving the young girl alone with him.

Jaxon watched, amused, as a slim hand was placed over the older woman's in reassurance. As if he was the problem, please!

Regina did not seem convinced, but she reluctantly rose off the stool, and slowly came out from behind the counter. She nodded her head at the younger woman, and sent a threatening look in Jaxon's direction, as she moved aside to allow her to take her place. '*Be nice,*' the look seemed to say. '*Or else!*'

Jaxon wanted to smirk in amusement at the thought that Regina could be a threat to him, but did not. Instead he cocked one dark eyebrow, and gave a slight nod of his head in acknowledgment to her message. He turned his head slightly and followed Regina's progress to the curtain. As the mystery behind the curtain swallowed her up, Jaxon heard the same smoky voice address him. But this time amusement was heavy in the tone.

"Now then, sir," the voice said, "would you like your fertility charm in a box or just in a bag?"

Chapter 9

Jaxon lowered his dark eyes to focus on the object he held in his hand. For the first time he really looked at what he held. Uncurling his fingers, he let the object lie in the middle of his palm and almost felt panic. The small figure was a pregnant female with hands cradling an obviously bulging belly.

"Oh shit," he mumbled to himself, trying to keep it together long enough to lay the charm carefully on the glass counter top. He wanted to rub the palm of his hand on the leg of his shorts, but refrained, not wanting to give the girl anything more to laugh at.

Maybe he should sanitize to make sure no bad juju rubbed off on him and had him impregnating the next woman he slept with. *'Oh crap!'* he thought, wondering if that was even possible. Remembering his visitor last night, he was pretty sure anything was possible.

As the husky, knowing laughter coming from across the counter finally penetrated the fog of male panic in his head, Jaxon raised his eyes and got his second jolt of the day. He had been correct in thinking she was young, barely a woman, but that was the only thing he had been right on.

The hair he had thought of as medium brown was actually the color of a tiger eye stone, with the same generous shots of gold, red, and even dark brown or maybe black. He could not tell which. Standing in a ray of sunlight that was coming in through the front window, her hair sparkled with health and beauty. It lay thick over her shoulders and down her back in soft feathers that curled around her chin and framed her long neck. It looked soft and touchable, and that is what Jaxon wanted to do, touch. He wanted to bury his hands in the thick richness, and feel the softness run through his fingers like warm satin.

Next, his dark eyes found her mouth and settled on it, studying it, memorizing it. It was soft and naturally pink and, at the moment, spread in a grin that had dimples creasing her cheeks.

'*Sexy as hell*,' Jaxon thought.

Her cheeks were high and had the natural peaches and cream coloring that was unique to youth. Her face seemed flawless to Jaxon, as he let his eyes roam where they would. Her brows were dark and formed slashes over her eyes that, at the moment, were still looking down, focused on what had been in Jaxon's hand. He noticed they were lightly outlined in black, and had long, dark lashes lying like butterfly wings on her soft cheeks.

When she raised those eyes to meet his, he felt an icy chill crawl up and down his back, making him want to shiver and step back. He allowed his reaction to those eyes to show for only a split second, before he dropped a veil over his emotions and returned her stare, flat, cool, and assessing.

'*Those eyes,*' he thought.

Those eyes made his mouth go dry, even as he tried to swallow the spit that had pooled there in the first seconds of contact. Flat, almost black eyes met and clashed with eyes that were the impossible deep red of old blood. They reminded him of the blood he had spilled every time he had dispatched an enemy, pooling underneath and running in rivers to be drank up by the thirsty, waiting earth.

Odd and strange things like this did not usually creep him out, but this did. As they continued to stare at each other, Jaxon felt a power coming from the girl. It was nothing he could put his finger on, but he felt it none-the-less. If he had to describe it, he might say that it was a warm feeling, kind of like waves that washed over him, through him. Or he might have said that it was an intrusion into his mind. Or maybe his soul. Or maybe he had just been out in the sun too long, and it had finally fried his brain.

Jaxon continued to look into those strange eyes. He got the feeling that she was not so much looking at him, as looking in him. Her eyes had gone slightly out of focus, and she appeared to be seeing something only she could. Jaxon did not like it. He did not want to be studied, probed, violated, or whatever you wanted to call it.

His muscles tensed as he bent at the waist until his eyes were level with hers.

"Get out of my head," he ground out, low and threatening. "You weren't invited and you're not welcome." His dark eyes shot fire as they reinforced his words.

Jaxon watched her face lose its color, until it was chalk white and beads of sweat dotted her upper lip. He caught her by the shoulders as she started to crumple forward over the counter. Jaxon could feel the coldness of her skin as it seeped through her shirt to his hands. He shook her until her head fell back and her eyes were once again centered on him.

"Whatever you are doing, stop it. Stop it right now. You've gone too far!" he spat into her face.

He supported her until color leeched back into her face, and she brought her hands up to the counter to brace herself. It took several deep breaths before she pushed herself upright and stood on her own two feet with no help from him.

"What the hell was that all about?" Jaxon demanded. "Are you trying to kill yourself? It sure looked that way to me." He watched those smooth cheeks pinken and her posture become stiffer with every word he barked at her.

"I'm sorry if you have been inconvenienced," she said, the same smoke in her words. But this time there was brittleness in the tone, a cracking in the voice, as if it would take very little more to break her.

"Thank you for your concern," she said, her eyes still lowered, having remained that way since their connection had been broken. "I think I will have to ask you to leave now. I believe we will be closing the shop for the day. Did you want to purchase this charm before you go or not?" She pointed at the forgotten charm on the counter and waited for Jaxon to answer.

"I didn't come in today to make a purchase. So no," he answered. "I came in to see if I could meet the owner and talk to her."

Those same blood-red eyes flashed up in surprise that turned to questioning, as they found and held the dark brown ones across the counter.

"Who are you, and what do you want?" she asked, suspicion in her voice. "I don't believe I know you."

Jaxon took a step back from the counter and let his eyes travel up and down the woman before him. No conflict showed on his face, even though he was a volcano on the inside. '*You have got to be kidding,*' he thought, '*this just keeps getting better by the minute.*'

"Ms. Priest?" he asked, cocking his head to the side. "Ms. Hannah Rose Priest?"

"As I said before, I don't know you. What do you want?" Hannah asked, also taking a step back from the counter. She needed to put some distance between them, even if it was just one step. She wasn't going to like what he had to say, she knew it.

Jaxon didn't know of any other way to tell her why he was there, except to just say it.

"My name is Jaxon Riley," he said, and looking her straight in eyes he changed her world forever. "I've been sent here to save your life."

Chapter 10

Hannah opened her eyes to the first rays of what promised to be a scorching sun. She lay in her soft bed and, as she did every morning, took a moment to let her eyes wander the bedroom of her apartment.

The apartment was located right over her shop. 'Her shop,' she thought, relishing in the same tingling feeling that she felt every time she said that. At the young age of 23 she was her own boss. Not out of the burning desire to exploit her talents, but more of a necessity.

Since her earliest memories, she remembered being different. Not so much by her actions, but by her looks. The color of her eyes made her the mark for cruel remarks by children and adults alike. She had been called a freak, a witch, a monster, and adults thought she was evil.

Her parents had shielded her as best they could. As she prepared to enter school, they realized they couldn't be with her every moment of the day, or drown out the voices that drifted her way. They had looked at her with sadness and endless love the day she had asked for contact lenses. They knew why, and they hurt for their daughter.

She had picked out a beautiful soft brown pair, brown being the only color that the deep red of her eyes would not show through.

Her life was as normal as she could make it. It was not only the strangeness of her eyes that made her stand out, but an ability she had been born with that made those she called her friends so rare.

It had taken her many years of working with another who could do what she did, before she was able to control it and live with it. Christine, her mentor, had been in her early thirties when they had first been paired up. In the countless hours they had spent together, she had made the very young Hannah see that she was special, not a freak.

By the time their training was over, Hannah had a firm grasp on her talents and was able to function in the everyday world without screaming in terror.

Hannah's gift was that she was able to see a person's true character just by looking at their face. The good one's faces did not change a lot, but carried a glow about them. The changes she could see in them were small, not so scary.

The bad ones used to give Hannah nightmares, before she had learned how to control her gift and interpret what it meant when a person changed into a gargoyle or a monster right in front of her eyes.

As she got older Hannah would wonder why she could not have a cool power, like flying, or invisibility, or reading minds. No, she had to be able to see the evil that people hid from each other. She saw it all. From what she thought of as normal, like warts, or long noses, or sagging skin, to the really bad ones that looked like towers of runny sores, puss-filled pockets, or had liquefied skin dripping from their bones. Things that no horror show could even come close to imitating.

In her late teens she had helped the police identify the worst criminals society could produce, sending them to jail. She pointed the way and the police did the rest. But she had pulled back from that when her life had been threatened too many times, and attempts came too close for comfort. The police had tried to keep her identity a secret, but things leaked out to the wrong people. The danger was brought home when Christine had been killed by a suspect in a multiple murder case she had been helping with.

At that point Hannah had withdrawn from everything, giving up the sham of a normal life as she retreated into herself. It had taken many years for her to feel safe enough again to venture out into public. Until she was sure she had been forgotten by the evil ones.

It had taken the death of her parents to make her change her life, to want to seek out contact with humanity again. She had traveled until she had found a safe place to live, a place far from her home. Golden, Colorado. She had lived there for a while now, making sure she was in no danger, seeing no recognition in the faces she passed on the street.

She became bored doing nothing, wondering what she could do with herself, when the idea of opening a small shop came to her. She decided to offer a small but unique selection of mystical and magical products for those that believed. She, herself, believed that there was more than what the eye could see in this world. Good and evil.

She hunted for rocks that spoke to her, as she wandered the Rocky Mountains day after day, until she had collected enough wares to open her doors to the public. She did not have to advertise. Her business had grown steadily by word-of-mouth from those that had stumbled in her front door and been more than pleased as they carried away good fortune and good luck with their purchases. She did not offer anything harmful or evil, and turned away those that asked for such things.

She remembered the first time she had used her talents to help a customer, as if it were yesterday. A thirty-something female had entered her shop, setting the bell above the door to dancing and bringing Hannah out from the back room. Hannah had stopped short as she looked at the male that was with her. As she watched, his face had become black in color, his eyes had turned to bottomless pools of red, and fangs had grown from his black cavern of a mouth. He watched the woman with possessive eyes and guarded her like a dog with his bone. The fists that hung from arms, long and roped with muscle, were used to give pain, not comfort.

Hannah knew that he was wrong for this woman, who looked beaten down, and whose appearance, to Hannah, was one of gray colors and drab browns. Hannah also knew that should this woman escape this man, she would change to bright colors and radiate warmth and peace.

Hannah had broken out in a cold sweat and her hands had started to shake. Should she say something, offer advice that had not been asked for? As the two looked around the store, Hannah had made up her mind. She made her way around the shop until she stood beside the woman, offering a smile and receiving one in return. She felt the woman's need to be free rolling off her like the heat rising up from the street in the midday sun. She also felt the woman's fear that chained her to the man, making her too afraid to do what she needed to do.

Hannah had taken a deep breath and, looking the woman straight in the eye, she had dropped her smile and whispered in dead seriousness, "Not this one. This one is not for you. Get away. Get out now."

The woman did not even pretend not to understand, but had returned Hannah's look with helplessness.

"If you don't, you'll die," Hannah hissed into her ear. "Do it."

The woman had backed up from Hannah and almost ran from the shop, leaving the man behind. Hannah had felt drained for the rest of the day. When she'd closed the shop that night, she'd been more than ready to call it a day.

A few weeks had passed, when the same woman came back into the store and sought out Hannah straight away. Her appearance was as Hannah had known it could be, glowing and warm.

"Thank you," she'd said, when the two were alone. "Thank you for telling me what I already knew, for giving me the courage to act before it was too late."

"You're welcome," Hannah had said, and had turned to move on. A hand had reached out and rested on her back, making her turn around.

"How did you know?" the woman asked. "How could you have possibly known?"

Hannah had been reluctant to admit anything, but knew she could not play ignorant either. "I just do," she said, trusting her secret once again to another.

The woman had just nodded and, after clasping Hannah's small hand in hers for a moment, turned and left the shop. Hannah had spent an anxious time wondering if the woman would tell all who would listen about the strange woman in the little shop who had powers to help. But the hoards had not come and Hannah had relaxed into her regular routine.

Every once in a great while she would see someone in need, and tell them what she knew. And once in a while, she knew those she had helped had sent another in need to her.

She started to think of herself as a matchmaker of sorts. She looked at men and women that came to her and asked, "Is he the one? Is she the one?" She could not see if they were meant to be together, but she could tell them if their partner was good or not. That was all. It was enough.

She put minds to rest or voice to nagging fears. Everything had gone well and Hannah had found a measure of happiness in her everyday life. Until today. Until this stranger had walked into her store and into her life. Until he had said he was sent to save her. Until she felt the chill of the truth reach into her chest and paint her heart with dread. Until she looked into his eyes and once again knew fear.

Chapter 11

While Saul had been busy watching over the humans assigned to him, guiding them along the path Destiny had written for them, Roman, his counterpart from The Dark, had been busy himself, but for a very different reason.

Roman had been consumed with the need to find a soul he could turn from its path, until it fell into darkness and would do The Dark's bidding with joy and relish. It had taken more hours than Roman could count, but gazing into the Inferno of Torment had paid off. Roman had finally made his choice. He chuckled as he rubbed his hands together in glee at having so many souls to choose from.

Everywhere Roman looked he found greed, lust, perversion, and the hunger for power boiling inside the hearts of mankind, until he fairly drooled with pleasure at the course the humans were heading. Heading straight to him and his army, dying to join their ranks, lining up to pay the small price with their souls, if only they could have what they desired in their lives.

It would have been easy for Roman to choose one of these masses, but he was looking for more. He took his time. After all, he had an eternity to find a human with true evil in his soul, just waiting for it to be given a reason to be released.

Roman watched carefully, day in and day out, until today, the day he finally made his choice. He chose a man, even though he had had his pick of females that were also bad to the bone. He knew that males had the strength that females did not, having been bred since the beginning of time to hunt and kill. When it came time for a baby to be born that was of use to him, he would choose a female. But for this bit of mischief, he would stick to a male.

Roman backed up from his place in front of the icy beast he referred lovingly to as "The Flame" and made his plan.

He had chosen a man that was the General Manager of a casino, knowing that he would have plenty of subjects to pick from when it came time to practice, before getting down to the true work to be done.

Once again Roman would whisper into a human's ear, whisper instructions and encouragement, building this man's confidence until he believed he could do anything, be anything, and get away with anything. He would guide, giving him the names of his victims, staying by his side as he caused death, spreading fear as each deed was reported and exploited by every media outlet available.

Only when the Dark's newest instrument of despair was ready, would Roman set his true plan into motion.

"It's time," Roman said out loud, to no one but himself. Taking the form of nothing more than a dark wisp of smoke, Roman prepared to meet his new best friend.

He let loose a long chilling moan, as he disappeared into the shadows. His hordes of minions hearing it, responded in kind, knowing that a battle cry had been given and that death was about to follow.

Chapter 12

Simon Small scratched his skinny ass as he made his way into his bathroom to take a shower, after his alarm had gone off, signaling the beginning of another useless day. He paused, as he did every morning, to admire his body in the full length mirror he had installed in the bathroom. From the neck down he was satisfied with what he saw, muscles that were defined in his arms, legs, chest, and abdomen. He worked out every day after he came home, feeling the need to be toned and fit just in case he ever found a woman that he deemed worthy of his attentions. So far they had been few and far between.

Those that he had approached had not been able to see past his thinning, limp, dirty-blonde hair, his small mud-brown eyes, the too-small chin, and the overly large nose. He could see it in their eyes and in the lurking sneers on their lips, when they noticed he stood only five feet four inches tall, that his chances with them ranked somewhere between not a chance in hell and you have got to be kidding.

His attitude did not help, since he was the poster boy for the little guy syndrome. He came off as arrogant and obnoxious, trying to make up for what he lacked in looks and in height. He was pushy and had a mean mouth when he was turned down. No one really liked rejection, and he took things personally when a woman turned her back on him or giggled with her friends at the nerve he showed in approaching them. He made sure to loudly point out any flaw he could find, embarrassing them the way they had him.

He made up for his lack of size in the most typical way, by having the best car, the best apartment, the best clothes, and a very well paying job.

He had started out in the casino industry as a dealer, been promoted to Pit Boss, then Shift Manager, and finally worming his way up to the General Manager position at the biggest casino in Colorado, "The Underworld."

When he had started his casino career, the name 'The Underworld' had failed to attract high rollers, as the games they offered were the boring, dime-a-dozen variety offered in every casino. The casino had been in trouble, failing financially. But when Simon was named General Manager, he had pitched his idea for a drastic change in the décor. He had spent hours coming up with a slogan he thought would be interesting and pull in the money.

'Come play at Colorado's best Casino, The Underworld. Anything you want, anything you desire, anything you hunger for can be yours. Yours for the taking. Why wait to have it all? Come play with us today and leave a winner. Everything has a price. All we ask for is your money and the small price of your soul.'

He had put in a stream with a bridge over it at the main entrance, the water flowing not as a normal stream, bubbling and blue, but black and boiling with stream rising up in angry hisses, leaving the guests with the impression that they indeed were crossing the river Styx and stepping into Hell itself. The décor was dark, making each gambler think of the sins that were buried deep within their soul as they entered and stayed. The laughter on the lips of fun-loving visitors died as they moved deeper into the casino. Their darkest desires seemed to be pulled from hidden corners where they had been buried until they lay bare and could not be ignored. The desires seemed to take on a life of their own, demanding to be freed and allowed to flourish, to be tried once more or be experienced for a first time.

Simon made sure that all vices could be bought for a price, and The Underworld soon became the busiest and most profitable casino in the country. And stayed that way. He catered to the wealthy or, for that matter, anyone that produced the money to pay for their sins. He never forgot who asked for what and, as the hordes came back over and over again, he made sure that before each left they were hooked on the pleasures that could be purchased if you had the price.

It gave Simon great pleasure to bring the high and mighty to their knees, where they stayed as they begged him for just one more taste of the forbidden, sometimes illegal, fruits that he provided. It gave him the power he could not get on his own, elevating him to a position above those who looked down their noses at him, thought themselves better than him. He showed them who had the power, every time he made them come to him with their secrets. He kept records, for he was not above using black-mail if he were ever to find himself in a jam. But mostly he kept records so he could crush all those that had more power than him, more money, more friends, or a life that he envied.

Simon could not believe how his life had turned out. He had gone from being a nobody to being a very powerful man. Not being sure what he had done to have all this good luck, Simon had long ago decided not to over analyze each bit of good fortune, convincing himself he was just getting what he deserved. And this had worked out well until recently, when he had begun to feel antsy and restless. Usually when he felt a little off he would just escape from his office and wander the floor of the casino, until he found an unlucky employee to jeer at and berate until he had ruined their day, thus making him feel better for having stomped on some peon's fragile ego, flexing his power.

But lately even being an asshole had not satisfied him. He needed something more. But what? Shrugging his shoulders as if trying to dislodge an unwanted hand, Simon got in the shower to start his day. It was going to be a long one, he could feel it.

"No it's not." a small voice in his head said, "Today is going to be the best day of your life. Today is the beginning of everything. After today the world will know who you are and cower before you in fear. Today you and I become partners, partners in your own secret sin. Partners in murder."

Chapter 13

Roman was satisfied that the first contact with his chosen human had gone well. He'd expected to have to calm Simon after he introduced the idea of murder to him, but was more than happy when it was accepted with the thrill of anticipation and excitement. In fact, he had left Simon alone in the shower, whacking off with more enthusiasm than ever before, as the idea took root and began to grow.

Yes, Roman was more than satisfied with the choice he had made. This little runt of a human was going to more than make up for his lack of size by becoming huge with his foul acts of killing.

Roman spent the few minutes until it was time for Simon to leave for work, slinking around Simon's home. Today Simon would not be traveling alone. Today he was going to be joined by the little voice in his head. The voice that told him to choose a weapon and bring it with him in his briefcase. The voice that stroked his ego, telling him how good it would feel to have another's life in his hands, another's blood to bathe in. The voice that wormed its way into his mind and would not leave him until his body was dead.

Roman liked the black place he now occupied in Simon's mind. It was dark and held so much cruelty and evil, just waiting to be unleashed, that Roman almost felt like he was on a vacation. This was not going to be work as much as it was going to be fun.

Roman dug his nails in deep, firmly planting himself in the mind of his killer. A killer of his own making. With each act of violence committed, Simon would be remade into the Dark's image. An image that would be visible only to those already in the Dark, and a few humans with the power to see into a person's soul.

Roman wiped the dark drool from his lips and his eyes glowed red as he thought of these special mortals that had put a stop to his plans in the past before they had been fully recognized. Fully completed. This time he would be more careful and show his subject how to hide what he did not want seen and to be craftier while perfecting his trade. This time he would go after those who would expose him and add their lives to the list of his victims.

There was only one obstacle that stood in Romans path, and he had a plan to take care of that on his own. This time when their paths crossed, Roman would not be playing a game. This time Roman planned on putting an end to the foe he called Saul. A very painful and very permanent end.

axon stood across the counter, arms crossed and legs planted firmly apart, giving Hannah time to digest his statement of being in her shop for the sole purpose of saving her life. He could read by the paleness of her face that she might have an idea of what he was talking about. He doubted she knew who sent him and, at this time, he had no intention of enlightening her as to the identity of his, for lack of a better explanation, partner.

As the minutes ticked by Jaxon became impatient. When he couldn't stand there doing nothing anymore, he moved to the door, flipped the open sign over and, with finality, clicked the lock on the door. Whether Ms. Priest liked it or not, she was closed for the day. They had things to talk about, plans to make, and he had orders he wanted followed to the letter.

He wanted to know who this Regina was. Even though she didn't seem to be a threat, he wanted to do a rundown on her. It would help to know if she had any skeletons in her closet that the killer could use against her to influence her to help him get to Hannah.

"Do you have a back door?" Jaxon asked when enough time had been wasted.

"What?" Hannah asked, coming back to the present at the sound of his voice. "Back door?" she repeated.

"We need to lock the back door," Jaxon told her. "Now."

"My employee, Regina, will need to get in," Hannah said, putting a hand to her forehead. "We can't just lock the door without telling her why. And what gives you the right to tell me I am closing anyway? I have a business to run and can't just close the doors for the day because you said so," she countered, even though she had planned on doing just that when he left.

'Well, well, well,' Jaxon thought to himself. It would seem that this little slip of a woman had a bit of a bite to her after all. His first impression of a quiet, meek, shy person was going to be proven wrong.

He watched as roses bloomed in her cheeks and a storm built in her eyes. She could dig in her heels and bluster all she wanted he decided. He had a mission to see through, and she was just going to have to suck it up and do what she was told. He was not used to having his orders questioned, and now was not the time, and she was not the person to be the first to try.

Planting his hands flat on the counter, Jaxon bent down until his nose was level with hers and he was staring her right in the eyes. "I just told you that I was sent here to save your life and, to be able to do that, you have to do what I say, when I say it. Kapiesh? Understand?" His dark eyes took on the familiar cold, flat, blackness he showed to his enemies as he dared her to sass him. "Now, Hannah, where is the back door, because I am going to lock it right now."

"You seem to know my name, but have failed to introduce yourself. Who are you?" Hannah demanded, not giving an inch to this man trying to tell her what to do. This was her shop and, no matter how his words chilled her, she was not going to give her life over to someone she didn't know from Adam. *'Really!'* she thought, *'Did people actually do what he said, just because he said so?'*

"Forgive my manners," Jaxon said, the sneer on his lips betraying the fact that he could not care less if she forgave him or not. "My name is Jaxon Riley and, as I said a couple of times before, I am here to keep you from getting killed."

"Well, Mr. Riley, why would anyone be interested in killing me? I am no one special. I think you have been given some bad information. So if you don't mind, please show yourself out." Hannah pulled herself up to her full five feet six inches and raised her chin into the air. She would show him that she was not going to fall in line with his plans just because he came into her store and tried to be all bad and commanding.

"It's just Jaxon," he replied seeing her get her back up and try to stand up to him. "And you are lying to me about not being special. I told you that I know all about you, and it is because of your "special talents" that your life is in jeopardy. So you will have me in your life, whether you like it or not, until the threat to you is over."

"No one died and left you in charge of me!" Hannah shot back, fighting with everything she had not to believe him. "I can take care of myself. And if I need help, there is always 911. I don't need you, nor do I want you. So just march your happy little ass out of my store before I find out how long it would take before the police get here to help you leave." Hannah's chest was heaving with her emotions by the time she was finished and her fists were clenched at her sides.

'Oh my god!' she thought, *'I do not need a body guard. And if I did, it certainly would not be an over-bearing, full of himself, it's my way or the highway, boob.'*

Hannah still panted as she let her eyes roam up and down the six foot five inch man standing still before her. Her eyes gave her thoughts away, as they shot fire and smoked with indignant, impotent rage.

Jaxon stood quiet and still, letting her fuss and fume at him, knowing that all her posturing would be for her benefit alone. He was not budging. He was willing to let her get her anger out. After all, he would be pissed too if some stranger came into his life and dropped a bombshell on him as he had her. But it still didn't change the fact that without him she would end up dead. And according to Saul, this was unacceptable.

"Hannah," Jaxon began, but was interrupted when the curtain to the back parted and Regina came marching in. She looked like a mother hen coming to the rescue of her chick, as she made straight for Jaxon, veering off just in time to miss the counter as she came to stand beside Hannah.

"Is there a problem, Miss Hannah?" she asked, though her expression told them she knew she had walked in on a situation.

"Jaxon Riley," Jaxon said, sticking his hand out for Regina to shake, even though she looked at it like it was something offensive to her.

"Regina Jensen," she finally said, taking the hand offered and making sure she squeezed it as hard as she could.

Jaxon let a twinkle enter his eyes for just a second, as he recognized the squeeze she had given his hand as a warning that she was here to protect Hannah from him.

"Nice to meet you, Regina," Jaxon said, as he finally let her hand go. "You must be Hannah's sister."

Regina blushed and brought a hand up to smooth her short white hair as she fell under the spell of Jaxon's black Irish charm and handsome good looks. Those dark eyes of his had her remembering what it was like to have a good looking man begging for her attention.

"You're a handsome one, aren't you?" she asked, not expecting an answer. "And you have a silver tongue too. But that still doesn't explain what is going on here. I won't have you or anyone else coming in and giving Hannah a hard time. What is your business here?" she snapped.

Jaxon let his instincts rule his decision as he felt in his gut that there was no threat in the form of Regina Jensen. He could use an ally. He was not above taking help when and where it was offered.

"Do you want to tell her or should I?" Jaxon asked Hannah, giving her a chance to spin the story anyway she liked for Regina.

"Actually, Regina, there is nothing going on here, and Mr. Riley was just leaving," Hannah said, thinking she had a way of getting rid of this man. She was sure he would not want to make a scene with a witness. After all, his story was one very few people would believe. He didn't know that Regina knew all about the "gift" Hannah possessed and she was not going to enlighten him.

"Actually, Regina, I am not going anywhere until Hannah and I talk." Switching his gaze from Hannah's face to Regina's, he dropped the twinkle from his eye and, once again, a cold frost seeped into the dark orbs. "Someone is out to kill Hannah and it is my job to stop him and keep her alive."

Jaxon leapt into action as, with a small squeak, Regina effortlessly headed towards the floor.

Chapter 15

Hannah spent the better part of the next hour watching as Jaxon fussed over Regina and Regina flirted shamelessly with the dark stranger. She had tried to help but got her hands batted away for her efforts.

It took another half hour for Jaxon to reassure the older woman that he was going to protect Hannah and, without giving details, managed to escort her to the back door. He finally got her outside, leaving the poor woman starry eyed and in a twitter as he shut and locked the door.

Jaxon came back into the shop and again stood in front of the counter, as Hannah puttered behind it, trying to ignore him.

"I'm not going away, so you might as well take me up to your place and let me check it out. Then we can sit down and talk this out." Jaxon said, looking sternly at Hannah, knowing she was still thinking of ways to fight him at every turn.

At her raised eyebrow and pursed lips, Jaxon just smiled brightly and let his eyes dance with amusement. *'She has no idea who she was dealing with.'*

Giving in, Hannah put the money away in the safe and turned off the lights. Both doors were already locked, she thought with a pout. Finally doing as Jaxon asked, she led the way up the stairs and opened the door to her apartment. It felt strange having a man follow her into her home, as she had never invited one in before.

Jaxon put his hands on slender shoulders and, without much effort, moved Hannah out of the way. He went from room to room, checking to see that windows were locked. He looked outside to see which ones could be accessed if someone wanted to get inside. He checked for trap doors leading to the roof and, in the closets for hidden doors that could allow the occupants to get out without using the front door. He checked everything. He did not rush. He made no mistakes.

By the time he completed his inspection, he had a firm plan of what needed to be done to make the house a safe zone.

"Sit down," Jaxon said, moving past Hannah to plant himself on her couch. *'A little frilly for my taste,'* he thought, as he looked at the pastel flowers that graced the throw pillows. The least of his problems.

"I'm not getting rid of you, am I?" Hannah asked, dropping down in a chair across from Jaxon. "Is there nothing I can say to make you leave me alone?"

"No, nothing," Jaxon confirmed, leaning back against the couch, stretching out his legs to their full length, looking to anyone like he was planning a nice long sit down.

"Even if I were to tell you what I see when I look at you?" Hannah asked. She was trying to scare him into freaking out and leaving. It had happened before without her even meaning it to. People tended to be scared of her and her abilities when they became aware of them. Most left with their tails on fire and dust rising from the tracks they made as they exited.

"Don't." Jaxon said, low and gruff. He sat up and his posture was no longer relaxed and casual. "I know what you're able to do. If you think you can intimidate me into backing out, then you had better think again." Jaxon had read Hannah's intentions correctly, and smiled without humor as her face pinkened and fell.

"Look," he said, scooting to the edge of the couch, "I took this job, if you want to call it that, because I was asked to and because I was the best for the job. I never fail. I am sorry that I have been forced on you. I cannot say I would react differently if the tables were turned. But until the person who is a threat to you is caught or killed, you are stuck with me and me with you. So how about if we just put the bullshit aside for a few minutes and discuss what needs to be done?" He paused for a moment, looking at her with one eyebrow raised before continuing. "First, I'm going to make sure you are safe for the night before I leave. Come tomorrow I will be camping in that spare bedroom you have down the hall. And I will be there, under your feet, wherever you go, until this situation is resolved to my satisfaction."

"Speaking of bullshit!" Hannah started out, angry all over again. "I did not hire you, nor did I ask you to be a guest in my house. You are not staying here!" she said with finality in her voice. One look at Jaxon's face made her grind her teeth and flare her nostrils, as she could tell her words had fallen on deaf ears.

"I don't remember asking if I could stay here" he said, his calm tone in direct contrast to his knotted jaw and burning eyes. He wanted to beat his head, or hers, against the nearest wall in frustration. *'How could someone not want help in staying alive?'* he wondered. He laced his fingers together between his spread knees, trying to keep from placing them around her throat and shaking her until she saw reason.

"Look," he tried one more time to get through to her, "I did not go looking for this job. But once I said I would accept it, there is no turning back for me."

Hannah tried thinking of all the reasons for Jaxon to be on his merry way, but one long look at his face left her with little doubt that she might as well be talking to a wall, for all the good it would do her. *'Should she play along?'* she wondered. After all he did say he was leaving for the night. That would give her a chance to decide what to do—stay or take off for a few days until her self-proclaimed protector got tired of waiting for her and moved on to his next damsel in distress.

"Say what you have to say," she finally told him. "I will listen to your plans and then I will decide if they are worth considering."

Jaxon drew in a long slow breath and counted to ten. He knew what she was thinking, and he needed to calm down before speaking or he just might say something he would regret. Reaching ten, he opened his mouth to calmly lay out his strategy, but one look at her tight mouth and cocked eyebrow had him snapping his lips shut and deciding ten was not nearly enough. One hundred was more to his liking, so he set his sights on that goal and slowly started counting.

Chapter 16

Jaxon pulled up in front of his apartment well after the sun had sank behind the Rocky Mountains in the west. He was bone tired and wired up all at the same time.

He turned off the motor and sat behind the wheel trying to breathe himself into calmness. But it did not seem to be working. With each breath he recalled a part of the long day he had endured with his "assignment," Hannah Priest. For being so young Hannah was as stubborn as they came. She fought Jaxon at every turn and it took him all day to wear her down.

Jaxon wished he could instill in her the urgency he felt and the need to take every precaution to keep her safe. But even after spending all day with her and going over and over details, he was still not convinced she would comply with his orders. Stay inside unless he was with her, keep away from windows, don't answer the door, don't answer the phone, keep the store closed until he was with her, and stop fighting him at every turn. *'Damn that woman,'* he thought, *'why was she being so hard headed?'*

With a deep sigh Jaxon got out of his car. The heat hit him like a punch in the gut, suckling the air out of his lungs and burning his skin, leeching out all moisture in what felt like seconds, until his mouth was dry and he felt like an autumn leaf, dried up and ready to crack.

Wanting to get inside, Jaxon wasted no time in climbing the stairs to his front door, unlocking it, and going inside. The air inside was cooler than outside, but he had not turned on the air before he left so he had very little relief. Crossing the living room, Jaxon cranked on the ancient air conditioner, that he was sure had been one of the first ever made. He stood in front of the unit, enjoying the cold puffs of air it hiccupped out on his heated skin.

He stayed where he was for a full five minutes, resting his hands against the wall, letting his head droop, turning his mind off and closing his eyes. He was content to have just a few minutes to himself, to take a breath and set his problems aside.

A few minutes was all he got before he felt a tingling between his shoulders. Going from relaxed to full alert in the blink of an eye, he spun around, fists clenched, teeth bared, eyes cold, ready to show the intruder the error of his ways in breaking into his apartment. After the day he had just had, his feelings of frustrations were about to be unleashed, and he looked forward to it. He was feeling mean.

But once again he had to pack his frustrations away as the intruder turned out to be none other than Saul.

The Guardian stood motionless and quiet across the room, letting his warrior unwind his taut muscles and beat down the urge to fight, until his hands unclenched and fell to his sides. Only then did Saul move closer and, taking a seat, motioned for Jaxon to do the same.

"I've come to see how your day went," Saul said, his voice low and soothing. "I have kept my promise to you and not entered your mind to see for myself what progress you have made. So I need you to tell me what happened. Then I'll answer any questions you have or offer any help that I can."

Jaxon finally did as the Guardian offered and sat down on the couch facing Saul. He stared at the robed figure until Saul finally arched a fine eyebrow and had to ask "What?"

"I think I get what you are." Jaxon began, "But if you and I are going to be in this together, you are going to have to do something about the way you look."

Jaxon could see puzzlement written all over Saul's handsome face, and he had to let a small smile tip the corners of his mouth before enlightening Saul as to his meaning.

"You need to change out of those robes and look a little more, well, normal. It is just too distracting trying to deal with you the way you are now. I assume you can change your clothes, right?" Jaxon asked.

"Well, yes," Saul said, surprised at the request put to him. "I have never been asked to do this before. I find it interesting that my appearance should bother you."

"I didn't say it bothered me." Jaxon countered. "I said it distracted me."

"What would you have me, um, change into?" Saul asked, turning the tables and making Jaxon choose a look he would be comfortable with.

"How the hell should I know?" Jaxon shot back. "Can't it be something more . . . ?"

"Human?" Saul supplied.

"Works for me," Jaxon said, waiting to see what Saul would come up with.

Saul shrugged his shoulders and rose to his feet. "I think this is a strange request, but one I will comply with if it will make dealing with me easier for you."

Jaxon did not rise to the bait, swallowing the denial that he could not handle something out of the ordinary. His life was one big out of the ordinary, as far as he could tell. He relaxed back and waited for the outcome, enjoying being the one in control for the moment.

Saul closed his eyes and the light he emitted all but blinded Jaxon, until he had to close his eyes to its brightness.

When he could not see the unusual brightness through his eye lids, Jaxon cracked his eyes open. Being satisfied it was safe, he opened them fully to see the new Saul.

"Not bad," Jaxon replied, nodding his head at the choice the Guardian had made. Where before had stood the white-robed figure, now stood what looked like a man in blue jeans and a deep red polo shirt. The Immortal's strength showed in the muscled arms that stretched the sleeves tight, the wide chest that left no room to spare in the shirt, and in the jeans that bagged nowhere. The face still held the same sinfully beautiful appearance, and the black hair still hung down his back, falling between the great wings that grew from his shoulders blades.

"Is this better?" Saul asked Jaxon, never having done this before, he was anxious for the humans approval. Not needing it, but wanting it anyway.

"Works for me," Jaxon said, again nodding his head and putting the matter behind them.

"Good," Saul said, once again taking a seat. "No more distractions. Tell me how your first meeting went with the human, Hannah."

"We've got work to do," Jaxon said, settling himself on the couch. This was going to take awhile.

Chapter 17

Hannah waited until Jaxon finally got up and left to go home before she would allow herself the luxury of falling apart. She walked on watery legs to the door and locked it, as he had instructed her to do. Not because he had told her to, but because she always locked the door and tonight she definitely wanted privacy.

She made it into the bathroom before her stomach rebelled at the tension she had harbored all day, and its meager contents came out with impressive force. She really hated throwing up and, once again, confirmed the fact that it was not on her top ten things to do list.

When her legs would hold her again, she made her way to the sink and brushed her teeth, trying to rid herself not only of the sour taste in her mouth but of the taste left behind from her day with Jaxon Riley. That taste was of defiance, rebellion, denial and white hot fear.

She knew that her gift made her a target of evil men, just as it had made a target of her friend and mentor Christine. If only Christine had had a protector like Jaxon, then maybe she would be alive today instead of dead, having died by the hands of the same evil that was now tracking her.

Having Jaxon come to her and tell her she was to be protected had made her feel guilty that she was to be spared instead of her friend. She had wanted to yell at him that he was too late! Why her and not Christine? Was she more special than her mentor? She had wanted to beat her fists against that rock hard chest of his and make him apologize for being too late in his protection of the innocent.

But she had not. It had made her acceptance of his help almost impossible to stomach. She had dug in her heels and made every attempt he had made to help her like pulling teeth. Not that she did not see the truth in his attempts, in the need to do as he said to be safe, but her guilt at being alive rose up, making her almost want to be left alone, unprotected. To let what ever was to happen, just happen.

She had stopped helping the authorities and had turned her back on that life. So why now would someone want her out of the picture? It made no sense to her.

And why, when she had looked at Jaxon, trying to see his true self, did she only see a bright light outlining his body? No slight shifting in the bones and skin, not warts or open sores. Nothing at all.

He had told her a little of his background when she had asked him what made him think he had what it took to stand between her and harm. She should have been able to see his past deeds. But she could not. The deaths he had caused and felt no remorse for should have made him almost unbearable to see. But instead she had only seen the bright light around him.

She had been standing with her sudsy toothbrush forgotten in her hand while the water ran down the drain, while she tried to figure out the puzzle that was Jaxon Riley. She got nowhere.

She finally rinsed her brush and swished the bubbles out of her mouth before turning off the water, leaving silence as her only companion. She dried her face, hung up the towel, and finally turned to meet her eyes in the mirror. The deep, rich blood-red of them never failing to make her want to turn her face and hide from her defect, as she thought of it.

She should have been used to it by now, but she was not. In fact, she wondered if she would ever get used to the eyes that made her different, or as her parents had said many times, "special". She did not want to be special. She just wanted to be normal, be accepted, have friends, and have a man look at her the way the men on TV looked at the ones they loved.

The pain that washed through her each time she witnessed these looks rocked her to her soul. Always leaving her with the knowledge that she would never be looked at or loved that way. The hurt left her isolated and broken, with no one to help pick up the pieces and heal her. Just herself. Always just herself.

Even buying the pretty brown contacts had not helped, because people did not forget. It seemed with long memories came the need to point out others failings, instead of having the spotlight shine on their own. If they made her the focal point of their scorn and laughter, then they were safe from the same treatment.

'*Water under the bridge,*' she told her twin in the mirror. '*Stop feeling sorry for yourself and figure out what you are going to do.*'

Hannah turned her back on the mirror, turning off the light as she left the bathroom. She did not see the deeper black of a shadow in the far corner. Nor did she see the two glowing red eyes that, so unlike hers, were bright red like a lava flow staring out at her. She did not hear the wet chuckle that the shadow gurgled out, or the whisper of triumph that seeped into the tone, as with glee, a Dark minion had done as it was ordered.

Before it left to carry its news to others, it could not resist gloating to itself. *'How good am I?'* it thought. Out loud it left a warning of what was to come, if there had been anyone to hear it. "I found you!" it hissed. "I found you."

Chapter 18

Simon parked his car in his reserved spot and turned the motor off. He sat with his hands gripping the wheel, thinking about what he had in his briefcase. Before he'd left his house he'd gotten a terrible urge to choose a wickedly sharp knife from his kitchen and bring it with him.

He had hidden the weapon under some paper work in the briefcase. As he drove to The Underworld his eyes kept shifting to the case, his fingers itching to open it and take out his secret, hold it in his hands and imagine what it would feel like to use it. He was consumed with it.

Since the moment in the shower this morning, the instant when the idea of what he could do with it, wanted to do with it, it seemed to be all he could think of. As he sat there in a trance the same voice that had been talking to him since this morning came to his rescue.

"Get out of the car and go to work," it instructed. "You must not let others know what you are thinking. What you are planning."

"I don't know what I am planning," Simon confessed. "I don't know what I am thinking."

"I will tell you what to think," the voice commanded. "We are partners now. Let me do the thinking and you do the acting. You just have to act normal until I tell you differently. You can do this," the voice said. "You are strong, and only I know how strong and powerful you really are. Only I will share in the glory of your actions. I will never leave you."

Simon felt, as the voice said, strong, as if he could do anything. The feeling he got when the voice talked to him was one of strength and confidence. It was very good for his ego. It fed his need to be noticed, to be important. It was as if someone was finally taking notice of him, believing in him for what he could do.

"Yes," he said out loud, "I will go about my day as if nothing was different. I have a secret," he said, and giggled like a little girl to his empty car.

Grabbing his briefcase, he got out of his car and locked the doors with his remote. As he made his way into the casino, no one bothered him, no one noticed him, just like any other day. Even though he was the General Manager of The Underworld Casino, people did not see him.

He walked with a slight glaze to his eyes until he had almost reached his office. Two employees, males, were walking towards him and, on this awful day, one made the mistake of bumping into Simon, almost knocking him into the wall.

"Sorry," the tall, fair-haired man threw over his shoulder as he kept walking. He didn't even bother to look back to check on the condition of his almost accident victim. He just kept walking.

Too bad for him. Too bad that he did not pay attention where he was going. Too bad that he did not give the little man the respect he thought he deserved. Too bad that Simon Small had brought a weapon with him on this day. Too bad that today was now going to be the last he would live.

Simon burned with anger and hate for the half-assed apology that the man threw his way. He was this man's boss, after all! He had the power to fire him for what he had just done.

"No," the voice said to him, "we are not going to fire him. Not today. Today we are going to pull out our little secret and we are going to show him, show everyone, what happens when they ignore us. When they do not see us. Today we take the first step on our journey to fame," the voice said, all smooth and stroking. "Today is the day we become one and finally let the world know what we can do. Today we kill."

Chapter 19

Harvey was only a floor person. He had only been with The Underworld for a few short weeks. He had been walking with his trainer down a hall before his shift. He was paying close attention to what he was being told, when he bumped into someone. Not wanting to miss what was said, he quickly called a short, distracted "sorry" to the person, not even bothering to see who it was that had almost got mowed over.

He kept going. Going down to his section of the floor, concentrating on his new job. He liked the job. He needed the job. If he had known who it was that he had run into, he would have stopped and apologized properly. He had heard horror stories of the temper of the General Manager. He had no way of knowing today he had made a fatal mistake. Small in his way of thinking, but huge to his killer.

Harvey worked his shift. When it was time to clock out he gave a sigh of relief, thankful that he had made it through another day without making any big mistakes.

Harvey made his way out to the parking garage, making a beeline for his car, wanting nothing more than to get home and go to sleep. The long days on his feet were something he was not used to and his legs were crying out for him to get off them.

As he made his way down the row of cars, he did not see the short, little man fall in behind him. Nor did he see the shadow of the arm raised, or the tire iron being swung down on his head.

Harvey did not feel himself being dragged quickly back to the trunk of a fancy car and stuffed inside before the lid was slammed down into place. He did not feel the car start up or the motion of the vehicle as it drove up into the mountains, instead of down into the city. He barely felt the car slow down and turn onto a bumpy road. He was just coming to when the car halted and the lid of the trunk was opened. He did not have his senses back completely, so he did not put up much of a fight when his hands were duct taped together and he was yanked out to fall to the ground.

Harvey started to panic when he saw the sharp knife in the hand of a short man. He tried to fight, but being small did not hinder the strength of the man as he knocked him down. Grabbing him by the hair, the man began to pull him into the thick pine trees that stood on the side of the road.

Harvey could not help the tears of fright and pain that leaked from his eyes to fall on his cheeks, as he finally was brought to a halt and made to kneel on the fragrant piney carpet of needles. The sound of the breeze singing through the tree tops was lost to him, as he begged his captor to let him go. He asked him over and over why he was doing this.

He knew what was going to happen seconds before the first swing of the knife cut through the air and cut through his flesh. His scream was heard by no one except the one who would be his killer. And that one relished the anguish it caused, the pain it inflicted, and the life-taking power only he controlled.

Harvey's pleas for mercy and his begging for the knife to stop fell on deaf ears. The only good thing was that it did not take long for his blood to run out of his many wounds and for his pain to stop because of death. He was past the point of feeling when hands were dipped in his blood and it was smeared and rubbed all over his murderer's body. He could not be sickened any longer by the glee the one who took his life expressed over this senseless act. Or by the many more cuts his body had to endure until he was finally left in peace to lay alone under the trees with only the wind to dry his blood soaked hair and clothes, while his killer pulled an overcoat on to cover his own bloody clothes before driving away.

Harvey was past the point of feeling, but Simon was not. Simon was not and he felt good. Better than he ever had. His heart raced as he drove away, leaving his first kill to rot out in the open where it would not be discovered for many weeks.

He drove home, hyped up on his own power, as the voice in his head praised him for his deeds. It told him, "Now all will know how mighty you were. No one would ever dare to disrespect you again. Never again and live to tell about it." the voice stroked his frail ego.

And Simon wanted more.

Chapter 20

Simon entered his apartment like any other day, but all that changed the minute the door closed behind him. Tonight he carried a secret home with him.

The doorman, like always, opened the door to the building and greeted him as he walked in, but Simon kept his head down, not meeting anyone's eyes, in a hurry to be alone. The doorman did not notice anything out of the ordinary, as Simon never talked to him anyway. Always letting him know by his actions, or lack of them, that he considered himself far above the peon that opened the door for him and did not deem it necessary to acknowledge the greeting.

Simon made a beeline to the elevator and pushed the button to the top floor. He huddled in the far corner until the doors opened, allowing him to stumble to his front door. With shaking hands he opened it, falling in and slamming it at his back.

He flung the briefcase across the room and ripped the over coat from his back, letting it drop to the floor on his way to the bathroom.

Simon stopped in front of the mirror and stood staring at his reflection. He did not appear any different than he had this morning, except for the tell-tale streaks of blood that rose from his now limp shirt collar. That and the fact that his eyes were no longer limp brown pools. Instead they now appeared wild and feverish in his pale face. Simon raised his hand to touch his face, his gaze drawn to the dried blood that resided under each and every one of his finger nails. A dead give-away as to his recent activities.

Simon tore at his clothes until he stood naked, wearing only the blood of his victim that he had rubbed on his body as he had lain dying at his feet in the isolated cold mountains.

'What did I do?' Simon thought. *'I can't remember.'* It seemed like a dream to him, a TV show that had happened to someone else, surely not to him.

"It was real," the voice in his head told him. "Remember how the power flowed through you! How it felt to be in control of life and death. How you made the man pay for the disrespect he heaped on you. This will only be the first of many that you will make pay."

"Look inside yourself!" the voice commanded. "Look and see that this is what you want. What you have always wanted to happen. Payback to those who have not paid the homage to you that you deserve."

"It was good," the voice assured him. "It was right. It was why you have been put on this earth. You enjoyed it, didn't you?" the voice asked, sly knowledge in its tone. "Be truthful with yourself. Let yourself feel the glory in a job well done."

"There is no one here but you and I," the voice crooned. "Admit it now, out loud that you liked what you did. You liked taking a life and feeling the power flow through every part of you as you did. Admit it."

"Yes," Simon said out loud, staring at his reflection but not seeing it. Only hearing the voice that stroked his ego, fed his need to be important, to believe in himself and his right to avenge wrongs done to him.

The longer Simon stood listening to his voice, as he now thought of it, the calmer he became. His heart stopped pounding in his chest and his hands no longer shook with reaction. He felt good about his day and all that had happened.

Before letting himself relax, Simon retraced his steps and found his briefcase. He took it to the kitchen and gently set it on the counter. Opening the lid, he found the knife he had used only hours before laying alone on the blood stained silk lining. He could smell the metallic odor of blood spilt. He took the knife to the sink and cleaned it until no evidence was left to be found.

Simon turned the knife over and over in his hands, seeing his reflection appear many times in the mirror like finish of the blade. He marveled at how right the knife felt in his hands. He had meant to put it back in the drawer and leave it there, but he could not. He needed it with him. He laid it gently on the counter while he sponged the blood and bits of flesh from his briefcase, before wrapping it in a soft towel and once again closing it inside.

Feeling happy, Simon went back into the bathroom and climbed into the shower. And as he did every night, he took a long hot shower to wash the sweat from the day and the stink of the casino off his body, letting it swirl down the drain. But tonight it was not only sweat and stink that swirled away; tonight it was joined by the

- Diane Nielsen -

red of blood as it mixed with water, turning pink before disappearing down into the sewer.

Simon washed until the water stayed clear, before getting out and drying off. *'It was the best day of his life,'* he reasoned as he turned off the lights and lay down in his bed.

"This is only the beginning," the voice soothed and assured, as Simon slipped into a dreamless sleep. Smiling.

– 94 –

Roman rested along with his pawn. He rubbed his hands in glee as he reflected on the day's events. He really didn't have to do much persuading to get this pathetic human soul to do his bidding. To create the chaos that would be the beginning of fear and terror. He could see the future as he wanted it to be, with humans looking over their shoulders in fear of being the next victim of the newest face of terror, Simon Small.

His biggest challenge, as far as Roman could tell, was going to be to keep this one's urges in check. He could not let him run wild and be discovered before his mission was completed.

As Roman explored the twists and turns of his human, he found the hunger for revenge and power to be deeply rooted. He wondered if even he would be able to control what he had unleashed. Yes, he wanted what this human could deliver, but he had to keep him on a short leash or else he would run amuck and Saul would be alerted before he was ready for his plan to be discovered.

Keeping the Guardians in the dark for now was a way to poke at his equal from the light, to one up the great Saul, and to prove that the human soul was easily swayed to do the Dark's bidding.

Roman left the sleeping Simon to hit the streets, moving from shadow to shadow, watching the humans as they went about their boring lives. He loved creeping around in the shadows, dipping his fingers into unsuspecting minds, digging through the trash until he found something he could exploit.

With a small nudge he could start a fight between soul mates, making them say and do things that would rip their relationship apart. He could have life-long friends at each others throats, spewing pent up feelings at small irritations, until forgiveness was impossible. Small things really, but enough that it kept the Guardians running here and there trying to repair the damage, trying to keep the mortals feet on the path of their destiny.

Roman spent the night drifting down streets, sneaking into bedrooms and, just for fun, popping into the mind of the supposedly most powerful man on earth. Planting seeds of imagined greatness and a puffed up sense of self worth in the mind of the President was so much fun he almost could not stand it. He laughed uproariously as he started the ball rolling to make this mortal one of the most hated men on earth. Letting it be seen by the public how he thought of no one but himself, and how he did not care if he brought the great country of America to its knees as long as he thought himself great.

'*Let the Guardians try to fix that,*' Roman thought laughing.

As the sun began to peep over the horizon Roman headed back to Simon and, once again, dug in deep to enjoy the day with this mortal.

Simon had gotten a taste of power, ultimate power, the day before and he had more than liked it. He had bathed in its glory. Roman knew that he was going to have to take the reins and hold on tight or things were going to blow up in his face. Getting out of control was something Roman was not going to let Simon try out.

This was his plan, his game, and Roman had every intention of being the one in the driver's seat.

"Wake up," Roman tickled at Simon's brain. "Wake up and do my bidding!" he shouted, not letting Simon swim up from the depths of sleep. Instead he had him vaulting from his bed, as if a hot poker had been applied to his backside.

"It's time to get moving," the voice once again spoke to Simon. "Let's go see if Harvey still keeps our secret," it said, laughing at its own joke.

Chapter 22

It took Jaxon hours to tell Saul all that had taken place during the day. He went over the security measures he was going to have to take to protect Hannah, even if she did not want protection. He let his frustration pour out, pacing his small living room as he vented, until he had purged himself of wanting to get his hands around the neck of the stubborn one he kept referring to as "that woman".

Saul sat quietly until Jaxon had run himself down. He listened until he could sense that all that was left inside his champion was the bare facts, no emotions. Until all that was left was the cold need to do what had to be done to complete his task.

Saul did not let on that he also detected the small spark of attraction for Hannah that Jaxon would die before admitting to. Jaxon's grudging respect for the tough outer shell that she projected, even though he could see in those unusual eyes, the fear and denial that wanted to take over until she cowered and clung to him in weakness, had gotten under his skin.

The need to protect and take care of Hannah was going to give Jaxon many sleepless nights as his feelings grew and were denied. Saul almost smiled as he could tell, without using his powers, that these two humans were going to set off some serious fireworks with their clashes until feelings erupted and were acted upon. He almost envied them this future, until he remembered what the outcome would be if Jaxon failed.

"It sounds to me like your plan for this mission is in place. You have good ideas that just need to be implemented. What do you need from me?" the Guardian asked, spreading his hands wide in question.

"Can't you do something to make Hannah be receptive to the idea of my protection?" Jaxon ground out. "You know, get in her head, and bomb the hell out of her stubbornness until she sees reason."

At the look of returned frustration on Jaxon's face, Saul laughed and was rewarded with daggers being sent his way from black eyes. *'Humans were such large sources of amusement,'* he thought. *'Their natures were so volatile and their emotions were a constant roller coaster ride that he never tired of.'*

"No," Saul said, as he reined in his laughter. "Hannah needs to figure this out and come to terms with her situation for herself. Should I interfere, she would feel unsettled and sense deep down that something was not right. Her will is strong and would not bow down to being manipulated easily. This is one of the reasons saving her is so important. Her strength and her convictions will not let her be influenced or turned from the path set before her. The Dark has many plans that Hannah could and will put in jeopardy in her lifetime. She will unknowingly, to her, be a force for good."

"Fine!" Jaxon ground out, running his hand through his rich, long hair. "Fine. I will just have to keep at her until she sees the light. It's either that or chain her to her bed until someone makes a move. Can you tell me how long this will be?' he asked, hoping to see a light at the end of the tunnel.

"When what will be?" Saul asked.

"When the Dark will try something," Jaxon replied.

"No," Saul repeated. "I cannot tell what the Dark will do. I only know that they will come for her and you MUST stop them."

Jaxon huffed out a breath and finally relaxed into the couch. His couch he thought. "I'm going to miss this couch," he muttered under his breath, not meaning for the Guardian to hear.

"Why?" Saul questioned, having heard anyway.

"As of tomorrow I will be staying with Hannah until this situation is settled," he informed his partner. "I did not think to tell you, but I guess I should have."

"No need, really," Saul said, with a slight shrug of his shoulders. "I can find you anytime I need you or anytime you need me, but thanks for the information."

At the slight nod of the humans head, Saul stood up and prepared to leave. "Is there anything else you need from me or want to tell me?" he asked.

"As of tomorrow everything changes," Jaxon said, also standing. "Since I will be with Hannah, how will this work, you and I talking or whatever?"

"No one can see me unless I want them to," Saul said. "I do not see a need for Hannah to be made aware of my existence."

"That's great," Jaxon said. "I will just be talking to myself, as far as she is concerned and can tell. She is going to have more issues than she does now, trusting her life to someone who is crazy."

"We will find a time and place to go over problems that come up and discuss issues that need to be dealt with," Saul assured him. "Do not worry that I will reveal our connection."

"Good enough," Jaxon said, placing his trust, not something easily done for him, in the Immortal he called *Partner* now. "Just don't go far. I need to know that you will be close by when I find out who is the threat. I'll do my part, but to clear this all up, you will have to deal with your part too. You said you would handle the Dark."

"Do not worry," Saul said, his face turning stony and his eyes going to black. "I will be at your side when the end comes."

"Let's just hope it's not mine," Jaxon ground out.

Saul faded out, but not before Jaxon heard a faint echo of Saul's reply, "Nor mine!"

Chapter 23

Jaxon spent the night tossing and turning, his mind going over and over his plans, trying to see any flaws or weak links before it was too late. It was early morning before he shut down and let himself drift into blissful sleep.

His internal clock did not let him over sleep and, true to his word, he packed light and headed out the door before the smell of fresh coffee from other apartments had a chance to fade away.

He stopped and picked himself up a coffee and a breakfast sandwich to eat on the way over to Hannah's, feeling the need to fortify himself before beginning his day. He fully expected to meet with the same resistance as the day before, and braced himself mentally for having to go over the same arguments until he was satisfied Hannah was on board again.

Jaxon chewed slowly through his sandwich while he maneuvered around slow moving cars in the early morning traffic. He licked his fingers clean of the gooey cheese that had leaked out between the muffin halves and washed it down with swigs of hot coffee, loving even this simple pleasure that he no longer had to go without and could indulge whenever he wanted.

Feeling full and satisfied, he almost smiled as the cool wind tugged strands of hair from the tail he had groomed after his shower. The day was already warm, but not enough to cause the sweat to start dripping yet. Right now Jaxon was happy with his day.

The feeling lasted right up until he parked his car and turned the engine off, letting the early morning quiet almost lull him into a false sense of calm. It only took a few seconds for the reality of his situation to barge in and ruin his peace.

He parked his car in the small parking lot behind Hannah's store. Immediately his eyes began moving, taking in every detail of his surroundings, his focus totally centered on protecting his charge. Satisfied that everything was in order, he squared his shoulders and grabbed the door handle to let himself out of the car. He unfolded his body from the car, reached in and grabbed his bag and swung it over his shoulder. He locked the car door and began making his way to the small back door that led to Hannah's store.

He had already pulled the key to the door out of his pocket, holding it firmly between his fingers. He fully intended to use it as a weapon should anyone come at him before he was inside. He could lay someone's face wide open before they knew what happened with this key, and he had no problems fighting dirty to stay alive. It would not be the first time, nor would it be the last.

Jaxon's powerful legs ate up the distance, until he stood before the door that separated Hannah from him. He slipped the key in and turned it without making a sound. He opened the door, walked in, and closed it, still with out alerting anyone to his presence. He climbed the short flight of stairs and again used the key to let himself into the apartment Hannah called home.

Jaxon dropped his bag onto the couch and began checking the windows, satisfying himself that all was secured. All the while, he kept his hand on the butt of the gun he carried in the back of his pants. Retracing his steps throughout the apartment to where he had left his belongings. He grabbed the bag and deposited it on the bed in the spare room before going to the kitchen to rummage through the cupboards, waiting for Hannah to finish her shower.

It took another ten minutes of listening to the water run and Hannah's voice singing along with a radio, before the water was shut off and Jaxon heard his "assignment" moving around the bathroom.

He'd made a pot of coffee and had just turned with a full cup when Hannah made an appearance. Jaxon forgot the cup in his hand as he got his first look of the day at the clean, rosy-cheeked, fresh-smelling woman, clad only in a tank top and cut off jeans shorts, standing not five feet away from him.

Her hair was combed back from her face and hung wet and heavy down her back. No tie had been used to hold it in place and no make up had been applied to the face that it would frame when it dried. With nothing to shield them from his gaze, dark red irises became the focus of almost black as they locked and did battle, each trying to win the claim of alpha.

Jaxon waited, letting the seconds tick by, recognizing the challenge that lay between them. He waited and let his eyes go flat and cool. He waited for her to break, but took no pleasure in his victory when her eyes dropped and her shoulders sagged.

The twinge of pity he felt was surprising. He let the feeling run through him for a moment before crushing it and tossing it aside. He had a job to do and a life to insure, both of which needed his full attention. Soft feelings had to be set aside and ignored.

Ignored yes, but Jaxon swallowed hard when he knew, without a doubt, that they would not be forgotten.

Chapter 24

"I was hoping you wouldn't come," Hannah said, letting a pretty little pout turn her lips down at the corners.

"You can hope all you want," Jaxon said, wanting to roll his eyes as his secret wish of not having to go through everything again seemed one second away from being shot to hell. "If I tell you I am going to do something, you can bet your life that I will do just what I said. If you remember only one thing about me, remember that." Finishing his statement, Jaxon raised the cup of coffee to his lips and walked past Hannah to go make himself comfortable in the living room.

Hannah had tossed and turned all night, going over everything her self-appointed protector had told her. All the orders he had given her and, without question, expected her to follow blindly. The more she thought, the more she could find no way out of the situation. Her pillow had taken more than its fair share of punches before giving up.

When morning finally dawned, Hannah had flung the light covers back and made a beeline for the shower.

The hot water helped to calm her then, before getting out, she turned the cold water on full blast to get her going for the day.

The first thing that hit her when she'd opened the door after getting dressed was the smell of fresh coffee. Her heart jumped and her mouth went dry, her fear freezing her where she stood. On silent feet, Hannah made her way to the doorway of her kitchen and, with stealth, peered around the jam.

For the second time in a matter of minutes her heart jumped and beat a fast tattoo in her chest. Only this time it was not from fear. This time it was Jaxon that had Hannah on edge. During her long night Hannah had to finally admit to herself, in the darkness of her bedroom, that it was not only what Jaxon had told her that had made her dig in her heals. It was the strangeness of the sensations that started bombarding her the minute he had walked into her shop.

She had never gotten involved with boys in school, nor with the men who had approached her afterward.

It was too hard to try and explain her gifts, and it was too hard watching the horror enter eyes that only moments before had burned hot for her. It was so much easier, and hurt so much less, to be by herself, leaving no room for rejection.

All her feelings of self protection seemed to disappear the moment she laid eyes on the tall, dark stranger entering her shop.

She was shocked at the tingling in her body, the humming in her lips, and she wanted to bury herself in his arms and draw his mouth down to hers, locking them together in a first kiss.

She had made her way over to the counter thinking that up close she would be able to find flaws in what, from across the shop, had appeared as male perfection. But the closer she got, the better he looked.

She was surprised and nervous at her wanting this man, but was all prepared to jump right in and try her hand at flirting. That is until he told her why he was there. Then her world had turned upside down, the foundation of security she had so carefully built crumbling around her.

Now seeing him in her apartment, feeling funny how it had never seemed small to her until now, left her not knowing what to do. It was obvious she was not going to get rid of him any time soon. So what should she do?

Maybe she should just go about her business as if he was not there. *'Yeah, fat chance of that happening.'* she thought. Her eyes seemed to want to follow him wherever he went, and the smell of him was burned into her brain. She had never noticed how people smelled, unless they had worn perfume or cologne. Then why did he smell so good to her? Like something dark and rich that her tongue craved and her body needed to survive.

She did not want to believe that he would only be in her life until the danger to her was eliminated. She wanted him. She wanted him now, and she wanted him in her future. And these feelings scared the holy hell right out of her.

Doing the only thing she could think of, she put distance between them, fleeing to her bedroom and slamming the door.

The door to her room was easy to close. The door to her emotions resisted her efforts to do the same. No matter how she wished it, the lock she had placed on her heart lay forever broken, leaving her vulnerable. Vulnerable and scared.

Chapter 25

Saul grinned to himself as he watched Hannah run like a scared rabbit, hiding from herself and Jaxon in her room. It had taken a very small nudge on his part to make the attraction take root and grow in Hannah's mind and heart.

Saul had told Jaxon that he could not force Hannah into accepting his help, and he had not lied. She would have resisted his intentions at every turn, and his work as her protector would have been frustrating to say the least.

So the only thing Saul could do that would help was to dig up the feelings she had begun to feel, before Jaxon had revealed his mission to her, and let her focus on them instead of the danger she was in.

He had lied though to Jaxon when he told him he would stay out of his head unless he was called on for help. He needed to be kept in the loop of what was happening. So he would be checking in on a regular basis until the identity of the killer was revealed.

Checking in was how he became aware of Jaxon's buried attraction for Hannah. Jaxon had thought he had found a dark hole to shove his feelings into, but Saul would not let that happen. He wanted the deeper connection between the two to take some of the edge off, and to make their time together pass more quickly.

Having feelings for Jaxon would make Hannah more receptive to what needed to be done to keep her alive. Her life, so far, had been lonely and isolation was how she had dealt with the rest of the human race that could not or would not accept her. But Saul wanted to give her joy, to let her feel the pleasure of loving another. To fill her heart and mind with memories that could be carried with her always.

She deserved this small favor that he could give her, and Saul was happy to be of service. All too soon her life would be filled with danger and uncertainty. But for now Saul was going to give her this gift. The gift of love.

Saul stood beside Hannah's bed where she had sat after closing her bedroom door, thinking herself safe from intruders. Her chin rested in her hands and she rocked back and forth slightly as she tried to process her new feelings.

Reaching out his hand, Saul let it rest on the top of her head before trailing it down her back, letting himself feel the softness of her hair. That same hand took on a warm glow as he took into himself her feelings of fear for her safety and her future, until they became his. Until he wanted to cry out with her pain that was now his.

"Do not be afraid," Saul whispered into her mind. "Reach out with both hands and grab all the happiness you can. Life is short and someone as special as Jaxon comes along once in a life time. Do not waste a moment of your time together. Love and be loved," he encouraged. "Start living your life today. Don't wait for tomorrow, and don't give yourself a reason to look back with regret."

"Get up, Hannah," the Guardian said. "Go out and meet your future. It's sitting in your living room."

Saul waited until Hannah rose from her bed, squared her shoulders, and grasped the door knob, before fading away. He had given all the help he could for now. He would not go far, but he had other duties to attend to. So for now he left his two charges to get on as best they could. He crossed his fingers and sent up a prayer for their success.

Success and life.

Chapter 26

Roman stayed with his human killing machine, helping him to choose his victims, watching as the deeds were done, and praising him for his prowess and skills.

He watched as Simon killed a woman that, after rejecting his advances, was taught a lesson in turning up her nose when love was offered. She was not so pretty when Simon had finished with her. Finished with her and dumped her lifeless body again in the cold mountains to feed the wild animals and lay alone until discovered.

He watched as Simon picked a beautiful blonde woman, Julie by name, not even caring if she agreed to go out with him or not. Secretly hoping that she would say no so he could again experience the power that came with murdering.

As expected, she denied the small man's advances, and Roman cheered as Simon cut her to ribbons and removed her heart, a final insult to her to prove his point that she had no heart. He did not know that her heart was what Roman had been after in the first place. She was good and kind and would have been a safe refuge for those left with no hope for their futures. Julie would have been a turning point for lost and troubled souls. Roman wanted her gone and used Simon to insure this desire.

Simon tired of picking on people who he believed had slighted him. So he expanded his scope of hunting until he found two young men, boys really, that he plied with money and the promise of more, if they would run errands for him. His only expectation of them was that they keep his identity to themselves. They had, until Simon had tired of their boot licking and had murdered one, leaving the other to shoulder the blame.

Laughing to himself, as no matter what he did he was not caught. He felt larger than life, and more powerful than a God.

Roman pulled on the reins to slow down the carnage. He did not want anything to go wrong before he had a chance to discover the identity of the one he was really after. The one who would prove to be a huge threat to his current and future plans for chaos. He was not sure if it was a man or a woman, but he needed time to find out, and could not have his pawn unmasked before that time.

Roman had put his minions on alert, giving them orders to search the earth. They were to seek out this special person and report to him right away when they found him or her. There had been many false alarms. With each prospect, Roman was filled with wild glee, only to have his hopes dashed when the ordinary humans proved not to be the one he sought.

The disappointments left him filled with anger that needed an outlet. He found one by turning his wrath against the incompetent dark soul that had the misfortune of bringing the wrong information to his attention. Wasting his time. Those dark souls were punished in the most painful ways Roman could think of, screaming in tortured agony until their master ended their pain by ending their existence.

Each failure did nothing to dampen Roman's need. Instead they fed his hunger to be successful in finding his target. The frustration and disappointment consumed Roman, until he thought of little else except his need to pluck out and destroy this thorn in his side.

He swam around Simon's mind, biding his time until the next report was brought to him. And the one after that, and the one after that. It was little comfort that he had an endless amount of time to accomplish this task. He wanted instant gratification and patience was never one of his strong points.

With each passing day Roman's rage grew, and with it his plans for ending the human life in the most foul way possible. He wanted to hear this human scream until its fragile mind broke under the pain and horror of what the Dark Being had in store for it.

Roman wondered if Saul was the reason for his failure in finding one measly human. Maybe he was hiding the human. Maybe he was protecting this "pet" from the Dark's eyes. *'No matter really,'* Roman reasoned, *'he was going to be successful in the end.'* He had no doubt of this and, as an added bonus, he just might be able to finally get to do battle with Saul. The way he was feeling now, he had no problem visualizing his victory over the Guardian. He could even hear the roar that would go up from his hoards of Dark souls as his enemy lay dead at his feet.

Roman's victory would make all who encountered him cower in fear at his power. He wanted this power, so he spent his time guiding Simon. But always, always he was thinking of ways to get what he wanted. And what he wanted was more. More power and more death.

Roman's eyes burned hot as he smiled with the dank hole he called a mouth, because he knew he always got what he wanted! One way or another!

Chapter 27

Jaxon cooled his heels, drinking coffee and wandering through Hannah's small apartment. He did not know why she had escaped into her room. *'Nothing was said to make her angry,'* he reasoned. *'And nothing was in the apartment to scare her. So what gives?'* he mused.

The only answer he could come up with was that she was a woman. That certainly answered it all, as every man in the world could tell you. Females were a puzzle that no one of the male gender could figure out.

Jaxon shook the questions from his head, not liking the distraction that Hannah seemed to create in his mind without even trying to. He needed to be sharp and alert, not distracted and soft.

Putting the now empty cup into the sink after rinsing it, Jaxon made another round of the windows, pulling down shades and checking locks before feeling satisfied that all was secured to his liking.

He had just picked up the remote for the TV set, meaning to listen to the news until Hannah made another appearance, when the door down the hall opened and he steeled himself for another round of antagonism.

He was not going to give her the satisfaction of turning around until she spoke to him, but the silence stretched out until he huffed a breath out and glanced over his shoulder. What he saw in one sweeping glance had him rising to his feet and planting them wide.

Hannah had changed her clothes from tank top and shorts to a short sleeved pinkish shirt and light weight white summer pants. Blingy little flip flops let him see the pale pink toenails with each step she took, and right now they were heading towards the front door.

"You're not leaving!" Jaxon ground out, as he beat her to the front door and blocked it with his body.

"I have a business to run and I can't do it from up here, so please step aside," Hannah said, trying for a calm voice and demeanor. She was tense inside, wondering if she was going to have a fight on her hands, but her fears were unfounded. Jaxon took a few seconds to think about her request before deciding that maybe having her sort of out in the open would draw the killer out and his job would be over that much quicker.

"Okay," he said "but I will be coming with you. And you will not leave my sight without telling me where you are going and why. Understood?" he asked, not caring what her answer was going to be, as they were going to do things his way, and that was final.

Hannah's nails bit into her palms as she listened to the bossy oaf blocking her way, telling her what to do. *'Really?'* she thought. *'She would do what she wanted and to hell with her "protector".* But if it would get her out the door, she would have agreed, or appeared to agree, to almost anything.

"Fine," she said, sweetness dripping from her mouth. "Let's go." She reached around the hard body, still blocking her way, and pulled the door open. Well as far as it would go until it ran into an unmovable object, Jaxon.

Looking up to see what the hesitation was for, deep red eyes met and were held by luscious brown ones that looked deep into her soul and made her feel as if all her secrets were being laid bare.

Hannah wanted to shiver and cross her arms over her chest to keep her secrets and thoughts from being revealed. '*Stupid!*' she thought to herself '*Don't be stupid. No one could read another's mind.*

"What?" Hannah finally asked. Anything to distract Jaxon and end the scrutiny she was under. "Why are you staring at me?"

Jaxon arched a dark brow at her and finally blinked lazily, leaving his eyes half hidden with lowered lids and thick lashes. "I'm just trying to figure out what you have up your sleeve," he said. "You agreed far too easily for my peace of mind. You're up to something, or maybe you have a plan. So you might as well tell me what it is if you want to get out of this door."

Hannah wanted to rip the door open again, dreaming that it would knock Jaxon out cold. Of course she would be nice and step over him on her way out, even though she would like to step right on his fat head since he would be laying there like a good door mat.

At the picture her mind was conjuring up, humor brightened her eyes, making them dance with sparks much like the lights that shot up from a campfire on a crisp fall night.

Jaxon saw the change in those eyes and his breath was trapped in his chest. He had never seen anything so unusual and he experienced something he had believed long dead. Want. He wanted those eyes to sparkle because of him. He wanted to see those eyes burn for him until they scorched him with their heat.

In that moment Jaxon became a hundred times more dangerous to the person trying to kill Hannah, because that person now threatened something he wanted. And no one threatened what he wanted.

No one did that and lived.

Chapter 28

Hannah was surprised at how well Jaxon blended in, never making her customers suspicious or nervous. Never getting in her way, but never letting her out of his sight either.

Chrissy, her part time store clerk, was so totally under his spell that if he said he walked on water and could capture the moon, she would have sighed with longing and believed him without reservation.

Of course when he turned on the charm and smiled, Hannah was in the same boat as her helper. Her insides melted and heated up all at the same time, wanting him to smile at her and only her. When a few brave female guests tried cozying up to him, tried getting him to notice them, Hannah wanted to grab them by the hair and show them what the front door looked like from the outside.

But she did not. She was able to relax and concentrate on her work as Jaxon, time and again, turned the women away. He even accomplished this without being rude and causing trouble for her.

All and all, both Jaxon and Hannah were satisfied with the day as the final customer was checked out and the door locked behind them.

Jaxon took his time checking every window and every door, while Hannah counted the day's money. She got her deposit ready for the bank, hesitating before heading out the door to deposit it before the bank closed for the night. One look at Jaxon told her that he knew what she wanted to do and was weighing the decision, always thinking of Hannah's safety first.

"I'll get my car and pull it up to the front door. Make sure you do not come out until I wave for you to come out. Do you understand?" he asked, wanting Hannah to be perfectly clear on what was required of her.

"Why the front door?" Hannah asked, her eyebrows arched over eyes that chilled at being ordered around without even being consulted on the plan.

Jaxon paused in his checking out the traffic both on the street and the sidewalk when he picked up on the ice that edged the tone of Hannah's voice.

It had been a good day, with Hannah seeming to accept his presence. He hadn't minded spending the day listening and learning the business. When Hannah had finally stopped killing him with her eyes, Jaxon found his job much easier and his concentration much more focused.

Jaxon was not used to explaining his decisions and balked at doing it this time. Instead he took a breath and tried to see things from Hannah's point of view. He would not like to be told what to do without some kind of explanation either. So he backed up from the front window and turned to face his pain in the neck.

"You want to go to the bank, correct?" he asked. Waiting for her silent nod, he continued, "I will be driving you so the front door will be the safest exit to get you into my car. The front door has an awning covering the door, so if someone were to be in a building across the street aiming a gun at you, they would have a very small window of opportunity to get a shot off before you are safe inside. There will be traffic on the street and people walking by, so they too will give cover to your exit from the store."

"I will go out the back, get my car, and pull up to the front. I will get out and, when I think it is safe, I will escort you to the car. I will walk in front of you, shielding you until you get in the car. That is my plan. Any questions?"

The color in Hannah's face drained a little more with each word Jaxon spoke, until the only color remaining was the dark red of her scared, disbelieving eyes.

"Do you really think someone is going to be out there waiting for me to go to the bank?" she asked, doubt and disbelief heavy in her voice.

"Do you want to take the chance that they are not?" Jaxon countered. "Because if you are wrong, all you will remember is walking out the door. That's it, nothing else. You won't remember getting killed or lying on the sidewalk, or how I stood over your body and said I told you so. Nothing! Are you so anxious to have your life end that you are willing to question my every plan? I will, and can, keep you safe if you just stop fighting me at every turn."

"For God's sake, just do what I tell you and this will go a lot easier. Please," Jaxon ground out, wanting to gag on having to say the word to get what he wanted.

"Fine," Hannah spit out, no longer scared, only angry at having been talked to like she were two and had not brain one in her head. "I am not used to being told what to do and I am not used to having someone dogging my every move. How sure are you that your source is for real? Can you trust what he or she tells you is the truth about someone coming after me?" she asked, anger in her words.

"I will bet my life on this information," Jaxon said, no frills in his voice. "The thing I am not willing to gamble with, is yours. We have gone over this before, but I am telling you again. If you do not let me do what I came here for, you are going to die." Jaxon was winding up for another go around with Hannah on the finer points of his plan, when he was cut short with her next comment.

"OK!" she said, "You win! I will not ask again. I am just having a really hard time wrapping my mind around the fact someone hates me enough to want me dead."

"They don't hate you," Jaxon said, more kindly now that he was finally getting through to Hannah. "You are a threat to them. They want to eliminate that threat any way they can."

"Now let me go get the car and wait for me to tell you to come out. Stay by the front door, but away from the windows. I will only be a minute." And with that, Jaxon's long legs ate up the distance to the back door. Hannah heard the lock click into place, leaving her alone in the now quiet shop.

Hannah was afraid. Jaxon's words had made her that way. Every time he went through his speech, she was afraid. Hannah moved to the side of the shop's front door and peeked out. She would watch until Jaxon came to get her, and she would hurry to his car. '*This can't be happening*!' she thought for the thousandth time. '*This just can't be happening*.'' That was the last thing she thought before the window in front of her exploded. The only thing she could do was scream.

Chapter 29

Jaxon walked out the back door of Hannah's shop, never letting his eyes stay still. He took in everything, and he missed nothing. His eyes told him there was no one hiding, no threat to be seen. He saw nothing, but his instincts told him, warned him, that not everything was as it appeared.

He felt on edge the second he locked the door at his back. Jaxon stood for the few seconds it took to scan the back parking lot, before moving smoothly towards his car. He opened the door and slid in, jamming the key in the ignition at the same time he closed the door. He did not bother with a seat belt, as he shifted gears. He did not waste time going around the block. Instead he cruised into the alley and was just pulling onto the street when he heard the familiar sound of a shot being fired and glass exploding.

His instincts and reactions had not dulled in the few months he had been out of Special Forces. He went into defense mode, ducking low in the seat, presenting a small target. He stayed that way until he screeched to a halt on the sidewalk in front of Hannah's store, having jumped the curb.

Jaxon took one second to assess the crowd of people that were running in fear or just standing still in shock or confusion. He saw no weapon pointed at the store or himself, but he still pulled the ever present hand gun from the back of his pants before leaving the car in a low crouch.

He did not bother opening the front door, but instead lept through the missing front window. Hannah stood frozen, her mouth open, as piercing screams boiled out of her throat.

Jaxon never stopped or slowed down as he grabbed Hannah by the waist and dove behind the counter. He pushed Hannah to the floor, putting himself between her and the exposed store front.

"Are you hurt?" he barked out, his voice gruff. He did not waste time trying to sugar coat his concern. His voice was stone cold, leaving no room for emotions to taint the mission he was charged with.

"I said, are you hurt?" he asked the shaking Hannah again, demanding an answer.

"No," Hannah said, her voice shaking and muffled with her face pressed into the carpet, her hair pooling around her head.

"Stay down until I get back." And with that Jaxon moved around the counter and out of Hannah's sight.

He inched his way through the broken glass until he could see out the window. Only when he heard the approaching police sirens, did he put away his gun and rise to his full height.

Rounding the counter, he had every intention of getting Hannah and taking her upstairs, but came up short. His eyes dripped ice and his lip curled up in a sneer when he saw Hannah was not alone.

The Guardian Saul was crouched down beside Hannah, who was now sitting up, but Jaxon could not see her. Saul had unfurled his great wings and wrapped them around the shaking human, giving her his protection and comfort.

Jaxon opened his mouth to blister the Immortal. Before he could get a word out, he heard Saul's deep voice in his head.

"She cannot see me," the voice said to Jaxon. "She cannot hear me. But should you start talking to me here and now, she will wonder what the hell is going on!"

Jaxon felt like a volcano ready to explode, but had no choice as he put a lid on his emotions and swallowed his anger.

'This is not over!' he thought, guessing correctly that Saul would be able to hear his thoughts. *'I'm going to take Hannah upstairs, deal with the police, and then we are going to talk.'* His brown eyes were almost black as they locked with Saul's. He could see the anger and rage that the Guardian too was keeping in check, as streaks of lightning tore through his irises, rivaling the most violent of summer storms.

He did not care what Saul was feeling. All he cared about was keeping Hannah safe. It frosted his butt that Saul had not given a warning as to what was coming down. Surely with all his power, he should have had some warning and could have passed the information along.

'Move,' Jaxon told the Guardian without making a sound. When Saul folded his wings and stood up, Jaxon moved in to gather Hannah to him and stood up.

"I'm going to take you upstairs. Then I am going to talk to the police. I have no idea what I am going to tell them, but they will probably want to talk to you too. Be prepared." he said, as he cradled Hannah in his arms and headed to the stairs.

Hannah did not say a word, only tightened her arms around Jaxon's neck, letting him, for the moment, take control. She felt safe in his arms and she wanted out of the store. The deep beating of his heart comforted her, assuring her she was going to be alright.

Jaxon could not help himself as he felt her arms grip him in reaction. He lowered his lips to the top of her head, letting them rest there for a second, feeling relief wash through him. For the first time ever he felt his legs want to shake and his stomach want to heave at the close call they had escaped.

'Someone is going to pay for this!' he thought, shaking off the feelings he considered a sign of weakness. *'Someone is going to pay, and I'm going to be the one to collect!'*

axon wiped a tired hand across his face, hearing the rasp of the stubble. It sounded like fingernails on a chalk board inside his tired brain. It grated.

It had been a long night, starting with the shot fired at Hannah and finally ending with Jaxon boarding up the front of the store where there should have been a front window. Boarding it up from the outside, and screwing a metal grate in place from the inside. All of this only after the police had covered every square inch looking for clues, talking to all the witnesses, including himself. As far as he could tell, they had no leads as to why anyone would target The Inner Self for what they called "a prank".

Right after it happened, Jaxon had carried a shaking Hannah up to her apartment and sat her on the couch while he checked the apartment to make sure all was secured. When he finished he had brought Hannah a blanket and told her to stay put while he went back and talked to the police. Brushing a hand over her hair, Jaxon had wanted nothing more than to stay and hold Hannah until she stopped shaking, but he had things to do.

Telling the police that he and Hannah had no idea why someone had taken a shot at the store and destroyed the window (at the store and not Hannah) was the story he told. Not exactly a total lie, but by far not the whole truth. He was pretty sure no one was going to believe him if he told the whole truth.

The whole incident had driven the story Saul had told him home, leaving no room for doubt as to the validity of Saul's claims that someone was after Hannah. He had taken in the story, but deep inside Jaxon knew that he had harbored doubts about the whole situation.

Having an Immortal Guardian come to him and tell him he had been chosen to protect another human from Dark forces out to kill her, was stretching his imagination to the breaking point. He was made a believer when Saul had shown him his powers and swallowed the whole story he had been fed. He had agreed to help Saul. But if he was honest with himself, he had wanted to claim it was all just a figment of his imagination.

That is until a shot rang out and his insides had frozen before he had gotten to Hannah to make sure she was alright. He had not seen who had fired the shot, but he knew it was as Saul had claimed. That an enemy of the Guardians had enlisted human help in carrying out its plan to erase Hannah as a threat.

Jaxon's plans for protecting Hannah from harm had not changed. He would do all he could, but he was not sure it would be enough. He did not know how to protect her from an enemy he could not see, did not know. He was used to going at a situation head on, knowing who the players were and exactly what was needed to correct a wrong. This was different. Waiting for someone else to make a move before he could react. He was beginning to feel like a puppet and some one he did not know was pulling the strings.

It was time he took back control and went on the offensive. Jaxon put away the tools he had used to secure the broken store window and, dusting his hands off, returned to the shop floor. Standing squarely in the middle of the room, Jaxon let go of the reins he had been holding on his temper and frustrations since this whole thing had started today.

"I know you're here," Jaxon ground out. "I know you know what happened today. No one is here but me, so I think it is time we talked. Let me see you and let's get this over with." Jaxon waited in the silence alone, until his temper flared and, like an inferno erupted, spilling anger that had been bottled up just waiting to be let loose.

"I am here," the familiar deep voice said. Jaxon had no need to turn around to know Saul stood behind him.

"Did you know what was going to happen today?" Jaxon asked, anger deepening his voice. "Did you know? Why didn't you warn me?"

"I told you that I can not read the Dark minds. I feel when something is wrong, but I do not have specific information as to what it is and what is going to happen. I could not issue a warning to you with nothing to go on."

Saul's explanation did little to curb Jaxon's anger. "You could have told me you had a feeling. I would have been more prepared."

"You would have tried to keep Hannah inside her apartment and she would have fought you. It is unfortunate, but the way things turned out today has been a good thing," Saul reasoned with Jaxon.

Jaxon's eyes turned to black pools, zeroing in on the Immortal and locking on him. He had always had a low tolerance for stupidity and he considered Saul's last statement just that, stupid. Stupid and reckless.

"You chose me to help you and, in doing so, made us partners in this insane venture. You put us at risk by not sharing all that you know when you know it. You jeopardize Hannah's safety and her life when you withhold even the most insignificant scrap of information."

Jaxon felt cold. His anger burned so hot that he turned to ice, even as the sweat trickled down his back, creeping and crawling over his skin.

Before he could blow, Saul reached out a hand and grasped Jaxon's arm. He held on tight when Jaxon tried to pull away, and ignored the snarl that curled the human's lips. Saul was not intimidated when a growl of rage rumbled in his protector's chest, clawing to get out. Saul held on, and Jaxon's eyes widened as the being before him began to glow. Softly at first, but as Saul took on the burden of Jaxon's rage the light around him grew brighter, until his form was almost obscured with its brilliance.

Saul did not stop until he was sure Jaxon was able to think rationally again. By taking into himself Jaxon's feelings, he knew that rage was not the only thing rolling through his body and mind. Of course he felt the anger, but he also felt the fear that was equally responsible for Jaxon's response to the situation.

Fear that he would not be able to protect Hannah. Fear that he would have to watch her die if or when he failed. And fear that the feelings he was beginning to have for Hannah would kill him, as no bullet had been able to, if she was taken from him.

Jaxon had begun to calm down as soon as Saul had touched him, but Saul wanted to burst with the intense feelings filling him up. His eyes turned colder than Jaxon's had. When he could stand no more, he threw the arm from him, unfurled his mighty wings, threw back his head and vomited up the rage, fear and frustration he had taken in. Saul did the only thing he could to rid himself of the avalanche of human emotions he had absorbed. He roared!

Chapter 31

Jaxon was amazed that his rage had ebbed away simply by having Saul grasp his arm. He felt better than he had in a long time. No stress, no being on edge, no anger. All he felt was focused and filled with strength.

He turned towards Saul, having every intention of thanking him and asking him his secret. Before he could get a word past his lips, he was stopped by the shear agony he witnessed on the Immortal's face. Saul appeared to be in unspeakable pain. Jaxon could not remember ever having seen such a look on a face, even ones that were suffering from gun shot wounds or those his unit had rescued from torture and starvation.

He did not flinch when Saul's muscles corded, his mouth opened, and black tendrils of smoke snaked from his being, purging his body of the bitter feelings he had acquired from Jaxon.

Jaxon steeled himself not to cover his ears and crouch down in protection mode when Saul roared with a voice that made the walls tremble and the ground heave. Jaxon experienced a deep guilt as he realized he was the cause of the pain this Guardian went through and bore on his behalf. He felt humbled. This was new to him and it did not sit well on his broad shoulders. He carried his own weight

"Get over it," Saul said. "This is what we do. You are not the first and you will not be anywhere close to the last human that I have helped or will help by shouldering the pain of feelings that have become too much to handle. Feelings that have gotten in the way of Destiny's path.

"I don't know whether to thank you or be mad at you," Jaxon replied. "I haven't felt this calm for a long time. That being said, you have taken away an important advantage I used to keep me sharp and aware. I purposely used my anger to keep me on top and on edge. I don't want to relax when lives are at stake," Jaxon explained to the Guardian.

"You don't need anger to have an advantage," Saul cut in briskly. "You have me! I am your advantage in this situation. So get used to my being by your side and right in the middle of things with you."

Jaxon smirked at Saul as he recognized the attitude the Immortal was displaying. He should, as it was his own. Saul must have picked it up when he sucked the feelings out of him without permission. '*Serves him right,*' Jaxon thought, '*for butting in.*'

"Ok, Saul," Jaxon said, "let's talk about what you know. Who shot at Hannah today? What can you tell me about that?"

Saul gave his shoulders a shake and took a deep breath to calm the lingering anger in his system. Jaxon had powerful feelings. More powerful than he had ever encountered before. He had chosen well when he picked his warrior.

"Very well," Saul said, back in control again. "I will need to do some checking with other Guardians to see which of their charges have been infected by the Dark. When I have found out something useful, I will come to you."

"I can check with my friend in the Police Department and see if they have any leads while you are doing that," Jaxon replied.

"No!" Saul said, his tone leaving no room for argument. "You need to take care of Hannah. Make sure she is safe and can handle what happened. Don't leave her side until I can give you some information."

Evidently Saul had not taken Jaxon's entire attitude, because being told what to do was rubbing him the wrong way.

"I can do both," Jaxon told his partner. "It will take five minutes to make a phone call. Then the rest of my time will be focused on Hannah."

"Very well," Saul conceded, having regained his own demeanor. "I will trust you to do what you must. Just be on your guard at all times."

"Don't forget to contact me when you have information," Jaxon said, starting to move towards the back staircase.

"I won't," Saul promised.

Before Saul began to fade out, Jaxon stopped and turned to face him. "I never said thank you for, um, helping me earlier. I saw what it did to you and I always pay back favors done for me. If you should ever need me, I'll be there."

"You are welcome," Saul said, inclining his handsome head. "And you have nothing to repay. I have already made my request of you. You did not hesitate with your answer to help. You are all I could want in a warrior for my cause. So it is my turn to say thank you."

Jaxon nodded his head in agreement. "Good enough," he said. "We're square. Good night, Saul," he said and, turning around, he left the Guardian to ponder and appreciate the beings known as humans.

Amazing!

Chapter 32

Jaxon made one more tour of the outside of Hannah's shop before feeling satisfied things were as safe as they could be. He made his way up the stairs, reverting to stealth mode, never making a sound.

When Jaxon entered the apartment he expected to see Hannah still sitting on the couch, huddled under the blanket, where he had left her. He should have known better. Instead of cowering in a ball, Jaxon simply had to follow the aromas coming from the kitchen to know where Hannah was. The aromas that filled the apartment made his stomach growl with appreciation. He had not eaten in hours and, without realizing it, he was starved.

He moved on quiet feet to stand in the doorway to the small kitchen and watched. Hannah moved with ease as she fixed salads and cut warm french bread into thick slabs to go with the Sheppard's Pie she had taken out of the oven and placed on the stove top to cool.

"Could you come and take these to the table?" she asked, without turning around.

"How'd you know I was here?" Jaxon asked, wondering what had given him away. He had not made a sound.

"I felt you," Hannah said, with a matter of fact shrug of her shoulders.

"Really?" Jaxon said, not believing her. "What do you mean you felt me?" he asked curiously.

"I can't really explain it," Hannah said, as she turned to hand Jaxon the two plates of salad and set the basket of bread on top of them. She loaded him up and pointed him in the direction of the table set for two. "I just knew someone was behind me and, since I did not feel any threat, I knew it was you."

Jaxon let the question die as he concentrated on setting the plates and basket on the table without spilling the whole lot. He managed without incident, as Hannah set the hot dish on a trivet and scurried back to the refrigerator for butter and salad dressing.

"Please sit down," she invited, as she, herself claimed a chair and helped herself to the dressing first. Passing it to Jaxon, she placed fragrant slices of bread on small plates and waited for Jaxon to follow her lead.

Conversation faded away as both dug into the food, feeling the hunger take center stage and demand their attention. Salads vanished quickly and large spoonfuls of the casserole, still steaming from the oven, were placed on plates.

Jaxon dug in and when the first forkful hit his mouth he could not stop the moan of pleasure that escaped his closed lips. "Mmmmm" he groaned, as his eyes slid shut on their own and he chewed, thinking that it had been forever since he had been served a home cooked meal.

His nostrils flared as he breathed deep, savoring the first bite and swallowing in total pleasure.

Jaxon finally opened his eyes and fought to not squirm, as he found himself under the warm scrutiny of the most unusual eyes he had ever seen. Eyes that were rich and warm, giving evidence of her pleasure with his reaction.

"I didn't know what you liked, so I took a chance and fixed one of my favorite comfort foods. I take it 'Mmmmm' means it meets with your approval?" Hannah said, looking for approval.

Jaxon immediately picked up on Hannah's need for comfort, not sure if she even realized what she had just told him. He wanted to pursue the opening she had given him, but he didn't. He would let her have her meal in peace. Squashing his desire to dive right in, he put another fork full into his waiting mouth and smiled at her.

"This is the best meal I have had in longer than I can remember. It's so good I could cry. Thank you," Jaxon offered heart felt praise to the cook with a big smile.

Hannah could barely understand what Jaxon was saying, so stunned was she by the smile he had flashed her way. She felt the jolt all the way to her toes. And when the zing hit her feet it traveled back up again to settle in her stomach, making it jump and quiver. She wondered if he even had a clue what his smile did to women when he let it loose.

Hannah had watched him smile all day long at the women who talked to him in her store, but the way he had smiled at her just now was as different as night from day. Yes, this one was different. This one had come all the way from his heart. It made dimples in his cheeks and his eyes had shone with pure pleasure. They held happiness that only she could lay claim to for being the cause. Hannah wanted him to keep smiling at her this way forever. It was exactly the way she had always dreamed a man would smile at her, before coming to the awful conclusion that it would never happen.

Hannah swallowed the food in her mouth with difficulty. She could not help the slight heat that crept into her cheeks as she tried to conceal her pleasure.

"I'm glad you like it," she said, trying not to stare at him.

Jaxon did not respond in words, as his mouth was kept full of the wonderful food that was disappearing at a steady pace from his plate. But he did spare a second to warm Hannah's heart a few more degrees with a wink from eyes that danced with undisguised pleasure.

"Hannah," he said, making himself pause with another forkful just inches from his waiting mouth, "this is truly one of the best meals I've ever had. You are a genius in the kitchen. I think I'm in love. Marry me," he said. Not being able to resist any longer, he opened his mouth and gave himself the pleasure of another taste of the home cooked meal he was enjoying. He failed to see the total shock that had frozen Hannah with her glass to her lips, but unable to drink.

Carefully setting her glass on the table before she dropped it, Hannah folded her hands in her lap. With earnest eyes fixed on the handsome man at her table, Hannah very quietly and, with calmness in her voice, said one word, "Yes."

She was immediately rewarded with a pea landing on her cheek, as Jaxon spit his food across the table in shock.

Chapter 33

Jaxon's total enjoyment of the meal and the company was brought to a screeching halt as his comment about marriage was met with a 'solid yes' from the meal's maker.

He was unable to stop his reaction of shock. He now looked at Hannah through the silence that blanketed the apartment. The lone pea still adorned her pink cheek. He felt the awful weight of guilt settle on his shoulders, making him want to squirm.

Jaxon met Hannah's stare. He could read in her eyes that she had not been kidding when she accepted his off the cuff proposal.

"Well this is a definite turn of events," a voice in Jaxon's head smirked.

Jaxon fought hard to hide his surprise from Hannah, the only tell being the hand that gripped his fork showing knuckles that were dead white.

"What are you doing here?" Jaxon asked Saul in his mind. "I have no time to deal with you right now."

"I check in from time to time and I thought it was a good idea to do so because of what had happened today.

I see the drama is far from over. What are you going to do?" the Guardian asked.

"None of your business," Jaxon replied, his nostrils beginning to flare and his eyes to narrow.

"Well think of something soon, because I believe Hannah is about ready to break and run in embarrassment from the lack of reaction on your part. My advice would be to let the question stand as legitimate, and go from there. You could do worse, you know," Saul chuckled, as he vacated Jaxon's mind.

Saul could not resist going to the Window To The World to watch the human drama play out. Humans were just too funny to watch. He wanted to laugh at the pickle Jaxon found himself in, but had to mentally pat himself on the back for having seen the feelings these two were beginning to have for each other, and for giving them a push in that direction. Still, in the end, it would be their decision as to where they went from here. Hmmmm.

After Saul vacated the premises Jaxon swallowed hard to give himself time to think, options flying through his mind. None of them were to his liking. Let it stand and go with it as a legitimate proposal, or try to let Hannah down easy and apologize for having to withdraw the offer of marriage all together? *'Think fast!'* he thought.

Jaxon laid down his fork and picked up his napkin. He reached out to wipe the small pea from the cheek that was beginning to pale.

"Why would you want to marry me, Hannah?" he asked softly. "I'm not an easy man to live with. I have been in the service for so long and on my own that it is not easy for me to deal with people. I think I have forgotten how to be nice and soft and in love. Can you tell me that you are in love with me?" he said, trying to think on the run. "Talk to me, Hannah," he said as she sat still and quiet across the small table from him.

Hannah had too much pride to break eye contact with Jaxon, as he sat doing battle with his conscience over the answer she had dropped in his lap. She refused to wipe the pea from her cheek, sitting quietly as she waited for his answer. '*What had made her say yes?*' she wondered. She knew it was not meant as a true offer of marriage.

Could she really see herself married to the mouth wateringly handsome man before her? A man who could melt her with just a smile, but could be so cold and distant more often than not. A man who she had known for only a few days. One who she argued with at every turn?

Hannah licked her dry lips and took a drink before she could make herself give voice to her feelings.

"You surprised me when you said you were in love, and would I marry you," she started quietly, her eyes looking inward more than at Jaxon himself.

"I know it was just said out of pleasure for the food you were enjoying, but it flashed through my mind, why not? I have never had anyone ask before and probably will never have anyone ask again."

Hannah held up her hand to stay the words Jaxon was about to say. "I have no false beliefs about the way I look and the way others see me. I know we have just met, and you really do not know me and I do not know you," she explained, pausing for a moment before continuing.

"Do I love you?" she repeated, finally getting around to answering Jaxon's question. "I have never been in love before, so I don't know. I do know that I feel something for you every time you smile at me. Every time we are close I feel something. I feel drawn to you like we are connected. I may be wrong, but I think we were meant to meet and be together. Does any of this make sense to you?" she asked, hoping he could explain it to her also. None of it made sense to her, but she had this gut feeling that she could not shake. This feeling they were meant for each other. The feeling she had had ever since they had first met.

Jaxon was the only person she had ever met that had not changed before her into something nightmarish. With what he had done in the past, she would have expected him to be the worst of the worst. But he only presented a glowing aura to her and she knew she was protected from seeing any more. This was also a plus for her, giving credence to her feeling that they should be together.

Jaxon had listened to all Hannah had to say. He knew the draw she felt towards him. He had felt the same pull, but had buried it deep down so he would not be distracted while trying to protect her and save her life.

Could he still be objective and do what needed to be done if they took a step forward and started a relationship? Could he be patient and use her as bait to draw out the one trying to kill her if she was to be his wife?

His wife! At the thought his body became hot and his tongue grew thick. Hannah deserved an answer to their dilemma. Jaxon finally opened his mouth to give her one.

With his decision made, Jaxon made a vow in his heart that should anyone or anything try to hurt Hannah, they would regret the day they were born. He had the means and, when his anger was unleashed, nothing was able to stand in his way or could stop him from opening up the dam of justice.

And all of Jaxon's enemies, if they could talk, would swear to the fact that Jaxon knew how to make it rain!

Chapter 34

Roman knew towering rage as he listened to his Dark follower tell him of the failed attempt on the human life of one Hannah Priest.

"And why was I not told of the identity of this human before you tried to kill her?" he asked, his quiet, soft tone being a clue to what was to come for the one who had failed him.

"I was trying to give you a gift," his minion groveled, almost crawling at what should have been his leaders feet.

"Did you not get my instructions that no action was to be taken before I was informed and had a chance to check it out?" Roman asked, moving slowly back and forth, not being able to be still any longer.

"Yes, I did," the black form choked out, "but I was so sure. And I wanted you to be pleased with what I had uncovered."

"Instead, you have now alerted the Guardians to our plans. It will now be much more difficult to have the plans for executing this human come to pass."

"Still, having our intentions out in the open will eliminate the need to be sneaky, and we can concentrate on the act itself," Roman reasoned, giving his follower reason to hope he would be rewarded for his efforts.

Stupid of him! He soon realized his error in judgment as Roman reached out a shriveled hand and laid it upon his bowed head. There was no caress of appreciation, no pat of well done, only rivers of pain as fire and heat moved from the Dark leaders hand into the form at his feet. The screams of agony and the death of his minion served to cool Roman's rage a small amount, but by no means lessen his resolve to kill Hannah Priest at the first opportunity. If she was the one he was after. He would leave immediately to see for himself if his target had at last been found.

If she really was the one, then his job had just been made much more difficult, as the Guardians would be on alert. He would have to do battle to be rewarded with her death. Still Roman looked forward to clashing with Saul. Every encounter they had brought Roman that much closer to ending his equal from the light's existence. That would definitely be a win for the side of Darkness.

Roman listened to the silence the dying Dark warrior's screams had brought about. There was no cheering and answering screams of victory to be found, as the rest of Roman's army scattered and sought cover from Romans wrath.

This pleased Roman and if he was able to smile he would have. But the dark hole he called a mouth was only capable of producing a horror inspiring grimace.

Roman chose to see for himself this human who was the reason for having to put a member of his Dark army to death. He began to fade out and, once again, the thrill of anticipation took hold of him.

'*Was his goal in sight?*' he wondered. '*Would he finally be able to move forward in his bid for chaos?*' He had a good feeling about this one.

And the feeling was the anticipation of murder.

Chapter 35

Saul watched his charges until he determined what Jaxon had in mind for himself and Hannah. He smiled his approval of the decision. But his happiness only lasted a short time, as the realization of what was to come crowded all else from his mind. Saul had seen the path Destiny had taken when Jaxon agreed to help save another human life.

It hurt him to know there was trouble ahead for two of his charges, due to the Dark's interference. It would do neither one of them any good to know that they had been fated to meet and fall in love. It would do no good to tell them that they had been fated to have two children and they would guide them in growing up to be wonderful human beings.

It would do no good for either one of them to know what their futures were to have been. Things had changed and now were going to change even more. Their lives would never be the same.

Saul might be able to nudge them in the direction of each other and make things happen faster, but he could not give them the time they would need to fulfill all that had been written for them.

Trouble was coming for Jaxon and Hannah and it was moving with the speed of a runaway locomotive!

Saul let the Window to the World go dark, to give the humans some privacy. He backed up a few steps and hung his head as he tried to think of a way to derail the Dark's plan without having to use Jaxon and Hannah. But he could not.

His frustration grew until he was no longer saddened by events to come. Instead, he was angry. Angry because even with all his powers he could not change the things to come. Could not protect his charges.

With fists clenched at his sides, Saul straightened to his full height and opened his eyes to reveal iris's molten and black.

Growling low in his throat, Saul issued a challenge, "Come out, Roman!" he challenged. "Come out from your hiding place! How weak are you that you have to hide behind the skirts of a human to do your dirty work? Coward! Face me now! Let's be done with this mess you have started!"

Only silence greeted his words. Saul could only lock his anger inside until his path crossed with the one responsible for this chaos.

'*Then!*' he thought, '*Then you will know the true meaning of wrath. Wrath and vengeance!*'

Chapter 36

"**I** will make you a deal," Jaxon said to Hannah, taking her hand that lay clinched on the table top and raising it to his lips for a brief kiss. "Once this business is over with and you are safe, if you still want to marry me, then I will be happy to claim you as my wife. What do you say to that?" he asked, letting a smile soften his lips and warm his eyes.

Hannah was not sure she had heard Jaxon correctly. Did he just say he would marry her? Looking at his smile and his dreamy eyes, Hannah began to believe her ears had not played a trick on her. The eyes that were blood red, deepened in color until they were almost black with emotions.

"Don't you want to take some time to think about this?" she asked softly, having found her voice at last.

"We have until this ordeal is over," Jaxon again pointed out, "to see how this feels. And if it feels right, I say let's do it."

Hannah looked deep into his eyes and tried to see more than was visible at first glance, but all she saw was the willingness to jump in with both feet and damn the consequences.

"I say yes," Hannah said, her voice growing strong with her feelings of rightness.

Jaxon again lifted Hannah's hand to his lips for a longer, lingering kiss. This time her fingers were not clinched with tension, but entwined with his. Both tested the feel of that first touch, and both found their hands fit together perfectly. His much larger and stronger, while hers appeared deceptively fragile and soft.

"I will protect you," he vowed, "I will keep you safe. I promise."

Giving her hand one last squeeze before letting it go, Jaxon returned the moment to a more normal mode by picking up his fork and again loading his mouth with her Sheppard's Pie and a healthy chunk of warm bread.

Hannah's hunger had totally left her, but she made the attempt to follow Jaxon's lead and took a small bite herself.

Small talk was injected between bites and, after serving chocolate sundaes for dessert, Hannah cleared the table and together the new couple washed the dishes.

Hannah could not remember ever enjoying the everyday chore as much as she did tonight. With her hands in the water and busy with the washing, she had no way of avoiding the small touches Jaxon surprised her with. Touching her hand as they both reached for a dish, walking close behind her as he put away the dishes, letting his arm brush her back, and tucking a stray strand of soft hair behind her ear when it fell over her shoulder. Her body sprouted goose bumps with every touch and she found the new sensation addictive, hunting for dishes to clean when no more were to be found.

Jaxon hung up the damp dish towel as the water circled the drain. "I need to check things out before I call it a night." He left her standing in the kitchen while he checked windows, not for just the locks but to make sure no one was watching from outside. He took his time, making sure he thought of nothing except his job.

When he was finished he found Hannah in the living room, standing with her arms wrapped around herself as the memories of what had occurred this evening swirled around her.

"We are safe for tonight," he said, trying to calm her fresh fears. "Why don't you call it a night? We will start fresh tomorrow."

At her nod, Jaxon took her elbow and guided her to her bedroom door where he stopped her from entering with a tug.

"Today was not all bad," he told her as he turned her to fully face him. "You are safe. We both are." Raising her chin, he paused for only a second before lowering his head and claiming her lips. The taste of them went straight to his head, making it swim. What he had meant to be a kiss of assurance, turned out to be the spark that lit a raging fire in his soul.

Her lips, so soft, stayed still at first, then came to life as he deepened the pressure. Each let their first kiss hint at feelings that were foreign and new, but maybe ready to be explored.

Pulling back, Jaxon felt his heart pound. He raised a hand that was, for the first time that he could remember, not steady to stroke Hannah's soft cheek.

"Get some sleep," he told her softly. "I will be right across the hall if you need me. I sleep light, so if you call I will hear you."

Hannah was unable to make her voice work as she gazed into the face of the man she was quickly falling for. She had only met him a few days ago and all they had done was fight since meeting. But the kiss of this man had undone her.

Jaxon watched as emotions flowed across the beautiful face so close to his, and had to rein himself in so as not to grab her and eat her whole.

"Go to bed," he said, and turned her around urging her inside so he could close the door between them.

Jaxon went to his own bed alone and lay down after putting his gun under his pillow, as was his routine. With only his boxers on and a light sheet covering his body, Jaxon lay for a long time listening to the night sounds that Hannah's home went through every night, as it settled for the evening. He wanted to be familiar with each and every creak, so any deviation would be obvious to him.

All thoughts of Hannah were pushed to the back of his mind, as he forced his body to relax and go to sleep. He needed to be fresh and alert, so that meant he needed some down time.

"Come on you bastard make a move," he thought, impatience making him flop over on his side one last time before he went under.

A shadow in the corner of his room deepened and two molten red eyes appeared, as a voice oily and sly whispered with glee, "As you wish!"

Chapter 37

The night air was hot and muggy, without a touch of a breeze to disturb the creatures that came out to hunt and kill in its blackness. Their success at hunting tasted sweet, as the ones who fell under their claws and teeth fed their hunger with flesh and blood as hot as the night air.

This was Roman's world. He lived in it, thrived in it, and ruled it. Tonight was no different. With eyes as red as the fires of hell, he watched his companions of the Dark scurry from shadow to shadow, showing no fear or hesitation as they did what they must to survive.

On this night Roman, too, was a hunter. He moved silently and unseen from one deep shadow to the next, until he hovered across the street from the place where he knew he would find the one he had been looking for.

Roman knew that Saul had been here not too long ago, he could smell him. The lingering odor of the Guardian made his insides roll and he wanted to gag on the sweet stench of goodness.

Roman stayed in the shadows, watching until he was sure there were no other Guardians protecting this place before he ventured out and crossed the street. No stone or brick or wood or steel could keep him out, as he moved through walls until he stood inside The Inner Self. All was dark and quiet, just as he liked it. He knew the one he looked for was upstairs. But he spent some time, not in a rush, looking at the human wares the store had to offer. They meant nothing to him. They bored him.

He did not find humans fascinating. They were only good for the use they could be to him and the Dark. Then, they were no more than a disposable means to an end for him and his army. Fun to manipulate, surely, but still disposable.

Finishing his inspection, Roman made his way to the apartment above to get his first look at his prey. What he found instead of one lone female was the female and a male who had Saul written all over him.

'So,' Roman thought, '*Saul has enlisted another human to protect this woman from her doom. So be it!*' After all Roman, too, had enlisted a pawn in this game, and his had taken to killing like a fish to water. Simon was sneaky and sly, and his hunger for respect and revenge made him easy to control.

Roman had the upper hand in this venture and he knew it. He was the one with a plan and Saul was left to try to figure it out. Of course he already had, but he had no idea of the how or the when. Two major factors that Roman had no intention of revealing before it was time.

Ah yes, time. It held no meaning for the Dark, as they had an eternity of it to endure. So Roman was content to hide and watch for now. And watch he did

From the deep shadows outside the windows Roman spied, as the two humans, Hannah and Jaxon, danced around their attraction for each other. He listened as Saul whispered advice to Jaxon. He felt a small thrill as he thought of a wee way to have a little fun before having to end Hannah's life. Really, "all work and no play," as the saying goes.

Roman watched as the two kissed and parted ways for the night. He was more interested in the man, as he considered the woman a done deal. So he was on hand as Jaxon issued his challenge before sleep drug him down to rest.

Roman smiled with his black hole of a mouth and gladly accepted. His eyes gleamed brighter and his mind kicked into high gear, as he used the night to set his play time into action.

All Roman had to do was make sure to avoid Saul while he tampered with destiny. A little twist here and a slight turn there should prove amusing. But first things first. He had been away too long from his Simon, so he needed to check in.

"But I'll be back," he crooned into Jaxon's ear. "Then we'll have some fun. Yup, then we'll have some fun!"

Chapter 38

Roman made the trip to Simon's in less time than it took to blink the human eye. He made his now familiar way into the mind of his killer, but what he found made him pause with the first twinges of unease.

'Someone has been busy while I was away,' he murmured to himself as he looked through memories of Simon's actions.

Simon had not lain low, as instructed but, instead, had gone on to kill four more humans. Roman watched the kills play out before him like a home movie. He relived it all through Simon's eyes.

Roman watched as Simon drugged two women. The first, brown haired Janet and then strawberry blonde haired Connie, not because of wrongs they had done him, but only for the pure pleasure of it.

Roman watched as Simon, once again, took them up into the mountains. He drew closer to the image as Simon woke them up to wallow in their fear as he brandished the wicked knife before their terrified eyes.

He approved as Simon first cut one, listening to the screams of pain and terror, and then the other, enjoying their cries in stereo. Simon was becoming a master at placing his knife perfectly, cutting arteries in the arms, legs, abdomen and finishing off with the ever fatal neck, jugular and carotid artery complex.

He watched as Simon played with them for hours, before finally ending their lives and leaving them lying in pools of their own and each other's blood combined, before driving away without a backward glance.

Roman took a moment to check on the bodies. He was satisfied with the glut their flesh had provided for the carnivores in the area. There was little evidence of the murders left to find but some bones and shreds of soiled cloth.

Roman returned to his entertainment to watch another set of murders committed. This time a man, Doug by name, and a woman named Crystal. Simon had taken the woman first, while she had been jogging. He stuffed her into the trunk of his car, and while driving to the mountains, he found a man stranded with car trouble by the side of the road. It was just too good to pass up! So Simon had clubbed him on the head and added him to his collection.

Roman saw what Simon saw, felt what he felt, every sense alive and on fire as he again cut and slashed his way until death was the only option available to the two tortured souls.

Roman watched as Simon evolved into an almost perfect killing machine. His only flaw being he loved to kill and could not stay away from it. At the rate he was going the police would find him soon. Just because of the rising number of disappearances and deaths, someone would see something. Someone would find him out.

Roman was not sure he could control the monster he had unleashed. Once the forbidden was tasted, it was almost impossible to turn back, to curb the urges, and to hold back.

While Roman contemplated his options, he felt the urge once again rise in Simon to taste the thrill of a kill, the power over life and death, and he stiffened at its strength.

"No!" Roman snarled, "You will not kill without my say so!" He sensed Simon's mild surprise at his presence, but it did not stem the rising need to do the deed.

Roman released an evil hiss, as he pitted his strength against the mortal mind he squatted in. He ground his heel down hard, finally making Simon's needs bow down before his command.

"You will do as I tell you!" he bellowed, making Simon clutch his head in pain. "You will await my instructions and do my bidding when I say. Do you understand me?" Roman asked, his voice carrying the frozen ice of command.

"Yes, yes, yes!" Simon whimpered, having fallen to his knees in surrender. "Make it stop! Just make it stop!" he begged.

Roman eased up on the pressure with which he held Simon's mind captive. Showing this human some mercy, when all he wanted to do was squeeze the puny brain until it exploded for having the nerve to try to defy him.

"Put the knife away," he instructed, then smirked with the speed with which Simon complied. "Now go to bed, tomorrow will be a new start and we have much to do."

Roman stayed with Simon as he fell asleep, making sure no dreams interfered with rest. He did not want any ideas popping up and lingering into the daylight.

This was **Roman's** show, and he would crush anything or anyone that got in his way. And that included Saul's human. His game! His rules! His way! And **he** planned on keeping it that way, or he would leave a trail of bodies trying.

Chapter 39

Jaxon came awake, instantly ready to fight, not knowing what had woken him up, just that he was needed. It was dark, but his eyes adjusted in seconds and he relaxed a fraction as he recognized the outline of the body in his bedroom doorway. He would not put the gun away until he knew for sure what was going on.

"What is it Hannah? Are you okay?" he asked, waiting for her to say something.

"I, I had a dream," Hannah stammered, as she moved jerkily into the room. "The shot today," she said for explanation. "It comes back every time I close my eyes."

Jaxon relaxed back onto the bed before lifting the side of the sheet closest to Hannah in invitation. Hannah hesitated before crawling in and curling into a ball.

Jaxon covered them both up before rolling to his side facing the trembling bundle in his bed. "Roll over," he said, not giving Hannah an option of what to do next.

She rolled slowly to her back, but kept going as a strong hand urged her further. When she was facing the door, Jaxon moved in behind her to press his big body to her back. Wrapping an arm over her, he pulled her close to share his heat with her chilly skin.

At first Hannah lay tense and unsure of what to do next, as she had never been in a situation like this before, so she had no experience to fall back on. Jaxon's heat seeped into her, making her relax. Maybe relax was not really the right word to use. She did heat up and her muscles turned to liquid from the heat she was receiving from Jaxon's hard body.

Hannah lay still, feeling the hairs on the back of her neck being stirred by the warm breath blowing there.

Jaxon's face lay snuggled into the fragrant hair streaming across the spare pillow on his bed. Hannah smelled fresh, sweet like a spring day in a meadow. *'Now where in the hell had that come from?'* Jaxon wondered. He was not one to have or let fanciful images cloud his mind. *'So what the heck was going on here?'*

He stiffened for a moment, but could not resist the small body curved so intimately to his. He was not going to take advantage of Hannah, no matter what his body was asking for. Not after the day she had just been through. What she needed tonight was comfort, so Jaxon forced a lid on his emotions and lay still, letting the warmth from his skin do its work.

Hannah felt safe and protected lying with Jaxon in his bed. His arm blanketed her and acted as an effective barrier to keep her bad dreams at bay. For the first time since having this man come into her life, Hannah felt at ease. The tension between them was immediate and constant since he had introduced himself and told Hannah why he had sought her out.

Tonight, right now, Jaxon did not feel like a protector. He was just a man she was interested in and, maybe if she was lucky, he in her.

Without meaning to, Hannah gave in to her stressful day and let her eyes slide closed. Her breathing slowed and deepened as she fell hard into sleep.

Jaxon was not so lucky. He lay awake listening to the sound of Hannah sleeping, feeling her body move with every breath, gritting his teeth when she shifted her position, snuggling her backside tighter against his lower belly.

He wanted to let his hand discover her body and let his lips learn the taste of her skin. But he refrained. He would not complicate his mission further than he already had by becoming her lover. The kiss he shared with her earlier had shown him it would take very little for him to lose himself in her and he knew she would welcome his attentions with warm and open arms.

"Do you really want to do that to her?" a mere whisper asked in his head. "Do you want to pull her into your world? The nightmare of your creating? Do you want her to learn about your darkest secrets and watch her recoil in disgust at what you have done?"

Jaxon stiffened as he heard his fears put into words. This was not Saul's voice he heard. This voice was dark and sly. This voice was mean and carried evil in its tones.

"Who are you?" he asked, without making a sound.

"Your conscience, maybe," it murmured. "Maybe just the voice of reason," it offered. "What do you think?"

"I think you are trouble," Jaxon countered. "I think you are the Dark Saul has warned me about."

"Maybe I am," Roman said, "but you know I am right. If you get involved with this woman, you will taint her life with the blood you carry on your hands. She would be able to see your true self. The one you think you are able to hide from the world. You won't be able to hide from her. Are you ready to see the disgust on her face, the shock and contempt in those eyes that see all? Eyes that are an abomination to mankind? You would do better to close those eyes for good, and save yourself the ache of rejection. You are meant to be alone. No amount of fooling yourself will change that truth. Better yet, do the world a favor and end it for both of you, now while she sleeps and can feel no pain. Take out the gun from under your pillow and do it," the voice cajoled, wheedled and commanded.

Jaxon smirked into the dark and with a sneer in his inner voice he did not hesitate in giving his response. "Piss off!" he said, and then he laughed. Laughed in the face of the greatest Dark Being in existence. Making an enemy for life.

And Roman meant for it to be a short one!

Chapter 40

Simon woke the next morning feeling groggy and hung over. He couldn't remember drinking, so it took him a few moments to recall why his head was pounding so hard he thought his ears would begin to bleed.

'It was the voice,' he remembered. 'The voice in his mind that had first told him what to do. Last night it had yelled at him and given him such pain that he had been unable to think of anything but obeying it.

Simon got out of bed and made his way into the bathroom. Maybe a handful of aspirins would at least take the edge off the pounding in his brain. He flung the cabinet open and popped the top off the little white bottle before tipping it into his mouth. Not bothering to fill a glass, he drank straight from the faucet, washing the pills down with the cold water.

Simon felt better, just knowing relief was on the way. Resting for a few seconds, Simon finally began to move, meaning to start another crappy day as he had started thousands of others. He caught his reflection in the mirror as he closed the door and it gave him pause.

What he saw puzzled him. His hair was spiky, standing out in clumps that went far beyond bed head. His skin was pale and sickly looking, and his eyes were rimmed in red, looking like he had been on a week's bender. When had he started to look like something that crawled out of a sewer?

"I thought you liked me," he said to his reflection, actually aiming his comments towards the voice in his head. "You showed me how to be great, how to make people respect me. Now you turn on me just like every one else has done? I thought you were in this with me. Helping me. Why have you turned on me?"

Roman listened to the drivel running from this mortal's mouth and wanted to give him another jolt of pain. '*Shut up!*' he wanted to yell. '*Do as you are told and keep the hell quiet.*' But he did not. He didn't do anything at all until Simon had run himself out of words and stood before the mirror, looking like someone had just crotch kicked him for no good reason.

"I am your friend," he finally said, trying not to gag on his platitudes. "I am the only friend you have. Remember?"

"Friends don't cause their friends pain!" Simon countered. "They help them with their problems and listen to them when they need someone to be there. You hurt me, and there is nothing I can do about it because you only live in my head." Simon whimpered back at the voice in his head.

"I am everywhere!" the voice said. "Do you think you are the only one I guide? If you do, you are sadly mistaken. I will continue to be by your side as long as you do as you are told. To cross me is to die!"

Simon actually smiled at the threat the voice in his head had just issued. *'My god,'* he thought, *'I just told myself I was going to hurt me if I do not tow the line and do what I was told. By me?'* "I'm going crazy!" he said out loud, feeling reality take a step back from his front door.

"You are far from crazy," Roman countered to his pawn. "I am not a part of you, but a separate being altogether."

A silly giggle slipped out of Simon as he ran a shaking hand though his already mussed hair. His eyes seemed out of focus as he tried to see himself in the mirror. His image was floating in and out, giving Simon evidence he really was losing it.

"I will make you a deal." Roman whispered to Simon. "If you promise not to scream I will show myself to you."

"What?" Simon asked. "How can you "show" yourself to me when you only exist in my head?"

Roman couldn't help himself. He wanted to have a little fun and, in the process, get his point across. Point being that he was running the show and not this mortal. He knew what would happen. What always happened when he revealed his true form to ones he was using. The screams and the peeing on themselves never failed to make him laugh and give him a jolt of power like nothing else could.

True, sometimes the fragile minds broke upon looking at the Dark Being, but no matter. He could always find another weak human if he must.

As Simon stared into the mirror, the image he saw began to change. It only took a few seconds for the small, pale, naked man to change into a dark wispy form with glowing red eyes and an oozing hole where a mouth should have been.

Charred skin covered hands with long yellowed nails reached forward toward Simon, until they came out of the mirror. A black cloaked body followed, until Roman stood before the shaking human in all his dark glory.

Simon did exactly as he was told not to do, he screamed.

Chapter 41

R oman moved around the puddle on the floor, sneering as he did, until he stood behind the human he had just revealed himself to.

Simon had finally stopped screaming and now stood in total shock. His eyes followed the horror that had stepped out of his mirror and was now sharing the bathroom with him. Its presence seemed to suck up all the light in the room, until everything was drab and gray, sinister and angry.

"I'm going mad," Simon whispered, a small stream of drool slipping down his chin to land as droplets upon his sparse chest hairs. "Oh my god, I'm bat shit crazy!"

"No such luck," Roman whispered, low and dark. "I am as real as you, only I am a God compared to you. I have the power of life and death and can bring hell to earth if I so choose. I have chosen you to help me in my latest bit of mischief."

"But you told me it was okay to take revenge on those that disrespected me. You told me it was okay to make them pay for the wrongs they all did to me. You said it was okay to kill," Simon wailed.

"And your problem with all this would be?" Roman shot back, wanting to bitch slap this human pansy. "I seem to remember you enjoying the freedom I granted you to carry out your revenge. Was I mistaken in assuming you wanted to commit these acts of murder to pay back those beneath you?"

"W-w-w-well, n-n-n-no," Simon stuttered, not sure where this conversation was going.

"I read your mind," Roman crooned. "I have seen your darkest wants and desires, and I have allowed you to be who you want to be. Now let's talk about the price I will collect for allowing you to commit these acts that could get you killed, should you be caught."

Simon paled at the mention of his dying. "What do you want?" he squeaked. "What price are you talking about?"

"You, up until now, have chosen who dies by your hand. But now it is my turn to give you a name, and you will kill for me," Roman told Simon.

"This is just a dream," Simon ranted, pulling at his hair, making it thinner as he pulled tufts out willy-nilly and watched them pile up on the floor at his feet.

"Stop that!" Roman commanded, his voice cracking over Simon like a whip. "Pull yourself together and stop making me regret my decision to allow you a place in history as one for the greatest, most feared humans to have ever lived."

"People may not know your name, but they fear your deeds none-the-less." Roman came closer and whispered in Simon's ear, all that he knew the fool needed to fall back into line and start acting like a man again, instead of a sniveling little rat.

By the time he was finished Simon could not feel his legs, as he had been standing in one spot for so long they had become numb and cold. But he again felt the power riding boldly through his veins, carrying with it the strength and desire to slice more victims until they screamed for him to make the pain stop. Prayed to their god to save them. Begged for help to come along at the last minute and end their suffering.

Simon stood straighter as he remembered he was the one to end their pain, and he was no savior.

Roman backed off as his work was done. His instrument of death was once more in full working order.

"Now to the order of business," Roman said. "As I said, I have the name of an individual I want you to eliminate in your usual way. The timing I will leave up to you, but you will not disappoint me and you will not misunderstand me when I say you will do this for me."

Simon had no problem killing for this thing that stood beside him, behind him, leading him in becoming great. In fact he would fall down on his knees and lick the crusty, blackened feet if Roman asked it of him. He was totally under the powerful Dark's spell, and he liked it.

"I will do anything you want," Simon assured Roman. "I will be loyal to you and only you. But I do have a question," Simon groveled.

"Ask," Roman commanded, granting Simon his question.

"What do I call you? What is your name?" Simon asked boldly.

Roman grew tall and his voice reverberated through Simon's soul when he answered. "You will know me as Master!"

Chapter 42

Jaxon swam slowly upward from the warm arms of sleep. He enjoyed the feeling of having had a good night's sleep for only a few seconds before reality set in and he stiffened at his lack of attention.

Jaxon never came awake slowly. He awoke fully alert and ready for anything. The deviation from his norm caused him to tense and mutter a mild curse underneath his breath. *'What the heck was wrong with me?'* he wondered, before the slight movement to his right jogged his memory.

He opened his eyes and slowly turned his head. Hannah's head lay on his shoulder, her hair spilling across his pillow, forming a deep brown waterfall, soft and beautifully mussed.

His hand rode her hip but he could not feel the soft skin, as his arm and hand had fallen asleep long ago with the unfamiliar weight pressing down upon it.

He remembered all that had happened yesterday, and figured he had slept so well because Hannah had come to him in the night, frightened, and shared his bed for comfort. Right now comfort was the last thing on his mind.

Waking up with a woman in his bed was new to him, as he usually sent them on their way shortly after his business with them was concluded.

Sending her away was not what Jaxon wanted to do with her. He wanted to trail his fingers and lips softly over her face and body until she opened those beautiful eyes and joined him in an early morning session of lovemaking.

He wanted to make her sigh softly as he touched her, learned her body, her desires and her needs, as he made love to her, forever driving all thoughts of other men from her mind. He wanted her so badly he could taste it.

"Saul!" Jaxon shouted in his mind, "This is your doing, isn't it? I know you can hear me so you might as well answer."

"Good morning, Jaxon," Saul said quietly "I trust you had a good night's sleep."

"What's going on here?" Jaxon asked. "I wanted to wring her neck two days ago and now all I want is to," Jaxon paused, swallowing hard, reluctant to voice his new feelings. "This is your doing isn't it?" Jaxon demanded. "Don't lie to me."

"I have no intention of lying to you," Saul said, his soothing tone doing nothing to calm his human warrior down. "You and Hannah were destined to meet and be together. I have given you two a nudge, but what happens from here is up to you. I do not control your emotions. I can not make you love her or visa versa."

"What's the rush now?" Jaxon asked. "Why give us a nudge, as you put it? Couldn't you have waited and let destiny play out?"

Saul wanted to take Jaxon by the shoulders and give him strength to bare the burden that was coming, but he could not. It was not allowed. With no regrets for this part of the job he had to do, Saul proceeded to lie to his charge.

"You two were not given the time to meet on your own, so I saw no reason not to speed things up." Saul answered, trying to be as truthful as possible.

Jaxon didn't know how to feel about this slight tampering, so he said nothing as he continued to turn the information over in his mind.

"What can you tell me about Hannah's future, and mine?" Jaxon finally asked, with no real hope of getting a straight answer.

"I have told you more than I should have already," Saul replied with a heavy heart. "What you do with the information, I will leave up to you. Tell her or don't tell her. You decide."

Before Jaxon could blast back, Hannah stirred in his arms. She stretched until her body quivered with the effort, and yawned until her jaws popped. She cuddled back up to Jaxon's side before her eyes opened ever so slightly for her first look at the new day.

What she saw was a new sight for her. A mile-wide expanse of gorgeous male chest, lightly covered in soft hair and sporting a healthy tan greeted her. Without thinking, her curled fingers loosened and began to stroke and touch the warm skin.

She shivered with the electric tingles traveling from her fingertips all the way to her toes and back again.

"That's my cue to leave," Saul said quietly to Jaxon. "Time is precious and should never be wasted. If you feel love for this woman, do not hold back. Tell her and show her every chance you get. Good luck."

With that, Saul left his two charges to what he hoped would be the start of a beautiful thing. Both had had more trouble in their short lives than most could claim and both deserved this time of happiness

"I wish for them great happiness and love everlasting," Saul said out loud, as he moved through the higher clouds. He hoped the Fates were listening and would grant his request.

"*Yep,'* Saul thought, '*some days his duties really did bite!'* He just hoped that today was not going to be one of them.

Chapter 43

Jaxon lay perfectly still as Hannah's small hands traveled over his chest. He felt every touch go straight to his heart and embed themselves there with roots that immediately went deep and permanent.

He treasured each touch, and held his breath so as not to give away that he was awake and aware. His heartbeat was not so easily tamed, as it picked up speed and drummed in his chest. His mouth dried up, but he felt the need to swallow hard at the same time.

He fought the urge to groan as Hannah moved closer to his side, letting her hand travel to his shoulder and down his arm. When she reached his hand, Jaxon's will broke and he laced his fingers with hers, bringing her delicate hand to his lips and placing a warm kiss upon it.

His eyes opened when she tried to pull away in guilt at having been caught exploring his body, but Jaxon had no intention of letting her or the moment slip away from him. He needed her like a starving man needed food to live, and he seated himself at her table, famished for the first taste that would end his hunger.

Jaxon rolled to his side, holding her hand captive so she could not flee his bed. His eyes slipped open and he held her gaze, drinking in her beauty in the muted light of the new day.

The sight of her uncertainty made his needs take a back seat and his passion cooled to a manageable level, as he wanted nothing more than to show her the beauty to be had between a man and a woman. A new feeling for him, but one he dove into wholeheartedly.

"Good morning, Hannah," he whispered, his face close to hers on the pillow. "Did you sleep well?"

Hannah could not make her voice work, so mortified was she at being discovered taking advantage of her protector that, all she could do was produce a small nod. Again she tried to pull her hand from the warmth of Jaxon's, but he again tightened his grip to keep it where it was.

"Don't go," Jaxon whispered, moving to close the gap between their lips. He pulled her hand across his body and placed it on his back, leaving his now freed hand to pull her flush against him, letting her draw from his warmth as she shivered.

But Hannah did not need warmth. She felt as if a furnace had been lit inside her, making her burn.

She had slowly surfaced from sleep to find herself in an unfamiliar bed with an unfamiliar pillow beneath her head. She had not wanted to move from the warmth at her side and lay totally content until, unable to resist, she had opened her eyes.

Last night it had been dark when she had fled her bed and stood in Jaxon's doorway. It had only taken seconds for him to come awake, without her having to make a sound. The dark had hidden her red cheeks as she admitted her fear of being alone.

When Jaxon had lifted the covers in invitation, she had only hesitated for a second before diving into the comfort he offered.

She had thought being in his bed would keep her awake, but the opposite had been true. She did not remember falling asleep, but knew it must have been quick as she remembered nothing else after laying her head on the pillow.

The light creeping in from the curtained windows was dim and gave the illusion of privacy, allowing for acts, before forbidden, to be tried and experienced.

Hannah had looked into the face of the man asleep beside her and boldly let her hand wander where it wanted. She marveled at the feel of the hard muscles, now relaxed, so different from her own, and the smoothness of the skin that covered them.

She took her time discovering the feel of the soft mat of hair that covered his chest and stroked it with wonder, having thought it would be coarse, but smiling with delight as it curled around her fingers as if in welcome.

Time slowed as she discovered the feel of the man who might someday be her husband. The thought had her eyes flying to Jaxon's face, and she jerked in guilt at seeing his eyes were open.

She tried to pull away but Jaxon brought his hand up to capture hers and hold her in place with that one touch, as no chains could have.

The words he spoke to her were hard to understand, as one thought blazed through her mind. *'Please don't let me go,'* she prayed. *'Just this once, please, please, please don't let me go!'* And then she thought no more, as Jaxon brought his lips to hers and she followed him on a journey to heaven.

Chapter 44

Jaxon had not heard Hannah's prayers, but he hadn't needed to, as his desires matched her own.

He brought his lips to hers, the pressure slight and questioning, wanting to give her a chance to decide if this was what she wanted. If he was what she wanted. Her sharp intake of breath and the added pressure on his back let him know that his attentions would not be turned away.

The taste of her lips filled his head, as nothing in his life had before. They were sweet, dark, innocent and seductive all at once, and Jaxon's world was turned upside down with her kiss. The feel of her body, even through the soft tee shirt and sleep shorts, added fuel to the already consuming fire inside Jaxon. Her hands left a trail of lava where ever they touched, but Jaxon wanted more. He wanted her to burn as he did, until the world and all its problems fell away, leaving nothing but two bodies waiting to taste the sweetness of passion and fulfillment.

Pulling away from Hannah was torture, but Jaxon wanted more, he wanted all. He rose to his knees and brought the dazed and starry eyed Hannah with him. The red of her lips drew him to her, but he resisted, but wanting to move back in to taste them again. Instead, he drew her between his spread thighs where he knelt on the bed. Ever so slowly, watching her eyes for fear or rejection, he placed his hands underneath her shirt and inched it upward, until her arms rose above her head so the barrier could be removed.

Her hair fell from the shirt, as it was tossed aside, to drape in rich waves across her shoulders and down her back.

Jaxon watched her cheeks warm as her arms came up to cover the breasts he craved to see. Taking her hands away, he placed them on his chest before he let his own begin their exploration.

He touched her shoulders, her back, every inch of the soft skin he could reach, letting her become accustomed to his touch. Finally ending both their torture, he cupped her pink tipped breasts in his warm hands. His eyes slid closed as he felt her draw in a jerky breath, caused by having his hands so intimately upon her.

His nostrils flared as he sucked in his own air as his hands were filled with perfection. His heart hammered in his chest and Hannah felt every beat, as she let her hands again run wide over his torso, loving the feel of her own heart as it matched his beat for beat.

Jaxon pulled her on to his lap so her legs surrounded him, letting her breasts rest against his chest, the dark hair there brushing them, teasing them until the peaks hardened with sensations and she pressed herself closer.

Again, he found her lips and drank from the well of passion, not slaking his thirst for her, but filling up his mouth with the taste of her growing passion.

He lifted her up, nestling her hips closer to fit his, letting her feel the evidence of his desire that had grown until he was almost insane with wanting her.

He felt the moisture that she could not hide of her own passion for him and he groaned low and deep in his throat, wanting the sweet pain to end, but knowing he could not rush their lovemaking.

Curling one arm behind her back, Jaxon lowered her to the bed following her slowly until he covered her completely with his body. He kissed her until her fingers formed claws and she urged him to take the next step.

He complied, easing the shorts from her legs and tossing them aside to be joined with his own just mere seconds later.

With nothing between them but the heat of their passion, Jaxon placed himself between her legs as his eyes again slid closed with the exquisite feelings running through his body. He waited until she cautiously moved her hips in invitation for more, before he allowed himself to enter her, burying himself deep within her to discover her warmth and the perfect fit each had for the other. He held back as long as he could, allowing her to feel all the pleasure he could give her with kisses and touches until he could stand no more.

He buried himself inside her again and again, going deeper and faster as he felt her arch beneath him. He caught her groans of release in his mouth before he allowed himself to join her in the dying embers of new love.

He lay joined with her until he had caught his breath. He then freed himself from her to roll to his back, bringing her to his side as he did so. Nestling her head under his chin, he contented himself with slow strokes up and down her back. His hand finally came to rest on her side, barely touching a breast that he caressed with feather light touches.

"That was wonderful," he whispered into her ear. Her slight nod was the only answer he received, and it gave him pause, wondering if he had hurt her or if she had been disappointed.

"Hannah, are you OK?" he asked, his heart beginning to beat faster, but for a different reason this time. "Is something wrong?"

Again Hannah's only answer was a slight shaking of her head.

"Look at me," he urged. He waited for her to raise her head. When she only snuggled deeper into him, he pulled back and raised her face so he could judge for himself if she was indeed OK.

Hannah gave mild resistance, but in the end allowed her chin to be raised by his strong fingers.

As Jaxon raised her head from his chest, the cool air touched his skin and he felt the moisture from her tears.

Rolling her to her back so he could see her fully, Jaxon froze in shock. For the tears he was expecting were not to be found. Instead he saw tears, tears of blood.

Chapter 45

Roman hissed out his anger when he got to Hannah's home, only to find the two entwined after having made love. He had planned on not letting that happen. He knew humans and he especially knew human men and their need to protect the ones they cared about. All he would have had to do was plant a seed in his brain that he had blood on his hands. The blood of those he had killed without a second thought, and make him see it being smeared on her skin when ever and where ever he touched her.

He would have pulled away in horror of the deeds he had done and the consequences he could not erase. He would never have touched her in passion if Roman had only been a few minutes earlier.

It was not like him to miss an opportunity to have fun and create chaos, but he had to be satisfied with the shock on Jaxon's face as he discovered Hannah cried tears of blood. *'Maybe he could work with that,'* Roman thought, beginning to perk up with the thought.

He could make Jaxon feel revulsion and feed that feeling until he would no longer be the warrior Saul enlisted to protect Hannah. He would gladly step aside when Simon came with his knife to drain the life from Hannah.

'OK,' Roman thought, *'I have a plan.'* Feeling satisfied at the small correction needed to his plan, Roman faded from the shadows where he had been spying. If he had stayed he would have, again, been enraged as he discovered his new plan did not stand a snowballs chance in hell of coming to pass. For he had misjudged Saul's mortal, and it would cost him.

Chapter 46

Hannah lay stunned, the weight of her new lover covering her like her favorite comforter. She had no idea that it could feel so good to make love to that special someone.

She had only had sex once before and it had been awkward. The young man had fumbled through the act, in a hurry to satisfy himself, not giving any thought to her needs. In the few minutes it took to complete the act, she had made up her mind that this was not for her.

She had read books that described the act of love as "ambrosia for the heart". She found it to be messy. It had, in no way, lived up to her expectations. Of course, if she had been even slightly in love with the guy it might have mattered, but she had not been.

Making love with Jaxon would have knocked her socks across the room, if she had been wearing any that is. There was not an inch of her skin that he had not touched, kissed, and loved. She lay there smiling all over, and at the same time, felt as if all her bones had turned to the warmest of puddings.

While they had been making love, Jaxon had stared into her eyes and she had seen no signs of revulsion. Only heat and want burned from them, making her relax and let him take her with him on the journey of her life.

When their lovemaking was over, she thought he had meant to get out of bed, but instead he rolled to his back, taking her with him to cuddle against his warm side. She lay still, savoring her new feelings. Jaxon continued to stroke her bare skin, keeping the fires in her simmering, banked but never going completely out.

The sound of his heart under her ear soothed her and she let herself drift, content in the moment. But it seemed that her feelings had a mind of their own. Without really knowing why, tears slowly welled up in her oh-so-unusual eyes before leaking out to form small puddles on the hard chest that was her pillow

Hannah began to panic. She never allowed herself to cry where anyone could see. Never ever! It seemed the color of her eyes was not the only thing to make her stand out from the rest of the human race. She had learned, at an early age, that her tears freaked out everyone who saw them. They were not the normal pearly drops of water that poets wrote about. But instead, were drops of blood that collected in her eyes, turning them pure red. Should they be allowed to fall down her cheeks, they ran in red streams, making anyone who saw them think she was dying, or something just as dire.

Hannah lay in Jaxon's arms and frantically tried to think of a way to get out of the room before he discovered another flaw in her and pulled away in revulsion.

Before she could come up with an escape plan, Jaxon was asking her if she was alright, wanting her to look at him. *'Oh my god!'* she cried inside, *'don't let him see. Please don't let him see!'* But it was too late, as he rolled her onto her back and rose above her to peer into her face.

She could not look into his face to judge his reaction. Instead her eyes were drawn to the small puddles of blood that had collected on his chest. She watched with feelings of dread and sadness, for she was sure that something beautiful was about to die, as the pools turned into streams and ran down his chest and finally dripped back onto her own body.

"Look at me, Hannah," Jaxon said, his voice low and deep. When she could not bring herself to meet his eyes, Jaxon placed his finger under her chin and brought her face up to meet his eyes.

What she saw in the dark brown depths was not what she had expected at all. There was no disgust, no horror, and no condemnation at all. Instead Hannah discovered sorrow and sweetness and maybe something she had to guess at. Was it possibly love?

"Tell me," Jaxon said with no frills.

"It is what you see," Hannah said, trying to act as if it did not matter to her at all. "Not only do I have strange colored eyes, but it seems I have been blessed with the talent to cry tears of blood. I don't know why and neither do the dozen different doctors that my parents took me to. So I have learned to live with my "special" gifts. I am sorry you had no warning of it. I would have prepared you, but I was not expecting to cry in front of you. I'm sorry!"

She closed her eyes after she had run out of words and waited for Jaxon to say something. The seconds ticked by with no sound in the room but the thundering of dread in Hannah's heart and ears. When she could take the silence no longer, she opened her eyes and again they were drawn to the dark orbs above her.

"Don't ever say you are sorry for being the most unusual woman I have ever met," he said, his tone filled with smoky acceptance.

Hannah let her mouth fall open in stunned surprise at the unexpected acceptance by the handsome man leaning over her.

She did not have a chance to voice her surprise, as Jaxon leaned down and kissed her sweetly. Sweetness turned to heat, and heat turned to passion. And Hannah, joining this treasure of a man, became their passion's willing victim.

Chapter 47

It was well past noon before Hannah and Jaxon emerged from the bedroom. Hannah floated on clouds, with a dreamy, sweet smile on her face and in her eyes, as she prepared to take a shower. Looking at herself in the mirror she saw a new image. No doubt, no regrets, just a warm feeling of Love for this man who had just rocked her world.

Jaxon, slipping back into his familiar protector mode, performed his morning check of the apartment and outside perimeter before surprising Hannah under the cool stream of water in the shower.

Hannah reveled in yet another new experience. "I have never shared my shower," she giggled, as she felt her body temperature go well above the water temp, "but I vow to make this a habit, whenever possible." she whispered sweetly in Jaxon's ear.

Jaxon pulled her wet, soapy body firmly against his as he whispered, barely audible over the flow of the water, "I promise to oblige you." and they kissed deeply, sweetly and without reservations.

- Dark Secrets -

Saul had picked this moment to peek in on them, but quickly exited when he found them engrossed in each other. He patted himself on the back for a job well done in bringing the two together.

He knew all the differences that Hannah possessed and was prepared to aid Jaxon in accepting them. But, as it turned out, Saul was not needed. His choice in the human was indeed a good one.

Saul moved around the apartment, meaning to kill a little time until Jaxon was free to have a conversation with him, but came up short when he detected the lingering stench of a Dark Being in the very bedroom where Jaxon and Hannah had spent the night together.

Saul prowled the room until he was certain where the Dark had hidden in the shadows. It was Roman! Saul knew it. '*So they really have figured it out,*' he thought. He had hoped that maybe the gunshot the day before was really a human coincidence after all, but now he positively knew differently.

Killing time was not so easy now, as he itched to interrupt the lovers and inform Jaxon of his findings. He needed to warn him and put him on guard that things were heating up. But Jaxon and Hannah seemed to be in no hurry to end their explorations of each other.

Saul growled low in his throat. "*Damn the Dark for the constant interference I am made to deal with. For the human destinies that were derailed, and for the happiness lost because of them.*"

Usually the most patient of beings, Saul found he could not stay in the apartment doing nothing, so he faded outside to watch the humans moving through the heat of the day. Each one could be the one that would threaten Hannah's life. But which one was it?

Saul slipped into the minds of those that stopped to look into the window of Hannah's closed shop, or lingered on the street, or even those eating within sight of his charge. But not one of them turned out to be the one he sought. If he could give Jaxon the name of the would-be killer, he knew that Jaxon would move heaven and hell to protect his new love.

Saul had done all he could outside, so again he entered the apartment. He was relieved to find the two humans dressed and sitting at the table eating.

"I need to talk to you," he murmured for Jaxon alone to hear.

Jaxon did not jump in surprise, as he was getting used to Saul's voice popping up unexpectedly.

"Can it wait a few minutes?" he countered. "I can't just jump up and leave Hannah without her wondering why."

"We should talk now," Saul said, anxious to impart his information to Jaxon.

"Not a good idea," Jaxon said, in a tone that left no room for argument.

"Very well," Saul conceded, "but it is important." With that, he withdrew to the kitchen to look around. Not much to see here, he thought, eying the strange things humans ate. Sometimes he wondered what food tasted like, but his curiosity was not to be fulfilled.

Saul paced around the small area with his hands in the pockets of his jeans. He found he loved pockets. Finally Jaxon came in carrying the few dishes to be washed.

"We have to make this fast," Jaxon thought, knowing Saul was in his head. "What is it?"

"I have discovered the lingering presence of a Dark Being in the bedroom you used last night," Saul disclosed.

"What?" Jaxon asked, giving his full attention to what Saul was trying to tell him.

"Last night you had a visitor. A Dark visitor. So I am here to tell you that the secret of Hannah's identity is out in the open. You must be on your guard and be ready for an attack on Hannah. And now that they know about you, they will come for you also. I came to tell you to be ready."

Jaxon said nothing as he dissected each part of Saul's message. "Let me get this straight," he finally said. "We were spied on last night. The Dark knows who, where and what Hannah is. So they are going to try to kill her and me for standing in their way, right?"

"Correct," Saul replied, surprised that Jaxon was taking the news so well.

Maybe on the surface anyway. Inside Jaxon was on fire for having their most intimate moments spied upon. On the outside he reined in his anger, so as not to have his judgment clouded with feelings.

"When?" he growled. "I want to know when."

"That I cannot tell you," Saul said. "I only know that she has been found out and from now on you must be ready for anything."

Jaxon's hands balled into fists with frustration. "OK," he said "Do you think it will be sooner than later?"

"I don't know," Saul said again, sorry he didn't have a better idea at this time.

"Guess!" Jaxon barked.

"I do not usually guess, as you say," Saul said calmly.

"Well do it this time!" Jaxon said. "If it was you carrying out this deed for the Dark, what would you do?"

Saul was hesitant to "guess" as Jaxon put it, but could feel Jaxon's barely controlled rage, and decided not to bait the beast anymore.

"I would say that it will not be immediate," Saul began, "as they know you will be expecting it. I should think it would be no more than a month or two, when they suspect that you have let down your guard. That is the best "guess" I can give you."

Jaxon thought this over for a minute before nodding his head in agreement. "I believe you're right," he told Saul, without making a sound. "Now leave it to me."

"I will help all I can," Saul said in a voice intended to help Jaxon stay calm.

"Just take care of the Dark. I got the killer," Jaxon said, cold and deadly. "This time they have to deal with me, and I'm going to make sure the tables are turned and the outcome they want is far from what they will be getting."

"I will die before I let them harm Hannah," Jaxon vowed.

And Saul's soul wept.

Chapter 48

Roman went back to Simon and resumed his place in the dark, little hole he had made in his mind. He slithered through the memories of what his pawn had been up to since their last visit and was delighted to find the urge to kill was now an addiction which he had been feeding on a regular basis.

He accompanied Simon as he drove to work, listening in on his thoughts as the day wore on. Roman found even he was slightly alarmed, as almost every person Simon encountered met with thoughts of how he would kill them and the pleasure he would find in doing so.

As Simon was driving home at the end of the day he passed a man walking along side the road with his thumb out, hoping for a ride. As he began to slow down thoughts of murder flooded his mind, but Roman was having none of it.

"Keep driving!" he growled. "You have done enough damage for now!"

The car jerked, as Simon was startled in hearing the voice, that had been absent for days, plow through his plans.

"But . . ." he began, only to be cut off by his Master.

"I said no!" Roman repeated with force. "We need to get home to make plans for your next conquest."

Simon stuck his lip out in a pout but did as he was instructed, leaving the lucky man alive and unaware of his close brush with death along side the mountain road.

Simon tried to keep his thoughts free of resentment as he drove to his home, but Roman found all he tried to hide, and chuckled as he flexed his power over Simon's will.

Simon parked his car and was in a particularly foul mood as he made his way past the doorman. He envisioned pulling out his knife and, in one swipe, running it across the cheery man's neck, leaving a gaping hole gushing blood on the pristine floor of the lobby.

"Walk!" Roman commanded, reining in Simon's need for blood.

Simon did what he was told until he reached his door, flinging it open and tossing in his brief case before slamming it with force.

Once inside, Roman extricated himself and appeared across the room. The dark and sinister shadow, with eyes glowing red as hot coals in a campfire, did not fail to scare and intimidate, giving him the thrill he anticipated.

"It is time for you to do something for me," Roman began. "This will take planning and, to be successful, you will have to listen and do exactly as you are told."

"What is it you want?" Simon asked, still sounding like a spoiled, pouting child.

"I have a human that I want you to eliminate for me," Roman divulged.

"You want me to kill someone?" Simon asked, his mood becoming brighter at the prospect of action.

Roman wanted to bitch slap him for asking the obvious. But instead his eyes only glowed brighter, the only evidence of his anger.

"Very astute of you," Roman sneered, contempt dripping from his voice.

Simon licked his lips in anticipation and took a seat, giving Roman his undivided attention.

"There is a woman that needs to be removed," he began, only to be interrupted by Simon.

"Why?" Simon asked, eager for details.

"Because I said so!" Roman replied. "Do not question me again!"

Simon cringed back in his chair, finally hearing the controlled wrath in his mentor's voice. "Of course," he groveled, "I'm sorry."

"Yes you are," Roman wanted to fire back. All humans were only good for adding numbers to his army of the Dark.

"This woman's name is Hannah Priest and she owns a shop called The Inner Self. She poses a threat to future plans that I and my followers are making, so she must be taken care of."

"I can do that," Simon gushed, eager to get on with it.

One dark look from eyes filling with hate silenced him effectively. "As I said," Roman continued, "she is to be eliminated. But there is one problem with this undertaking."

Simon again wanted to ask what, but held his tongue with the look Roman leveled at him, daring him to ask even one more question before he was finished.

"She has a protector. A man. I do not know anything about him. It will be your job to find out about him and to see how much of a problem he will turn out to be. Once you have done this you will report back to me and we will come up with a way for you to be successful in this task I am allowing you to perform. Now, let me hear how you plan on getting the information needed?" Roman more demanded than asked.

"I have trusted employees at The Underworld that are experienced in finding out things about people, even if they do not want them found out. I will need to get a photo of this man and also the woman, for that matter, before I am able to go any farther," Simon stated, a frown creasing his pale brow as he thought out loud. "Once that is done, it will take very little time to uncover everything we need. How is that?" he asked, sure praise was going to be given to him.

Roman knew what he was thinking and he wanted to berate him, but could find no reason to do so. Praise was not in Roman's vocabulary, so Simon had to make due with a nod of his Master's head.

"I will check back with you in a few days. Do not disappoint me!" Roman warned, before leaving Simon alone in his apartment.

Simon itched to begin, but after the long hot day he was tired and sweaty. So after some quick thinking, he decided to take a shower and call it a day.

He rinsed off and lay down in his bed, content to dream about his past deeds. Deeds that he had enjoyed committing and for his reward, had won him a permanent place in hell.

Chapter 49

Jaxon debated on whether to tell Hannah that the threat to her was very real, and the time table for the attack had been set in motion. After much consideration he decided it was the only way to insure Hannah would cooperate with any plans that needed to be made.

"Hannah," he called from the living room, "could you please come in here for a minute?"

Sticking her head around the kitchen doorway, Hannah smiled at the handsome man she was beginning to think of as her own. "What's up?" she asked, her eyes sparkling with her happiness.

Jaxon almost didn't have the heart to give her bad news and burst her bubble, but he really had no choice. He took just a few seconds to memorize how beautiful she looked with her hair up in a messy bun, flour smeared across one flawless cheek, and her mouth curving in a smile that made his heart ache.

He could not remember a time when he had been so happy or so in love as he was right now. This unusual woman had come into his life and made him realize how empty it had been. All he had to do now was make sure she stayed alive.

"Can you spare a few minutes?" he asked, loving the way she nodded her head while holding up one finger.

"Give me one minute," she said and ducked back into the kitchen.

Jaxon paced twice across the room before Hannah came bouncing in, carrying a plate of warm chocolate chip cookies and two ice cold glasses of milk.

"I baked," she said, stating the obvious as she sat down on the couch and looked up expectantly, waiting for Jaxon to join her.

He did not want to sit. He wanted action and results. He wanted this assignment to be over so they could get on with their lives. A life that they would make together.

Jaxon knew what he wanted and he ground his teeth because he could not make it happen. He finally sat and helped himself to a cookie from the plate Hannah offered him. At her anxious look he could do nothing else but take a bite. A low, small groan of appreciation escaped his lips as the sweet treat melted in his mouth "Mmmmmm."

"Oh my god," he said, finishing the cookie in two more willing bites. "This is amazing!" he praised as he reached for another before washing it down with the cold milk. "YOU are amazing," he said, leaning over to kiss her smiling lips.

Her cheeks pinkened with pleasure at Jaxon's words of praise and his kiss. Oh that kiss! It was all the reward she could hope for.

"I like to bake. But besides Regina, Chrissy and myself, there is no one to bake for. I'm glad you like them," she said, nodding her head to the now almost empty plate.

Jaxon stopped eating as his gaze locked on the half eaten treat in his hand. "It's been a really long time since I've had homemade cookies," he admitted. "And I've never had anyone but my mother want to make them for me. Thank you, Hannah," he said over the lump in his throat.

'I can't lose her!' he screamed in his mind. *'Not now that I have found her. What if I'm not good enough?'* he asked himself. *'What if I fail in this, my most important mission? Can I go back to being alone, being without her?'*

He was brought back when Hannah laced her fingers with his. "It's just cookies, Jaxon," she said, thinking he was getting choked up over a cookie. "If you like these, wait until I bake you cakes and pies. I am a pro at making deserts." She bumped her shoulder against his, trying to lighten the mood.

Jaxon put his half eaten cookie back on the plate and wiped his fingers on a napkin Hannah produced. He turned so he was facing her and waited until she copied his actions.

"I have something to tell you," he said, watching the joy and playfulness dim from her face.

"You look serious," she said into the quiet of the room. "What's the matter?"

Jaxon picked up her clinched fist and worked at her fingers until they came open so he could lace his fingers with hers. He brought their hands to his lips and kissed the back of the soft hand before patting it and taking a deep breath.

"I have received information concerning the threat to your life," he began. "I have reason to believe the time table for the attempt will be within the next few weeks. At the outside, maybe a month or so."

As he watched Hannah, her shoulders slumped and she let out the breath she had been holding.

"Are you OK?" he asked. "I promise you, I will do everything in my power to keep you safe. More than that I cannot guarantee. I am very good at what I do and I will die before I let anyone harm you. I swear. I need you to promise me that if I ask you to do something, you will do it without question," he said firmly, but with a reassuring tone in his deep voice. "It will only be to keep you safe, I promise." Jaxon waited for Hannah to say something, to argue, anything. But she sat quiet and still.

"Say something," he urged. "Tell me what you're thinking."

Hannah hesitated, not wanting to tell Jaxon what she had been sure he was going to say before he began to talk.

"I will do what you tell me to do," she said, trying to avoid telling him what she had been thinking, what she had been afraid of.

"Thank you," Jaxon said, "now tell me what you were thinking."

Hannah wanted to refuse, but she knew he really was putting his life on the line for her. She did not want to deny him what he asked for.

"I was afraid," she finally said. "Afraid that you were going to say you did not want to be with me. That last night was a mistake and you had changed your mind about us."

Jaxon's heart squeezed no harder than the arms that wrapped around Hannah and held her close to his heart.

"Oh Hannah," he sighed, "you have no idea how much I want you. I know it's only been a few days, but you have become everything to me. I have been alone most of my life. Now that I've found you I cannot imagine spending even one day without you in it, by my side and in my heart. Do you believe me?" he asked, needing to hear her say she did.

But Hannah could not speak, she could only nod her head. And for the second time in two days, she cried.

Chapter 50

Simon spent the next day at work itching to begin tracking down this "Hannah Priest" and her mysterious protector. He wanted to find them, study them, and get to the good part of what Roman wanted. Killing them.

But first he had to handle the small problems that cropped up at work on a daily basis, which ended up taking the better part of a week. It wasn't until the weekend that he found the time to visit The Inner Self and finally meet his next victims.

Once he'd found the little shop, he spent time walking up and down the street, checking out the rear of the building, and getting to know the routine of the businesses around it. Much the same as Jaxon had done, only Simon was at the other end of the spectrum. The one that measured good and evil.

He watched who went in the shop and who came out finally pinpointing which woman was Hannah. His guess that the mystery man would not leave the shop had been right on too. A smirk crossed his face as he congratulated himself at being right. Proving, once again, that he was so much smarter than his victims.

Before he could make a move to enter the shop, Hannah came to the window and turned the open sign around. He watched from across the street as her protector came up behind her and wrapped his arms around her. He sneered as he watched the man bend down and kiss her neck, before turning her around to kiss her lips.

Before he could spy further, they moved back into the now darkened store and out of his line of sight. He stood rooted to the spot, oblivious to the people that almost ran him over in their hurry to get where they were going.

He didn't feel the sweat crawling down his back from the heat of the setting sun, nor did he care that his face was contorted in contempt. He was focused on the two people he was going to get a chance to kill.

'How dare they!' he thought. *'How dare they be so happy and in love, when he had no one to do with what he was imagining they were up to behind closed doors.'*

He was going to take great pleasure in making them watch, as he cut one and then the other to pieces.

Simon finally moved from his spot, climbed into his car, and cranked the AC up full blast. The cold air did little to cool his temper, as he made his way, without conscious thought, to his apartment.

Simon called work and told them he would not be in the next day, directing all calls and questions to his assistant. He sat, with a strong drink in his hand, as he planned the next day. He needed to get some pictures of his two victims without the couple catching on to him. Not a problem, he reasoned, as cell phones could do everything but make you a meal now-a-days. He would pretend he was talking into the device, when he would actually be getting as many pictures from as many angles as he could.

When he was done he would print the pictures on his computer and get them to his staff at work. Then, like he told Roman, all he had to do was wait for information and the wheels would start turning to end their enviable existences.

Simon drank more and more as the night grew old. A new day threatened to appear before he finally fell onto his bed, passed out and snoring like a buzz saw.

It was past sunrise before Simon stirred from his drunken slumber, opening bloodshot eyes to contemplate the day ahead. His feet hit the floor quickly and his heart sped up in anticipation, as memories of the tasks that lay ahead flooded his brain.

After a shower to wash the stink off, he downed aspirin and ate a stale bagel before gathering his briefcase, with his trusted 'friend' inside, and left his apartment. He did not give the doorman a second glance, as he was focused on his goal for the day.

The drive to The Inner Self was uneventful. Before he knew it he was, once again, parking across the street, watching and smiling. He knew he was not going to have any problems getting what he wanted from the two, soon-to-be dead people inside the shop.

The tiny doorbell tinkled as he entered the cool store, pausing for a moment to let his eyes adjust from the summer sun outside.

There were only three people inside, an older female behind the counter and two customers. He wandered the store, pretending to be interested in the items on display, waiting for Hannah to appear. It took less than five minutes before she came out from the back of the store. The man followed her, carrying a box of merchandise to be put on the shelves. The two never gave him a second glance, as they worked together, laughing and touching often.

He took pictures, many pictures, the couple totally oblivious as to who he was and what he had planned.

Simon was almost ready to leave when Hannah moved to stand behind the counter, giving her employee a break. He picked up a small stone beside a hand written sign that promised it would bring him good luck, and moved to the counter to purchase it. Finally he'd get a close-up view of the woman.

When it was his turn, he placed the stone on the counter and gave Hannah what he assumed was the innocent smile of an interested customer. But when she looked up and their eyes met, he gasped at the strangeness of hers, fighting the urge to run outside and never come back.

The smile on his face froze and he felt dizzy, as her gaze seemed to reach far into his being and touch his soul. He felt violated by this woman and hatred bloomed in his heart at being probed without his permission.

"What are you doing?" he croaked, his voice dry and harsh. "Stop it!" he demanded, holding up his hands as if he were being attacked.

Hannah had looked up at the next customer in line. Looking into his eyes, a familiar feeling came over her as her "gift" took over without her wanting it to.

She opened her mouth to scream, but no sound came out. Only in her mind did she hear the horror of what she was seeing ring out and fill the store.

In reality, the only sound she could make come out of her mouth was one word, "Jaxon!"

Chapter 51.

Hannah was amazed that everyday she spent with Jaxon was better than the last. Even though he kept a watchful eye on her and never let her out of his sight, she did not mind. It gave her an excuse, not that she needed one, to spend every moment she could with this man.

'HER man. How great did that sound?' she mused' It never failed to send her heart beat racing and turn her breathing into shallow gasps every time Jaxon entered the room, or her thoughts for that matter. Even though she tried not to let him, he had quickly become the center of her world. She did not want to be dependent on anyone for her happiness. But, try as she might to be reasonable, her heart won out over logic and she slipped deeply into love with her rescuer.

The world, her world, seemed to be brighter and filled with joy. 'If she had to die, she would die happy,' Hannah thought. Of course she had Jaxon by her side to make sure that did not happen.

On this day Jaxon accompanied her to work in her shop. He never complained when she needed a strong set of arms for carrying things, or just wrapping around her. He appeared to be as happy as Hannah. So life, as far as she could tell, was pretty much perfect.

Leaving Jaxon to finish with some things that needed to be put away, Hannah relieved Regina at the counter for her break. There were several customers in line, but she didn't mind. Since it was not too bright in the shop, no one seemed to be aware of her unusual eye color. So everything went smoothly.

That is until a small stone was placed on the counter for purchase. Hannah picked up the stone, lifting her eyes at the same time as she opened her mouth to ask if that was all, but never got that far.

For two heart beats the short, balding, dishwater blonde-haired man was visible to Hannah, and then he was gone. As if in slow motion, his body turned into a black form, wavering and shapeless. His face morphed into a black hole, with eyes red as fire and tongues of flames dancing where eye lashes should have been.

His mouth, with its pitch black lips, pulled back into a grimace that revealed yellowed, sharply pointed teeth, and the breath that reached her was hot, smelling of rot and decaying flesh.

Hands with talons instead of fingers reached for her, reflecting the light from their razor sharp edges, threatening her life as surely as if a gun were pointed at her.

She felt death roll off this monster like the heat waves that boiled up from the street during the hottest part of the day. Wavering and distorting objects caught in its path, melting anything in its way that was weak and vulnerable.

Hannah knew that this beast was the one sent to kill her. She knew it would not stop until it was successful.

The stone fell back to the counter with a clatter that sounded like a gun shot in her brain. Her hands moved to clutch at the counter as her world tilted and spun out of control.

She wanted to run! She wanted to scream out a warning to Jaxon, but she was frozen, unable to protect herself or those she loved!

Her eyes, that had been radiating happiness not a moment before, opened wide. The red irises growing deeper in color. Like blood that had been shed hours before, it was turning black and ugly.

They saw too much and there was no way to unsee what was standing before her! She had to escape or die.

Once again she tried to scream, but only one word escaped her lips. It was enough. It was power. It was salvation. It was all she needed.

It was Jaxon!

Chapter 52

Jaxon had spent the day, as he had every day for the last week, watching over Hannah. Watching over her and their future. So far he had found nothing to kick his senses into high gear. Still, he watched and he waited.

As much as he wanted action, he was content to spend each day with Hannah. He loved the way her eyes lit up when he walked into a room. How her smile was easily given when he looked at her, and how she asked for his touch just by being near.

Jaxon knew it was dangerous to have feelings for Hannah, but he could no more stop the flood of emotions than he could stop an earthquake from happening. And that is exactly what it felt like every time he was with her. The earth moved under his feet, the tremors reaching into the deepest part of his being. He loved, as he did everything in his life, giving one hundred and ten percent of himself.

Knowing disaster could happen if he let down his guard made him more watchful, more protective. He had vowed to Saul that he would save Hannah's life or die trying. An option that did not appeal to him, now more than ever.

They had started the day before the sun had risen, making slow, sweet love until they were both spent and happy. As much as the idea appealed to him, Jaxon hadn't showered with Hannah because he knew it would make them late opening the store. Instead he'd made her breakfast and when they had finished eating, he grabbed a quick shower and dressed for the day.

The store had opened on time. Jaxon liked the way Hannah hummed to herself as she prepared for the onslaught of customers, knowing he was the reason for her contentment. He couldn't find much wrong with the way things were going so far himself. All in all, it was looking like the beginning of a great day.

They were adding the contents of a box of crystals and rocks to the shelves when Hannah deserted him to man the counter. He winked at Regina as she passed by him to take her break, and had to laugh a little when her cheeks turned pink and she winked back.

Jaxon stopped what he was doing when the hair on his arms stood up and alarms began to sound in his brain. The room turned cold as ice, even though sweat began to run down his muscled back. He didn't know what was wrong, but something was, and he knew it had to do with Hannah.

He turned slowly, surveying the store and its occupants without being obvious, trying to appear casual, as if he were just passing time. He wasn't sure what was wrong, but he hunted like a wolf, sniffing out his target. When he found it, he would not hesitate to kill if he had to.

His eyes found and assessed each patron, moving on when he was satisfied there was no danger. That is until he looked upon a small man. He didn't look to be a threat, as he was dressed in summer shorts, a prissy-collared shirt, and useless sandals. The watch on his arm was expensive, but his hands were soft, like they hadn't seen manual labor, ever.

Jaxon noticed everything, every minor detail down to the single drop of moisture that left a track on his pasty skin as it crept down his face and hung suspended on his weak jaw.

'*This one was bad!*' he thought, '*Bad to the bone!*' He didn't have any reason to think so, but the warning bells in his gut were going off big time, and his muscles were tensing for action.

He watched as this man moved to the counter, preparing to purchase a rock or something. Again, without knowing why, Jaxon started to move quietly towards Hannah, needing to be close to her, to protect her. Her face stopped him for just a second, as she turned pale and a look of utter horror covered her face.

He began to move quickly, when Hannah drew in a sharp breath, then appeared unable to speak even though her mouth was moving.

She finally managed to squeak out one word. It went, like an arrow, straight into his heart. It was his name, "Jaxon!" she spoke, fear and need popping out of every pore on her body as she did. It was all he needed to spur him into action. He jumped across the room, making a grab for the man. But he was like a greased pig, slipping out of Jaxon's grasp and escaping out the door, leaving the bell swinging wildly in his haste to be gone.

Jaxon gave chase as far as the front door, not taking his eyes off the little weasel until he climbed into a fancy car and tore off down the street.

Jaxon closed the front door and walked to the counter, where he wrote down the plate number that he had seen as the car and its driver disappeared. *'I've got you, you bastard!'* he thought, as anticipation of the hunt and the scent of his prey kicked adrenalin into his blood stream.

"Saul?" he asked in his mind. "Are you here?" His inner voice was calm, but the tone was ice, letting the Guardian know the situation was serious.

"I'm here," Saul answered. "What has happened?"

"Wait a minute," Jaxon replied. "I need to take care of Hannah, and then we need to talk."

"Very well," Saul agreed. "I will go nowhere until we have talked."

Jaxon reached Hannah and gently guided her into a chair before ushering the remaining customers to the door. They left, but all were curious as to what they had just witnessed.

He locked the door just as Regina came back, explaining to her that Hannah was not feeling well and telling her she was free to go for the day. As she gathered her things and Jaxon escorted her to the back door, Regina turned to Jaxon saying, "I know about her gifts. I know the look she has on her face right now, and what causes it. There was someone evil in the store when I was gone, wasn't there?" she questioned him.

"I don't know," Jaxon replied, anxious to get back to Hannah, but needing to hear what Regina had to say.

"I do," Regina said, "and I'm telling you whoever it was, was bad. I've only seen her this way a couple of times, and she was right each time. They showed up on the news for committing terrible crimes. Don't take this lightly!" Regina warned him, "She's never wrong!"

"I won't," Jaxon said. His face was stone cold and his eyes were black as night.

Regina knew he told the truth. She trusted in her heart that he would keep Hannah safe. She walked out the door and listened as Jaxon set the lock in place, before crossing herself and shivering, even though it was close to a hundred degrees outside the experience had left her cold inside.

She knew Hannah would be safe with this man, because she had seen the promise of death in his eyes. Someone was going to die, and she said a prayer of thanks that it would not be her.

"God help the one that he is after, because they are dead. They just don't know it yet." Regina whispered as she made her way to her car.

Chapter 53

Jaxon checked every window and door before returning to Hannah, even though he itched to assure himself she was ok. He only had to remind himself once that she was his first and only priority, before all else was wiped from his mind and he could do what needed to be done.

He spent a few extra minutes spying out the front window to see if anyone else was taking an interest in the store, but the foot traffic moved at a steady pace. No one lingered on the street.

Satisfied, Jaxon returned to Hannah and pulled her up to snuggle tightly against his wide chest. "Are you ok?' he asked, his voice low and soothing.

Hannah had regained much of her composure, but still found comfort in the arms that held her so tightly. "Yes," she answered, "I'm fine now."

"Are you listening?" he asked Saul, wanting to make sure the Immortal heard the answer to his next question.

"Yes," Saul whispered, "go ahead and ask."

"What happened?" Jaxon questioned Hannah. "What did you see?"

Hannah moved to pull herself from his arms, but Jaxon held her tighter until she relaxed and heaved a sigh of defeat.

"Nothing you say will make me love you less, or think less of you. I promise," Jaxon assured her, being correct in his assumption of what was going through her mind.

"You can't promise that," Hannah said, sadness in her voice. "You don't know."

"Tell me," Jaxon again gently prodded.

"I saw something," Hannah said quietly.

"I kind of figured that," Jaxon said, letting amusement enter his voice to let her know she could tell him anything. "Tell me," he said again when she remained quiet.

"The man at the counter," she began, "He changed when I looked at him."

"What did he look like?" Jaxon asked. "I know what I saw, but what did he change into?"

"He was black, all black," Hannah whispered, seeing in her mind the hideous form. "His eyes were red, with flames surrounding them. His hands were claws and they reached for me. He was reaching for me!" she said, her voice becoming panicky and high.

"Its ok now," Jaxon reassured her. "I won't let anything happen to you. You believe me, right?"

Hannah didn't answer him, but began to talk again. "I think he was the one sent to kill me. He was so evil," she said, conviction in her tone. "His hands reached for me and if he had touched me," she paused, catching her breath, "I think I would have died."

"It's over now," Jaxon said, rubbing her back to calm her. But he felt anything but calm. "I got his plates. I will find out who he is and take care of it."

"How?" Hannah asked, fearing for Jaxon and what could happen to him if he went after the man who's evil image was still stampeding through her mind.

"Don't worry about it," he said, evading her question. She didn't need to know the details of what Jaxon wanted to do, would do, when he caught the man out to harm Hannah.

"Come on," he said, finally pulling away, "let's go upstairs and get something to eat. OK?"

Hannah didn't feel like eating, but nodded her head anyway. She met Jaxon's eyes for a brief moment and a fake, little smile curved her lips.

Jaxon was not fooled but let it go, appearing to believe her act. On the inside he was a volcano, ready to erupt with anger and vengeance on his mind.

Taking her hand, he led her to the back stairs and up to the apartment, where she excused herself to retreat into the bathroom.

"You believe her?" Saul asked when the door was closed and they were alone.

"Of course!" Jaxon ground out, no longer holding in his wrath. "I saw her face. I saw the way she looked into that man and she saw something that scared her speechless. I trust her judgment. She has lived with this ability all her life. She knows better than anyone what it all means."

"Will you be able to identify this person?" Saul asked.

"Yes," Jaxon replied, "I wrote down his car plates. I will call my friend at the police station to get a name and address."

"Then what?" Saul questioned.

"Then I pay him a visit and convince him that harming Hannah is a very bad idea. Fatal to him if he continues to pursue her," Jaxon explained in a cold, quiet voice.

Saul heard the threat of death in this human's voice. He knew Jaxon did not threaten idly.

"Once you find a name, I will find the Guardian assigned to watch over him. Then I will handle the Dark that has taken him over. We must work together to resolve this issue," Saul said.

"So you said before," Jaxon stated. "Leave the man to me. You take care of the rest."

"Very well," Saul agreed. "Make your calls and I will be ready when you have the information."

"It will only take a few minutes," Jaxon said, "so be ready. Don't go too far."

Saul left Jaxon to his business. Like his warrior, he too felt the thrill as progress was made. He had not let on to Jaxon the intensity of his feelings. But as he traveled to the Window to the World, his eyes heated with purpose and his wings trailed fire with the speed he generated.

The final showdown between the humans was coming. Saul wanted to roar with frustration at not being able to help with the outcome. He had seen Destiny's paths for Hannah and Jaxon, and had ground his teeth at not being able to change it.

Saul gave in to his feelings. Lifting his head to the sky, he roared out his displeasure. But he found no relief for the pain that was coming.

The pain and the death.

Chapter 54

Simon made it out the door without looking back and dove into his car. He jammed the key into the ignition and, without checking traffic, tore out onto the street, not stopping until he was parked in his own garage.

He wiped the oily sweat off his forehead and tried to calm his racing heart. Getting out of his car, he almost ran to the safety of his apartment and the lock on his door.

He had not been prepared for the protector to figure out who he was, or what he had planned. *'How had he been discovered?'* he puzzled. *'What had given him away?'*

He saw, again, the strange eyes of the beautiful woman Roman had given him to kill. He remembered how they had looked right through him, right into his deepest, darkest, and most hidden corners of his mind. They had scared him. And he needed a drink, right now!

Walking to the liquor cabinet he poured himself a healthy glass of whiskey. He dropped into a chair and proceeded to gulp down half the bitter liquor before beginning to relax.

He had time to think now, but the more he thought the angrier he became. He had gone into this assignment, if you will, unprepared and over confident. But it was not his fault, he reasoned. Roman should have warned him about what he was up against.

"You looking for someone to blame?" Roman asked, appearing before him, seeming to tower over him as he huddled back into the chair. "Why blame me?" he asked softly.

"You didn't prepare me," Simon accused, feeling bold and righteous in his accusations.

Roman didn't say a word, as he twisted and turned before his human monster.

"You didn't warn me about her freaky eyes," Simon accused. "You didn't tell me the man with this Hannah Priest was special."

"Special how?" Roman questioned.

"He knew me!" Simon wailed. "He knew why I was there. Why else would he have come after me if he didn't know? And what was up with the way the woman looked at me? I swear I could feel her inside my head. It was creepy!"

"Which to answer first?" Roman wondered out loud. "Let's discuss the woman first, shall we?" he began. "What she looks like is of no concern to you. What she can do is no concern to you either," he claimed. "But I will tell you a little anyway. Her eye color is of no concern to me, or to you. As to what she can see, you are correct. She is able to see inside those she meets. She sees their innermost being, their darkest secrets everything they hide from the world."

"She knows?" Simon squealed. "She knows about me?"

"Not that you are a killer. Only that you have a soul as black as hell," Roman said, taking pleasure in making Simon sweat. "Beyond that I do not know what she knows about you. Do you think the extermination of this human is more than you can handle?"

"No, of course not," Simon assured his Dark Master. "I have taken out bigger and better than her. She will be no problem. But what about the man?"

"Ah yes," Roman said, "The man. What is it about him that bothers you?"

"How did he know about me?" Simon asked.

"I would have to say his instincts are well honed. He has no power to see beyond what his eyes show him. He does not know about you. I would encourage you to do your homework, as promised, and find out everything you can about him before you do battle."

"Battle? What do you mean, do battle?" Simon asked, trembling slightly again as his fear tried to resurface.

"I mean you will have to face him first before you may have your prize, the woman. Stick to your plan. Find out as much as you can about him. Then you can come up with a strategy to take him down," Roman coached his protégé

Simon felt a small measure of calm enter his mind at the assistance Roman gave him. He hadn't told him anything he didn't already know, but it helped to hear someone else say it out loud.

"Yes, you are right," Simon breathed out, "I will just stick to the plan for now."

Roman wanted this over soon, before he lost control and had to finish off his pawn before the task was over.

He hated weakness and Simon was weak, needing constant bolstering. Roman wished he had chosen the man in the store, the protector of the woman. Now there was a fighter.

'Maybe there would be a way to bring him over to the Dark when Simon killed him,' Roman mused, as his tongue came out to lick his illusion of lips in anticipation.

'Ah yes,' the Dark Immortal thought, *'this bit of mischief might have more perks than he had dared hope for.'*

Much more!

Chapter 55

Jaxon made the call to his friend, Police Chief Donny Mack, at the police department. "I need your help," he said, after pleasantries were exchanged.

"What can I do for you?" the Police Chief asked. "Did you finally come to your senses and decide to take me up on my offer and join the force?"

"Naw," Jaxon laughed, "I think I would be more trouble to you than help."

Donny laughed as he asked, "Well then what can I do for you?"

"I need the name and address that goes with a license plate I have," Jaxon explained.

"OK," Donny said, no longer laughing. "Why? Is there something I should know about?"

"It's better if you don't ask," Jaxon said, hoping his friend would not push the issue. He didn't want to lie to him, and he seriously doubted he would believe him if he told him the truth. The truth being that an Immortal Guardian, with wings, had sort of hired him to save a woman from the Dark. That this Dark guy was using another human to kill the woman he had fallen in love with. Why? Because she had powers to identify evil men and women, which put a serious crimp in the Dark's plans.

'Yup that sounds totally believable,' Jaxon thought, rolling his eyes at his inner explanation. Not one peep was going to come out of his mouth, now or ever.

The phone line buzzed with silence as Jaxon waited for Donny to make his decision. "This is not going to come back and bite me in the ass, is it?" his friend asked, still trying to pry some information from Jaxon.

"No, Donny," Jason assured him "I would never put you in harms way. You know that. You know me."

'Well that was a bust,' Donny thought, running his hand through his graying hair. "Alright," he finally conceded, even though he knew in his heart he had not heard the last of this. "Give me the number and then stay on the line while I get into the computer."

Jaxon did, bouncing his leg with impatience as he waited. He glanced in the direction of the kitchen, hearing Hannah moving around as she made a light snack for them. They were both too wired to eat a lot at the moment. But having something to do helped Hannah settle, and Jaxon needed her calm.

"You still there?" Donny asked, knowing full well Jaxon would be.

"Yes," Jaxon replied. "What have you got?"

"The plate came back to a Simon Small. I assume you have a pen and paper ready for the address, right?" he asked the unnecessary question.

"Go," Jaxon said. He jotted down the address as he listened quietly, recognizing a neighborhood that leaned towards the well-to-do.

"I got a little more for you," Donny continued. "He works at the casino called The Underworld. He's General Manager there. Never been in any real trouble, but I've heard a few of my officers talking about that place. They said it was pretty upscale. They seem to go there exclusively when they go up the mountain to play."

"Thanks, Donny," Jaxon said, anxious to get to his own computer. "I really appreciate this."

"Are you sure I can't help?" his friend offered one more time.

"Thanks, buddy," Jaxon said, "but I got this. I'll let you know if I need more."

"I've got your back if you need anything," Donny said before hanging up.

Jaxon sat down at the computer and turned it on. Before it could come up, Hannah walked in carrying a tray with sandwiches, chips, carrots, celery, and pop for them to share.

"I heard you on the phone," Hannah said, "Was your friend any help?"

Jaxon came over to the couch and joined Hannah there. He draped an arm around her and pulled her close for a kiss. He loved the taste of her, and let the kiss deepen until Hannah pulled away, laughing and pointing at the food.

"Let's eat first, shall we?" she said, her lips, red from the heat of the kiss, now forming a smile that was reflected in her eyes.

"Mmmmm," Jaxon hummed, as he wanted to capture her lips again and make her forget everything but him. "Are you sure?" he teased, nibbling on her soft neck.

Hannah giggled, then wiggled her butt closer to the edge of the couch so she could reach the food. "Let's eat first. We may need the strength later," she said teasingly as she handed him the tray with a thick turkey sandwich just waiting for him.

Jaxon accepted her challenge and proceeded to help himself to the sandwich from the tray. Showing his appreciation, he took a man-sized bite of the sandwich. His appetite sat up and took notice as he filled his mouth with the tasty food.

"This is great!" Jaxon said, grabbing a few chips that went the way of the first bite.

Talking was forgotten as they dove into the food with gusto. For two people with barely an appetite, they ate until all that was left on the plate was a few grains of salt from the chips.

Jaxon took the tray out to the kitchen and washed up the few utensils along with it. Hey, Hannah cooked so he cleaned up. Fair trade.

When he came back he found Hannah still sitting where he had left her, waiting to ask the questions on her mind.

He didn't make her ask but offered up the information he'd gathered. "I got the name," he said, sitting down at the computer, rather than beside her.

"Who is it?" she asked, rising to stand behind his chair.

"Someone named Simon Small. Does that ring any bells?" he asked, just in case.

"No," Hannah said, a light frown creasing her brow. "What else?"

"He lives uptown and is the General Manager of The Underworld Casino," Jaxon explained.

"I've heard of it," Hannah said. "People whisper about it like there is some kind of secret stuff going on there. Something off."

Jaxon's attention perked up as a picture came on screen and he stared into the face of the man he had seen today.

He felt Hannah tense and reached around to grab her hand, looking up into her eyes, which were now filled with tension, he said, "Let me do some digging and then we can talk about what to do next," he said, allowing Hannah to retreat.

And she did. "OK, I'll turn on the TV for some noise, and relax for a bit," she said, quickly turning away from the computer.

Jaxon gave her rear an affectionate pat as he let her go, then gave his full attention back to the screen. He stared at the man staring up from the monitor. He didn't look to be much of a threat, but Jaxon knew better.

Jaxon's fingers began to fly over the keys, as he did what he said he would do. He dug, and then he dug deeper.

He had no intention of stopping until he reached six feet.

Chapter 56

Simon headed into the casino early the next day, anxious to begin tracking down the man that stood in his way. He had downloaded the pictures from his phone and had sat, until his eyes had begun to cross with fatigue, studying them. He'd wanted the answers immediately, but had to wait for the sun to rise on a new day.

When that day began, he showered, grabbed his briefcase, and headed up the mountain. He made it to his office without incident. He'd barely sat down before calling and leaving a message for the head of Security to come to his office immediately upon arrival. He paced the floor as he waited, muttering to himself for a good half hour, before he was able to pass off the photos and put a rush on the results. It would not take long, he hoped, and he was right.

In just a couple of hours a knock sounded on his office door and an envelope was passed to him. Hurriedly he locked the door and immediately tore open the envelope, being careful not to tear the contents within. Taking out the papers, he began to read. He had to read them three times before all the information sank in. His heart dropped and his spirits along with it.

How was he to best a young, decorated, although retired, Special Forces operative and team leader? True, he had become very good with his knife, but with the training his next victim had, he was not sure he could pull off eliminating him. Or even putting him out of commission long enough to get to the girl.

He sat down heavily behind his large desk, the pile of information lying scattered across its gleaming surface, mocking him for being less than this man. This Jaxon Riley. And he had no one to talk to about what he should do.

"Are you dense?" the sly voice asked in contempt. "You have me. I am you ally. Remember?"

Simon jumped, as he did every time Roman appeared. He was getting used to the Dark Master's appearance, but the popping up when ever still scared the crap out of him. Now was no exception.

"I take it you have found out the identity of the man?" Roman pried.

"Yes," Simon said, still looking despondent.

"Well?" Roman prodded, impatient with Simon's refusal to tell him the news he had been waiting for.

"His name is Jaxon Riley," Simon mumbled, "and he is trained up the ass in the art of fighting and killing. How am I supposed to compete with that?" he whined.

"You will have surprise on your side," Roman told him. "You are the one that will decide when this will take place. You have become very good at wielding your knife. People tend to under estimate you because of your size and appearance," Roman reminded him in an attempt to bolster his confidence.

Simon winced at Roman's bluntness. But he was not convinced he stood a chance in a fair fight with Jaxon.

"Then you make it unfair," Roman said, reading his thoughts. "You stack the deck in our favor so we get the results we want. By the time you return to your home tonight I will have come up with a plan to aid you. Now stop worrying and be a man," Roman said, giving Simon a mental kick in the pants. "I don't make plans that fail, and I don't plan to lose."

Simon felt better as Roman left, having him say he would come up with an idea so their side could win. '*Still,*' he groused to himself, '*why did Roman always have to be such a bastard about everything?*' Every time they talked lately he was mean and snide, never letting a chance go by to cut Simon down and keep him down.

Roman showed no respect for his champion and Simon was beginning to resent it. All this had started because people did not show him the respect he deserved. Now the one friend he had in this whole situation was taking the same attitude as all the rest.

"Fine," Simon said out loud, "I will make my own plan! I will show them all!"

He would show Roman that he was smart and worthy of respect. He imagined Roman praising him when Jaxon lay dead at his feet. Praising him and recognizing him as his equal.

Roman listened in and gagged.

Chapter 57

Saul had stayed by Jaxon's side all day, waiting for Hannah to give them a chance to talk after Jaxon had discovered the identity of the Dark's human.

Saul watched as Jaxon dug up information and smiled, as many times he paused to tend to his love. His protection was no longer a job, but now came naturally because of the feelings that had quickly grown between the two.

Saul stayed in the house, trying not to dip into Jaxon's mind, but peeking every once in a while. He was warmed and saddened at the same time to find Hannah never far from Jaxon's thoughts. Jaxon's concern and love for this woman drove him, as no other motivation could, to make sure she was safe and her life would be long.

It was well into the evening before Hannah excused herself to take a long bubble bath. Saul finally felt safe enough to come out and talk to his warrior.

"What have you discovered?" Saul asked quietly, having appeared beside Jaxon as he sat thinking on the couch.

Jaxon turned his head to look at Saul, and the Guardian could see the intense concentration in his eyes, as plans were considered and then discarded. Looking for the perfect fit to the situation.

"The man is a weasel," Jaxon flatly stated. "He seems to be unhappy with his lot in life. Small person, small mind. He uses that unhappiness to crush everyone that has gotten in his way to get where he is now."

"And where would that be?" Saul asked

"He's the top dog of The Underworld Casino. I checked on this place and it seems there are many questionable activities taking place there. He has knowledge of them all, and I would venture to guess that he encourages every one of them."

"What else?" Saul asked.

"I'm going on my gut here," Jaxon said before continuing. "I think he is the one behind all the murders that have been happening lately."

"Really?" Saul asked, sitting forward in his interest. "Why do you think that?"

"Like I said, it is just a feeling, but I've learned that my feelings are usually right." Jaxon stated with confidence.

"It would make sense," Saul agreed. "The Dark would allow him to hone his skills before setting him on Hannah's trail. They would be protecting him also if the business of the casino was to their advantage. Namely collecting debts owed, with the payment being the unfortunate one's soul."

Jaxon remembered what Donny had said about some of his officers gambling there. That would lead him to believe they were dirty, and had him wondering what favors they had agreed to do to keep their debts a secret.

He was going to have to put a bug in his friend's ear to do some investigating, before the situation got out of hand and the police force got hit with a scandal.

"How much does Hannah know?" Saul asked.

"She knows his name and where he works. I have not told her my suspicions about him being a serial killer yet. I honestly doubt if I will," Jaxon replied.

"What are your plans?" the Immortal asked.

"I don't know yet," Jaxon said, frustration evident in his voice. "This is not something I will rush into. The outcome is way too important. What about on your end?" he asked, "Have you found the Dark Being that is behind this?"

"Yes, I have," Saul said.

"And?" Jaxon prompted, as the answer he wanted was not coming fast enough.

As Saul stood and began to pace the living room, Jaxon could have sworn he saw little sparks, like angry bees, coming from the Guardian, and wondered at their cause.

"The one behind the murder and chaos is none other than Roman," Saul finally divulged.

"That means nothing to me," Jaxon said. "Who is this Roman? I take it he is important?"

"He is my equal," Saul said, coming to a stop in front of Jaxon.

"He's a Guardian?" Jaxon asked surprised.

"No he is a powerful being from the Dark. In fact you could say he is the leader of all the Dark souls," Saul told him.

"Our agreement was that I would protect Hannah and erase the human coming after her. It was, and still is, your job to take care of the Dark Being behind all of this. Can you do it? Will you be able to end him?" Jaxon asked, concerned that when he completed his part Saul would not be able to complete his, leaving Hannah once again in danger.

"Don't worry," Saul said, "I will hold up my end of the bargain. Hannah will be safe and off the Dark's radar."

Jaxon was not satisfied. He wouldn't be until both Simon and Roman lay dead at his feet. But he had no choice and no reason not to trust Saul, not to take him at his word. So for now he dropped the subject.

"It may take me a couple of days to find a solution that I am comfortable with. I am not going to rush this," he told Saul. "I know who Simon is, what he looks like, and I can keep an eye out for him."

"Very well," Saul said, "I will leave the details to you."

Preparing to leave, Saul turned one last time to Jaxon and met his eyes. "Even though you have all this information, do not let your guard down. The Dark is sly and will look for any opening to exploit. Keep Hannah close to you. Watch your back."

With that he disappeared from sight, leaving Jaxon alone to deal with his mounting need for action.

Action and blood.

Chapter 58

Simon sat alone in his home, the shades pulled down and the windows closed. Roman had not come to him in almost a week and he felt adrift in a sea of depression. Drowning with no one to come to his rescue.

He had no one to keep him company but his one true friend. He picked up the knife that lay on the coffee table in front of him, his only true friend. This particular friend never disappointed him, never let him down, and was always close at hand when it was needed.

Simon stroked the blade as if it were a lover, slowly and softly. He left his finger prints on the mirror bright surface, marking it as his own. He looked at his reflection in the metal of his knife and was more depressed by what he saw. It was nothing like he wanted it to be. No handsome face staring back at him. No thick dark hair. No sexy dark eyes. Nothing that would make him attractive to the opposite sex.

As he stared at his reflection, it changed until he could not see himself at all. Instead, he was seeing the face of the man protecting Hannah Priest. Jaxon Riley was everything Simon wanted to be. Tall, dark, and wickedly handsome.

Simon wanted to throw the knife from him, but stopped with his arm cocked back. It was not his friend's fault that Jaxon was everything, had everything that he wanted and wanted to be.

"I'm sorry," he said, as he cradled the knife to his chest before picking up the soft cloth he wrapped it in, to carry it in his briefcase. He huffed hot air onto the smudged blade before wiping it clean, returning it to its shining, deadly glory.

"What are you doing?" Roman asked, having appeared undetected while Simon had been engrossed with his knife.

As always, Simon jumped in surprise. But this time he yelped, as a thin red line of blood appeared where the knife had cut him.

"Why did you hurt me?" he asked the knife.

"Will you stop talking to that thing as if it were alive?" Roman hissed.

Simon hung his head as weak tears pooled in his eyes. His mentor could do nothing but criticize him lately, and now his knife had taken a bite from his flesh. Truly he was alone.

Roman was drowning in the feeling of self pity that rolled off Simon like a lava flow. Hot, thick and destructive. He hated being connected to this human, or any human for that matter, as they were so full of drama and self destruction. But he had no choice except to use them if he wanted to have any fun. And by fun he meant causing chaos and death.

"Have you found out the information on the man with that Priest woman?" Roman asked, changing the subject to try and get Simon's mind on something else.

Simon sniffed discreetly and forgot his problems for a few moments. "Yes," he said, sitting up a little straighter. "His name is Jaxon Riley and he is retired Special Forces. He was trained in the art of hunting and killing. He has no fear."

"How do you know that?" Roman asked, curious at this statement. "Everyone has something to fear, as you well know from The Underworld. You just have to find it."

"He has no family and very few people he calls friends," Simon imparted. "He is probably totally focused on protecting this Hannah right now. She would be the only way to get to him. I already have a plan for that."

"Really?" Roman asked, moving closer with interest.

"Really!" Simon shot back sarcastically. He knew Roman thought he was stupid and inept, but he had proven he was smart and sneaky. So why did his mentor always sound surprised when he came up with an idea? He was no better than all the people he met everyday, or those who worked for him. None of them respected him.

"Be very careful what you think," Roman warned, his voice awash with anger. "Remember I can hear what you are thinking and I am not a forgiving being."

"You need me!" Simon said, not backing down. He opened his mouth to say more but the heat from burning eyes and a growl that sounded like thunder made his mouth snap shut and his insides tremble.

"I'm sorry! I'm sorry Master!" Simon groveled.

Roman felt the power inside him build, until he wanted to reach out and, with a single touch, watch this mortal burn to ashes.

"Do not try my patience again," he warned. "Tell me what you have planned so we may be done with this partnership once and for all."

Simon began to babble, whispering to Roman all he had planned, never realizing how close he had come to death.

But Roman knew. He knew and he never forgot. When this was over he vowed Simon's ass was his!

Chapter 59

Jaxon had a target now. The impatience to act crawled like ants under his skin. He wanted to take the fight to Simon, instead of waiting for him to make a move on Hannah.

He had thought about just plain old walking up to the man and snapping his neck with one twist. He could do it without uttering one word and he could do it without feeling an ounce of remorse. Simple and sweet. But then again, he did not want to spend the rest of his life in jail for murder either.

His attack would have to be more subtle and more private. He knew where Simon Small lived, worked, ate, and crapped. He just needed a way to get him alone to make sure he would never be a threat to Hannah or anyone else ever again.

He spent every waking moment thinking of ways to have this situation turn out to his advantage. Even in his dreams he worked on the problem, never getting farther than the death of Simon Small.

He didn't think he fooled Hannah one bit, as she saw through his attempt to appear unconcerned. He caught her staring at him with worry and apology in her eyes. He had no way to reassure her except to hold her close and make love to her every chance he got. Words were meaningless and could be delivered as lies, so Jaxon relied on actions. He'd always been more about action than words.

He had finally come up with a plan to get Simon and the Dark off Hannah's back. For it to work Jaxon was going to have to have Hannah out of the way. He knew he was going to have to tell her she had to go away, from him and the situation, so he could concentrate to be successful. Once he was done, they could be together and have a life like everyone else. Marriage, a house, kids, a dog, maybe even a cat. Jaxon allowed himself the luxury of a few minutes to picture what his life could be like when this was all behind them. He saw Hannah and himself playing with their two kids in a lush green yard. The laughter came easy, and the love they all shared was evident and real.

He saw them all gathered around the TV watching movies, eating popcorn, chips, and ice cream. He imagined Hannah and himself sitting in an audience full of other parents as plays and concerts were attended. And of course the graduations that would make Hannah cry and him burst with pride at the wonderful children they had raised.

Yup, he could see his whole life and he wanted it. He wanted it so bad he was willing to kill for it. But to be successful he had to convince Hannah to hide for a couple of weeks to make it happen.

Jaxon went to find Hannah, as today was Sunday and they had the day off from the store. He stood in the doorway of the bedroom and watched Hannah as she tucked in the clean sheets on the bed. He hadn't thought they needed changing but Hannah had looked horrified at the thought of going even one more day without the bedding being changed. He stepped forward and caught a corner of the sheet she was snapping out over the bed and returned her smile as she let him know she was glad to have his help.

Hannah laughed as she tucked her side in, watching as Jaxon tucked his in just like he had learned in the military. Perfect, just like he was for her. Perfect.

She looped her arms around his neck and brought his lips down to her level. She lightly kissed them and drew in a deep breath of his scent before she retreated. She loved the way he smelled, dark and sexy as hell.

"Do you want to do anything special today?" she asked, gathering up the pile of sheets to be washed and heading into the laundry room. She put them in the washer and added the detergent as the water filled the tub, her task complete for the moment.

"I'm open to suggestions," he said, following her into the living room.

"How about just going for a walk?" she asked. She did not tell him that she wanted to get out after being cooped up for the last month. She just needed to be out in the fresh air, even if the weather was still hot and sticky.

Jaxon thought about all the danger she would be in out in the open, but he looked at her eyes begging him and he caved.

"When?" he asked, tucking a stray, soft hair behind her ear and letting his fingers linger to stroke her jaw.

"Now?" she asked eagerly.

"Get ready," he said, smiling as she scampered into the bathroom to pull her hair back and pee before they took off.

As they left the apartment, Jaxon went on full alert, keeping his eyes moving and his senses open to anything out of the ordinary. He wanted Hannah to have her time outside, but his heart sped up at the danger they were exposed to.

He could detect no one paying attention to them, but still felt eyes on them. He pulled Hannah closer to his side, trying not to hurry her along, giving her time to window shop and just enjoy the day.

He felt the sweat trickle down his side where their bodies touched, but he did not pull away. He needed her close.

Hannah sucked in her breath as something in a window caught her eye, and pulled Jaxon into the store with her to hunt the item down.

Thirty seconds later Simon followed.

Chapter 60

Simon had spent the last week in the shadows, watching and waiting. He knew he'd have to take out Jaxon first before he could get close enough to Hannah to finish his job. He'd said as much to Roman, and his mentor had agreed.

He hid behind glasses, hats, and fake hair, trying to blend in, waiting impatiently to be able to seize the opportunity when the two separated.

He carried his "friend" in a sheath down the leg of his pants, and had practiced many times pulling it out until he could do it in one easy motion. His ideal plan was to creep up behind Jaxon and stabbing him in the spine to strike him down before he knew what had hit him.

He imagined how it would feel to drive the blade deep into the back of his foe. All the muscles in the world would not help Jaxon, as the pain crippled him. Simon would feel the tug of his adversary's flesh, reluctant to let it go as he pulled the knife out and then plunged it in, again and again.

He would not stop until Jaxon was not so pretty to look at anymore. Until he fell to his knees, weak from the blood that would flow from his many wounds. Until he finally lay on the ground, unable to stop his life from running out. Simon was going to look into his dark eyes and watch as the life left his body, leaving his eyes unseeing, cold, and dead.

Before Jaxon's body was allowed to cool, Simon was going to move in and grab this "Hannah Priest." He would take her into the mountains, where no one could hear her screams and take his time killing her. She would pay for the rift her impending death had left between himself and his Mentor.

Roman would be proud of him again. He would allow him to pick up where he'd left off in his killing spree. No more restraints would be in place. Simon would again be powerful. He would be the one his victims would pray to in their pain.

All these thoughts ran wild in Simon's head as he watched and waited in vain. The two were glued together. Each night Simon went home, no closer to his goal than he had been when he had set out that morning.

Today was different. Today the two had exited the building where they had been holed up and strolled down the street, holding hands or arms wrapped around each other, as if they hadn't a care in the world. Simon had followed behind, keeping far enough back so he would not be seen or detected.

Simon kept his eyes on his targets, following discreetly as the pair entered a store. He followed, staying on the opposite side of the store, ducking behind clothing racks whenever Jaxon let his eyes roam. He watched Jaxon and could have sworn the man sniffed the air, trying to find him by scent. He felt panic begin to slide over him and sweat drip from his body. *'Maybe the man really could detect him by smell,'* he thought.

"Don't be stupid," Roman butted into his thoughts. "He isn't a dog. He's just a man! So calm the hell down!"

Simon again felt the sting of Roman's criticism filling his head. In his distraction, he almost missed the two exiting the store, as they headed back out on to the street.

He was breathing hard when he pushed the door open and literally ran into a wall of unyielding flesh. He stumbled back a step, meaning to skirt the obstacle without saying a word, but his shoulder was caught and held in a grip of iron.

"What the hell?" he got out, before his eyes tracked up and met the cold, dark ones of his prey.

Jaxon grabbed him by the arm and dragged him into the first alley he came to, slamming him against the wall. He lifted the little flea of a man off his feet until his toes barely touched the ground, and still he had to bend down to meet him eye to eye.

"I know who you are," Jaxon ground out, his nose almost touching Simon's. "I know what you have been sent to do. Did you really think your pitiful efforts to tail us would go unnoticed? I know that Roman is the one behind this and I want you to give him a message for me." Jaxon tightened his hold until he felt the fragile bones of Simon's arms grind together in his hands.

"You tell him that the next time I see you, I will kill you. And there will be a next time," he promised, a fine mist of spit showering Simon's already sweat drenched face. "I'm coming for you. And if you even think of hurting Hannah, I will make it today, instead of giving you the few days I had planned on."

Jaxon bared his teeth in anger and the fire in his belly erupted from his eyes. "If you want to live, get out of town and never come back. Consider yourself lucky that I've given you even a slim chance to save your sorry ass, because all I really want to do is beat you to a bloody pulp before snapping your neck.

Jaxon slammed Simon against the wall again, jarring him all the way to his teeth. "You can thank Hannah for the tiny reprieve you are getting, because she asked me not to kill you. Today. So today you owe your life to her."

"Get out of town!" Jaxon said again, "Or you will be the one left to feed the wild animals this time, instead of your innocent victims."

With that, Jaxon threw Simon aside from him and turned to go to Hannah, who had followed them to the alley and stood watching from the street.

"Is it over?" she asked Jaxon, as she slipped under the arm he held out for her.

"No," Jaxon said, a bad taste in his mouth at having left Simon alive. "He's too stupid to take me at my word. He will be back and then I will have no choice but to kill him." Jaxon pulled Hannah closer as he felt her shiver, and they headed home.

"You dumb ass!" he told himself over and over again, as they quickly made their way home. Because he had been weak and let Hannah stay his hand, he may have just cost her her life.

FOOL!!!

Chapter 61

Roman separated himself from Simon and twisted in the shadows, as he waited for the weak mortal to gather himself so he could finally stand on shaky legs. The temperature in the alley increased to that of an oven as Roman's anger rolled off him, hot and thick.

Simon leaned against the wall, trying to stop his shaking. When he spied Roman in the shadows, he found an avenue for his anger.

"Why didn't you help me?" he screamed out. "You have all this power, so why didn't you just do your own killing?" He panted, unable to catch his breath as he fought a new fear. He could be the one to fall by Roman's hand for daring to stand up to the Dark Master.

Simon lost his battle with his nerves, as ropes of vomit spewed from his mouth. When he was finished and could heave no more, he wiped his mouth with the back of his hand. The stench from his eruption filled the alley. The heat magnifying it until Simon almost started again.

"Pull yourself together!" Roman demanded. "Go home and I will meet you there." With that he disappeared in a twist of smoke, leaving his pawn to make his way to his car and home the best he could.

Roman retreated to his dark hole of a home, where he let loose a moan of such magnitude that the walls of black rock trembled and his minion's cowered in fear. Roman moaned out his rage at having picked such a weak human to do his bidding.

He should have chosen Jaxon himself. Then there would have been no question as to the outcome of his mission. He would admit to no one that he could have done better. He was the leader of the Dark and he could not be seen as weak or his decisions as less than perfect.

Roman would admit to no one that he had hid in fear in the dark corner of Simon's mind. Not because of Jaxon, but because he had seen the mighty Saul standing in that same alley behind his warrior. He had seen Saul spread his powerful wings and give his protection to his human.

Roman hid because he knew if he had shown himself, the fight between the two humans would have been a mere hiccup compared to the fight that would have ensued between the two Immortals.

Roman and Saul had met and done battle before, with neither coming out as the victor. But Roman knew the time was coming when they would meet and fight to the death. He would not engage his enemy without stacking the deck and having all advantages on his side.

Roman was a master of detecting the fears of others, but loathed to admit his own, denying to himself that he even had one. But he knew in his black heart what his one fear was. And it had a name. The hated name of Saul.

Chapter 62

Jaxon closely escorted Hannah until they reached the safety of the apartment. Only then did he feel safe enough to leave her side as he secured the home from within.

Hannah did what she always did when she was upset, confused, or angry. She cooked. She left Jaxon to his business, entered the kitchen, and began to pull food from the refrigerator. She brought out pots and pans and more ingredients from the cupboards. She had no idea what she was going to make, but she needed to keep her hands busy and her mind occupied.

Jaxon finished his rounds, but did not join Hannah in the kitchen. Instead he went into the bedroom and closed the door.

"Saul," he asked "are you here?"

"I've never left you," the quiet voice answered back.

"Did you see what happened today?" Jaxon asked in his mind.

"I did," Saul replied. "I stood at your back to protect you. I warned you the Dark would take advantage of a situation if you were not careful."

"I was careful," Jaxon shot back. "I've been aware that Simon has been watching us all week. When Hannah wanted to go for a walk I knew he would follow and, if given a chance, try something. I chose to go on the offensive and I guarantee you he is only alive because Hannah asked me to let him go."

"A decision you regret," Saul stated, knowing his warrior well enough to read the signs without reading his mind.

"Yes," Jaxon admitted. "I only did it for Hannah. If she had not been there, the outcome would have been much different. Why didn't you let me know you were there?" Jaxon asked.

"I was protecting you," Saul said, not wanting to tell Jaxon all he knew.

"Why?" Jaxon asked, not letting it go.

After a pause, Saul admitted the truth. "Roman was there."

"Where?" Jaxon asked. "I didn't see him."

"He only shows himself to those he chooses." Saul explained, "Much the same as we Guardians do. Should he have decided to attack you, we would not be having this conversation. He knew I was there and kept his distance, letting whatever was going to happen, happen."

"I told you I would take care of Roman," Saul reminded Jaxon. "Do not doubt that."

Jaxon nodded his head in agreement and got to the meat of why he wanted to talk with the Immortal.

"I wanted you to know that I am sending Hannah away, but only until this is over," Jaxon said, sitting down heavily on the bed after putting voice to his plan.

"Where to?" Saul asked.

"Does it matter?" Jaxon countered.

"I will need to know so I can have one of mine stay with her and report back to me if there are any problems," the Guardian explained.

"Very well," Jaxon conceded, "She will be traveling to Wyoming to stay with one of my team. One of the members of my team from Special Forces. I have already talked to him and filled him in on what I thought he needed to know, and could handle."

"Very well," Saul said, "We will keep her safe while you take care of things here."

Jaxon released a heavy sigh. He had done all he could to keep Hannah safe. With her tucked away, he could finish this job, then bring her home. There was only one small problem.

"What now?" Saul asked.

"Now I have to tell Hannah and get her to agree to leave," Jaxon said. "I don't know if she will."

"Persuade her," Saul encouraged.

"Yeah," Jaxon said, struggling to close his feelings of loneliness and separation away behind a door in his heart. But try as he might, the door stayed ajar, leaking feelings that were too strong to be contained.

Saul felt his struggle and knew he had to help if Jaxon was going to be able to focus on what was necessary. He joined with Jaxon and, putting his shoulder to the door, added his strength. Together they pushed and the door closed. Closed and locked forever.

Saul took Jaxon's pain as his own, and wept.

Chapter 63

Jaxon felt calmer after having talked to Saul. He had no idea that he was functioning because of the Guardian that stood at his side. He was brought back to the present when he heard Hannah call his name.

"Coming," he called, as he made his way to the living room. The small table was set with dishes and supporting a meal that made his mouth water.

'Hannah has been busy,' he mused.

Air conditioning really was a marvel, Jaxon thought. It allowed hot meals to be made, served, and eaten, even on scorching days like today.

The table held a meal of fresh bread, salad, chicken fried steaks, peas, mashed potatoes, and homemade gravy. A small dish of dill pickles, radishes, and carrots waited to be dipped into a creamy ranch dip, if desired.

Jaxon grabbed Hannah around the waist and pulled her close to nibble on her neck. "Wow, babe!" he whispered, breathing into her soft hair, "This is amazing! You are amazing!"

Hannah snuggled in close and finally relaxed. This is where she wanted to be, where she needed to be.

"I hope you're hungry," she giggled, pushing Jaxon towards his chair and away from her flesh. He made goose bumps pop out on her skin and, as usual, she forgot what she was doing.

"Starved," he growled, making a grab for her but missing as she dodged his hands.

"Let's eat," she said as she sat down across from him. Jaxon followed her lead and gave her the courtesy of serving herself first. He loaded his plate when she had taken what she wanted.

"Oh my God," Jaxon groaned, as he tasted a fork full of the creamy mashed potatoes. "This is wonderful!" he said, before diving in in earnest. His taste buds did a happy dance, as he enjoyed the meal down to the last bite. When he had cleaned his plate, Hannah took the dishes away and brought back two plates of home made cheese cake with cherries dripping down the side.

Jaxon looked at his slice a moment before raising warm brown eyes to his lady across from him. "Hannah," he began, "have I asked you to marry me yet?"

Her eyes opened wide and their deep red clashed with the pink that flooded her cheeks.

"If I haven't," Jaxon said, "I am now." He scooted his chair back in one smooth motion and came around the table to pull her up from hers and into his arms.

"I'm serious," he said, his voice rich and reassuring. "I want to marry you Hannah Priest," he said, watching her eyes fill with her unique tears. "If you will have me, I promise to make you happy. I know I can be hard headed and bossy sometimes, but I will keep you safe and warm, and love you every day of my life."

Jaxon kissed her trembling mouth until her arms came up and clutched his neck. He kissed her until her tears stopped and her breath came in short pants. He kissed her until her lips demanded more from him and her body felt like a flame against his.

Hannah pulled back and placed her hands on Jaxon's face. "Yes," she said, "if you are serious and sure, then yes."

Jaxon hugged her close and buried his face in her neck. "Thank you," he said, over a lump in his throat. "Thank you."

"When?" she asked shyly, not knowing if she was rushing him or exactly what she should do. "I mean do you have an idea when you would like to get married?"

Jaxon tensed slightly, as the moment he was dreading had arrived. "How about the day I come to get you?" he said, trying to make his voice light and nonchalant.

Hannah pulled back to look in Jaxon's eyes. "What?" she questioned, sure that she had not heard right. "Get me from where?"

Jaxon swallowed and plowed ahead, "I'm sending you to stay for a few weeks with a buddy of mine in Wyoming."

"You're sending me?" Hannah asked, the light of happiness dimming in her eyes as she tried to understand what Jaxon was talking about. "You're sending me? What do you mean you're sending me?"

'Well crap,' Jaxon thought. Knowing Hannah the way he did, did he really expect her to just say OK without knowing the why of it?

"Come sit on the couch," he said, catching her hand as she pulled out of his arms. "We need to talk."

Hannah allowed herself to be pulled over to the couch before her legs gave out, and sat down with a bounce.

"I should have asked you before making these plans, but your safety is all I care about. Please keep that in mind while I explain what we need to do," Jaxon said, coming as close to pleading as he ever had in his entire life.

"This thing with Simon Small is coming to a head. I need to know you are safe and away from here before I can do what needs to be done. I called a buddy of mine that served with me in Special Forces and asked him to protect you for a week, maybe two at the most. I believe Simon will be making his move by then. After the situation is over, I will come and get you and we can spend the rest of our lives together."

When Hannah did not respond, Jaxon broke down and clutched her hands to his heart. "Please don't say you've changed your mind about marrying me," he whispered. "Please don't do that."

Hannah felt the heavy thudding of Jaxon's heart beneath her hands, and she knew he was scared. It didn't change the fact that she wanted to dig in her heels at having plans that concerned her being made without her knowledge or input.

She didn't want to go anywhere while Jaxon put his life on the line for her. She wanted to stay right here and be sure Jaxon was OK.

"Why can't I stay here, or why can't we both just leave and go somewhere so no one can find us?"

"If you stay, Simon may come after you," Jaxon said, trying to explain what was so clear to him. "I want him to come for me," he stated flatly.

It was Hannah's turn to have her heart jump in fright. She could hear the loud thumping in her ears and her mouth went dry with the plan Jaxon had in mind.

"I'm not going to leave here with you in danger," she said, flat and determined. "You stay, I stay."

"Saul," Jaxon yelled in his head, "Saul help me!"

Saul chuckled.

"What can I do for you?" Saul asked, laughter heavy in his voice.

"Make her agree to this," Jaxon demanded.

"Why?" Saul fired back.

"Because, it's the best thing for her," Jaxon said, frustrated that he had to explain it to Saul, also.

"I really think you should try again to reason with her," Saul said. "I try not to interfere if I can help it."

"Saul," Jaxon ground out, "just work your magic here, please?" he said, grumpy that once again he had to say please.

"Very well," Saul relented, "I will take the edge off, but you still must do the bulk of the convincing."

With that said, Saul stood behind the couple and placed a warm hand on Hannah's shoulder. He looked into her mind and saw not the stubbornness that Jaxon was hearing, but instead a deep fear that she was going to lose Jaxon if she were to leave. A fear of being alone again. Something she couldn't bear after having found this special man to love.

Saul's mighty shoulders, so broad and strong, sagged with the knowledge of Destiny's plan, and he took the fear away from her. He drank it into himself, his bones aching with the weight of her emotions.

After a moment Saul withdrew his hand and stood straight and tall. "I have done all I can," he whispered to Jaxon. "Try again. This time tell her everything. Tell her what is in your heart. Do not send her away without hearing all you feel for her. All you want for her, and with her. She deserves to hear it, every bit of it." With this done, Saul left the two to talk, but stayed close in case he was needed.

Jaxon took a deep breath before he turned to face Hannah. He looked into her eyes and saw the small spark of fear that remained, and his heart opened, releasing all he felt for her.

"Hannah," he began softly, "I have never, in my life, felt for someone the way I feel for you. At first I wanted to choke you for defying me at every turn. But then I got to know you and your strength impressed me. I know it was a lot to take in, when I told you why I showed up in your life. And I really can't blame you for thinking I was bossy and overbearing. But everything I have done, I have done for you, because of you."

"I never meant to fall in love with you, but I have. I want to spend the rest of my life waking up with you by my side. I want to build a life with you, and a family with you." Jaxon bowed his head, embarrassed to tell her the next part but wanting to hold nothing back.

"I've dreamed about having children with you, about how our lives will be with them in it. A part of you and I that came together to make two human beings that will grow strong and beautiful, because you and I love each other and will love them too.

I know I should have discussed your leaving for a couple of weeks before I made the plans, but I knew you wouldn't want to go, and I need you to go."

Hannah tried to pull away at this, but Jaxon held on, held on as if his life depended on it.

"Please Hannah," he said, "Hear me out." When she relaxed, he continued.

"I don't want you to go. I need to see you everyday like I need to breathe. But I have to give all my concentration to Simon Small. I can't do that if you are near by and in danger. You saw it today. He is getting ready to make a move and I believe he will try for me first. I need to do what I was sent here to do, before we can be free to spend our lives together. I need you to be OK with this. I need you to tell me you will still love me when I do what needs to be done."

There he had said it, said it out loud. He, the strong warrior, chosen by an Immortal Guardian, was afraid of her hating him, of her being repulsed by him when he had to end a human life to save her own.

How could she let him touch her again with blood on his hands? The blood he had on them now was before her time and he did not talk about it with her. Would never talk to her about it. But she would know about this. Could she, would she, still be able to love him knowing what he had to do?

Hannah gently pulled her hand from Jaxon's and used it to raise his face to her. Her eyes saw the agony he was going through, fearing she would reject him when he killed the man trying to take her life. This mountain of a man who oozed strength and power, sat beside her and showed her what was hidden in his heart.

Fear. Fear of being unloved by her.

Hannah raised Jaxon's face until his eyes met hers. She felt a pain in her heart she had never known before. His deep brown eyes were stained with tears and she saw the fight he put up to not have her see.

"No, Jaxon," she said, as he tried to hide his emotions from her. "I will tell you this—every morning when I wake up, I have to pinch myself to make sure you are not a dream. To have someone such as you love me, is almost more than I can comprehend.

Why? I ask myself a hundred times a day. Why would he want me, when he can have anyone he wants? Why would he want me, when I am strange and he will have to answer over and over the questions people will ask about me? But you know what, Jaxon? Every morning I push those questions away from me. I tell myself I am going to allow myself to love you. Every day I thank my lucky stars that you love me in return."

Hannah's throat closed up as she watched Jaxon lose his fight. A lone tear slid down his handsome cheek. Whatever its cause, the sight of that single tear tore through her heart, leaving her crushed and humbled. Hannah launched herself into Jaxon's arms and held on tightly.

"Promise me!" she said, "Promise me you will come for me! That you won't forget me!"

Jaxon's arms crushed her to his heart, as he shook with his love for her. "I promise!" he said fiercely. "I promise to come for you, and neither heaven nor hell will stop me. They'll have to kill me to keep me away."

With those words, dread filled Hannah's heart. Desperation was her companion, as she led the way into the bedroom, where she made love to and with Jaxon, storing up memories to last until they were together again.

Or if . . . .

Chapter 65

Hannah came awake the next morning, slowly at first, as she felt the furnace beside her and recognized it as Jaxon. She wanted to stay this way forever and put up a good fight to not remember what today was. Today was the day she was to leave Jaxon alone to fight a killer on her behalf.

Hannah's thoughts made her restless and her movements caused Jaxon to reach for her. She looked over at him, but he appeared to still be asleep. Her heart ached as she realized that even in sleep he protected her, took care of her, and comforted her.

She lay as still as she could, just looking at him, trying to memorize every tiny thing about him. She did not want to rely on memories to see his face. But she could not fault Jaxon's reasoning in wanting to send her away from danger. She did not like it one bit, having a deep down bad feeling that one or both of them was in serious trouble.

'It's not fair,' she thought to herself. 'It's not fair that after having found each other, they now had to go separate ways.

- *Diane Nielsen* -

Even for just a week or two, as Jaxon promised. That was just too long!'

She stopped thinking as Jaxon began to stir. She rose above him and welcomed him to a new day with butterfly kisses and soft, soft touches. She kept her eyes closed and let her sense of touch make memories that she would need when she was alone.

Jaxon had been awake longer than Hannah had known, lying still as he listened to her breathing. He knew that sound, as he had become familiar with everything about her, everything she did, everything she was.

He knew she fought an inner battle to do as he had asked and leave him and her home until he had made things safe. He knew his request caused her pain and he would give anything, even his life, to spare her from anything hurtful.

But this had to be. Jaxon stirred, as his decision did not sit well, and he still struggled with it, even though he knew he had no choice.

Jaxon kept his eyes closed as he felt her kiss his lips, his face, and his neck. He kept his eyes closed as he felt her hands, so soft and gentle, touch his skin, running them over and over his body until he could take no more.

He opened his eyes and, pulling her head closer to his, he kissed her. He too was trying to make memories to last while they were apart.

Jaxon prolonged the kissing and touching as long as he could, until he could take no more. He had to have her. And he did.

Jaxon made love to Hannah with his mouth and hands, slowly and deliberately giving her every pleasure he could. When they both had reached the breaking point, Jaxon lifted Hannah until she sat astride his body and allowed her to set the pace of their lovemaking. Jaxon groaned with the effort he used to hold back, until Hannah slumped down in satisfaction. He was not far behind. Then he held her tightly to his chest until their heartbeats slowed and steadied.

"I love you, Hannah," he whispered, kissing the top of her head.

"I know," she said, "I love you, too, Jaxon," she whispered, her voice shaking. "Don't make me do this. Don't make me leave you. Please!" she begged him.

Jaxon wanted to give in to her, wanted to say OK, stay, but he could not. He dared not.

"It won't be for long. Remember, I promised," he reminded her.

"Do you always keep your promises?" she asked, crushed even though she expected him to say exactly what he did.

"Yes," he said, "I do. Especially when it is so important, like this is."

"OK," Hannah finally said, swallowing her objections and arguments. She did not want to put added pressure on Jaxon. She knew he couldn't have his mind elsewhere when he needed to be focused on Simon Small.

"I'll go make breakfast," she said, getting out of bed and slipping on Jaxon's tee shirt. "You go jump in the shower. It will be ready when you get out." She quickly left the bedroom before Jaxon could tell her not to go.

Heaving a sigh, he got up as ordered, went into the bathroom and turned on the shower. But not before he heard her soft, muffled sobs coming from the kitchen.

Jaxon hung his dark head as he braced his arms on the counter below the mirror. He stared with unseeing eyes at the sink, feeling each sob tear into his gut. Being shot had not caused him half the pain he felt now, and he ground his teeth in anger at the turn his life had taken.

"Get in the shower!" he told himself, *"Stop thinking!"* He did just that. While he soaped his body and washed his hair, he kept his mind blank. The only thoughts he let trickle in were the ones about what he was going to do to Simon Small.

As he planned and plotted, he grew strong in his resolve. Tomorrow, after Hannah was safely away, he was going to call out this man and be done with it. He was going to fight and win.

By the time Jaxon left the shower, his training was back in place. The killer in him chomped at the bit to be let loose. He wiped the steam from the mirror and stared at his reflection. Cold, flat eyes stared back with nothing in their depths.

Nothing but the promise of death.

axon ate his breakfast. His gut burned as he listened to Hannah try to make small talk, pretending this was not their last meal together. '*No*,' he thought, '*it was only their last meal for a short while. He would get back to her! He would kill Simon Small, and then he would drive to Wyoming and get her. They would take a trip to Las Vegas, and they would get married.*' He had a plan.

He ate in silence. When the food was gone, he grabbed the dishes and hid in the kitchen. Dreading the coming hours.

When he could stall no longer, he went on the hunt and found Hannah in the bedroom, packing a bag.

"Can I help?" he asked, hurting as he watched her hands tremble every time she laid a piece of clothing in the bag.

"No, its OK," she said, a weak smile on her lips, but nowhere in her eyes.

He sat on the bed until she was finished and the bag was setting by the front door.

"Tell me about the man, your friend, who is coming to get me," she said, holding his hand and leading the way to the living room and sitting on the couch.

Jaxon sat beside her, gathering her close to his side. "His name is Brandon, Brandon Keller. I've known him for years and I would trust him with my life. I AM trusting him with my life." he admitted. "You are my life."

Hannah melted against Jaxon, her hand clutching his shirt for strength. "Don't," she whispered, "Don't talk about it or I'll fall apart. I'm tying my best to accept this plan of yours without breaking down. But if we talk about it, I'll break."

"Its OK," Jaxon assured her, as much as himself, "It's going to be OK."

"So," Hannah said, desperate to change the subject, "what is Brandon like? Tell me."

Jaxon took the hint. "Let's see," he said, trying to give her an accurate description, "he's six feet nine inches tall." smiling for the first time that day as Hannah's eyebrows rose in awe. "He has medium brown hair and the brightest blue eyes you've ever seen. All the girls fight over him. He has a good heart, and a soft one at that. We used to kid him that he was a push over for a sob story."

Jaxon's eyes lost their focus as he remembered his friend and teammate. "He's strong as an ox and steady, always protective of his friends. He is the best person you could have watching your back when things go south. I would trust him with my life. I'm trusting him with your life." he said, his eyes refocusing. "That's the best I can do."

Hannah heard the respect and trust Jaxon had for this man in his voice. She felt it in the idle stroking of his fingers on her arm and in the hard body that relaxed against her as he talked. He meant something to Jaxon, and she trusted him to pick the best to keep her safe.

She opened her mouth to ask more, but was stopped when a knock sounded on the door at the bottom of the stairs. Her heart picked up speed and she began to panic, as the time to leave loomed close.

"Stay here," Jaxon ordered her, as he switched into protective mode. He crossed, on silent feet, to the door. His gun appeared in his hand just before he opened it and disappeared from sight.

Hannah stayed. She tried to hear what was happening, but her own heartbeat was all she could hear, as it drummed in her ears.

In less than a minute Jaxon was back, walking through the door minus the gun but with a huge man at his back.

"Hannah," he said, reaching for her hand, "this is Brandon. Brandon, this is Hannah."

Hannah's eyes tracked up, up, and up, until she met the blue eyes Jaxon had spoken of. She looked into them, expecting to see the softness Jaxon had described, but it wasn't there. Instead she saw the same steel that lived in the brown eyes she was in love with. They bore into her, measuring her worth. Without her trying, she saw into him as well.

His face did not change, nor did his body. But an aura appeared around him, mimicking fire as it danced and twirled, never stopping. His eyes turned to chips of ice, and when he smiled, his mouth sported fangs that grew long and sharp. His fingers looked like claws, but were not raised to her in a threat. Instead, one reached for her. She felt no fear as she placed her hand in the large paw, letting it be engulfed and held.

"It's nice to meet you," Brandon said, the genuine warmth of his voice breaking through her vision, letting her see, again, the mere man before her.

"Come and sit down," Hannah invited. "Can I get you anything? Maybe something to drink or eat?"

"No thank you, ma'am," he said "I'm fine."

"Ma'am?" she questioned, her eyes sparkling with mischief. "Really? How about just Hannah."

Brandon smiled, and the warmth Jaxon spoke of came beaming through. "Thank you," he said, "Hannah it is."

"Jaxon," he said, turning to his friend, "We need to talk before Hannah and I get going. Your choice where."

"How about if I go to the bathroom and freshen up while you two talk?" Hannah offered.

"Thanks, honey," Jaxon said, kissing her lightly on her lips.

Hannah smiled and kept herself together until the door closed behind her, before sliding down its length. Scrambling to reach a towel, she muffled her sobs, muffled them until the towel ran red with her tears.

Chapter 67

Hannah stayed in the bathroom, crying until she could cry no more. She washed her face, then pulled out some spare make-up that she had not packed, and repaired the damage she had just done as best she could.

She paused a moment to take a deep breath and get herself under control, before exiting the room and rejoining the men.

Jaxon and Brandon stood facing each other, deep in conversation. They stopped when Hannah came into sight.

"Are you ready?" Brandon asked, turning a face to her that held no expression.

"No," Hannah said, panic taking ahold of her. She was not ready. No matter how many talks she had with herself, telling herself that Jaxon was right and it had to be. No matter how many times she repeated that it was only for a few weeks at the most. None of it mattered now that the time was at hand.

"How about if Brandon stays here and protects me while you do what ever you need to do?" Hannah begged Jaxon.

Brandon saw the war that raged in his friend. Jaxon had told him he was in love with Hannah. He had told him the whole story of how he had been hired to protect her because of a gift she had. How they had butted heads at first, and then how they had fallen in love.

Brandon watched as Jaxon's story unfolded and he saw the rage just below the surface directed at this Simon Small person. He felt no pity for this man that Jaxon was going to kill and, if the tables were turned, he would do the same.

He watched Hannah and saw her pain, but could do nothing to help. Well, maybe there was something.

"Hannah," he spoke up, "I've known Jaxon for a long time and my life has been in his hands more times than I like to think about. If he has a plan, you can bet that it is a good one and it is the best one for everyone. You have to trust him to know what he's doing."

The seconds ticked by with no one saying a word, but their minds working overtime. Jaxon weighing and rejecting Hannah's plea. Hannah holding her breath as she waited for an answer, not feeling reassured with Brandon's support of the plan. And Brandon, hoping he had not over-stepped his bounds by voicing his thoughts.

Jaxon broke the silence first when he turned to Hannah. "I can't have you stay close, baby." he said. "I need you to be safe. I need you to trust me with what I have planned. I'm asking you to believe in me and go with Brandon."

Hannah rushed into his arms, not caring that Brandon was in the room watching. "I'm scared," she said, admitting her fears to Jaxon. "I'm scared that if I leave, I won't ever see you again. I have a **bad** feeling."

"You will see me again," Jaxon said, raising tortured eyes to his friend.

"I'll meet you in the car," Brandon said, leaving the two alone to say their good byes. He had seen the torture, yes, but he had also seen the iron will beneath it, and he knew Hannah would be leaving with him.

Jaxon held Hannah close to him, savoring the feel of her in his arms. Even though the situation was not the best, he still could not pull away from her just yet. "Five more minutes," he begged, "just five more minutes."

Finally pulling away, Jaxon brushed Hannah's soft hair off her cheeks and bracketed her face with his hands.

"I love you, Hannah," he said. "I love you now and I will love you always. But," he stopped, swallowing hard before he continued, "I need you to go with Brandon, like I asked. Do this for me," he said. "Do this for us, so we can have a future without looking over our shoulders to see if someone is after us. After you. I can take care of this. I just need your help."

Hannah wanted to argue with all her might, but she knew Jaxon would be safer away from her. She had no way of knowing that an Immortal Guardian stood behind her and laid his hands upon her shoulders.

Saul could not stand by and watch them suffer any longer. He tried to stay out of the drama, but he could not. So he touched Hannah, the light it caused rivaling the sun. Saul drank her fear, not stopping until he knew she would be able to do as Jaxon asked. Walk away. He stayed, unseen by all, until he was sure what needed to happen would.

Hannah felt warmth come over her, her fears and doubts sliding away. She stepped back from Jaxon and, with a small smile nodded her head in agreement. "OK, Jaxon," she said, her voice only wavering slightly. "OK."

Jaxon let out a sigh of relief, as their parting became only slightly easier for him. He too had a bad feeling, but he had no choice. It would be as he said.

They walked side by side down the stairs and out the back door. Jaxon was sure they were safe, because Brandon would have made it so.

He opened the car door for Hannah to get in, but stopped her before she could climb in. "Remember, I love you," he said into her hair, as he held her close. "Don't go falling for Brandon. He is a lady's man, you know."

A small giggle trickled out the lovely mouth, before Jaxon leaned down and kissed her lips with all the fire inside him.

"I love you, too," Hannah said, clinging to him tightly.

The two only parted when Brandon cleared his throat, anxious to be gone. He didn't like sitting out in the open. Especially when the crawly feeling going up and down his back told him they were being watched. It was time to move.

"You know where to find us," Brandon said, as he started the car. "Don't be too long." The eyes of the two men met and locked, as they sent a message only they could read.

"Be safe," Brandon conveyed, "and get the job done! Your woman will be safe with me."

"Take care of her," Jaxon said, "I'll be seeing you soon."

"If you need anything," Brandon said out loud, "just call and I'll be back."

"Drive carefully," Jaxon warned him. "Call when you get there."

"Not!" Brandon said, "No communications until you call saying you are on your way."

Jaxon nodded his head in agreement and stepped back as the tires began to roll.

Hannah pressed her hand to the window and Jaxon waved until they were out of sight. The image of Hannah's flowing tears was burned into his brain, and those tears fed the hate in his belly.

He had twenty four hours to set his plan in motion.

"Twenty four hours," he promised out loud, "and then Simon, you're a dead man!"

Chapter 68

Roman had watched the whole touching scene from the deep shadows caused by the summer sun. He felt no fear of the tall man that had driven off with his human target. Humans did not threaten him. There really was no place for them to hide, so following them was not on his to-do list at the moment.

After the car had driven out of sight, Roman stayed to watch Saul's warrior as he stood in place, not moving. The hate that radiated off him was like a beacon to Roman, drawing him closer, making him want to claim this mortal for his army.

Roman let his snake of a tongue creep out and lick his lips in anticipation of just that happening. All he had to do was make sure Simon killed him. Then he would move in and claim his soul for the Dark.

Roman was jerked back from his daydream as a soft voice sounded at his back.

"Well, well, well," Saul said, feeling rather proud of himself that he was able to surprise the Dark Being. It was not often that he could do this, as Roman was always on the alert for an attack by the Guardians.

"What are you doing here, Roman?" he asked, not bothering to hide the contempt he felt for his opposite. "You have no business here."

"On the contrary, my age-old nemesis," Roman countered, "I do have business here."

"And just what would that be?" Saul asked, feigning innocence.

"I'm checking out your tool. So when my pawn kills him, I will be ready to scoop him up and make him one of mine." Roman answered indignantly.

"He is not now, nor will he ever be, on the side of the Dark!" Saul declared with heat.

"Really?" Roman taunted. "He is a killer," he said, gloating as Saul bristled. "He has killed many in his lifetime and is planning on killing again. Why would he not be claimed as one of mine?"

"He kills for the side of good," Saul said, calming down as he saw the way Roman fed off his reaction. "You will never claim him," Saul promised. "But why even discuss it. As we both know, he will best your Simon when they fight. He will be the one standing when the blood has stopped flowing."

"Would you care to place a small wager on the outcome of the fight?" Roman asked, even though he was not certain his human would win, but not wanting his rival to know.

"You have nothing I want," Saul said, waiting to see what bait Roman would toss out. Hoping it would be what he was looking for.

"But I do," the Dark Being challenged. "I have the life of Hannah Priest to gamble with."

"You have nothing," Saul said, following his words with a taunting laugh.

"Should my pawn win, I get to have Hannah Priest AND your warrior for my own," Roman said.

"What if Jaxon wins?" Saul countered. "What are you offering then?"

Roman twisted with seeming nonchalance as he thought for a moment. "If your Jaxon should win, then I will agree to leave him and Hannah to you. I will tell my followers to leave them alone. Forget about them. How is that for a wager?"

"Not bad," Saul said, having maneuvered Roman into offering what he wanted. He knew Roman would not want to appear anything less than confident, so would give him everything or nothing.

"I will take you up on your offer," Saul said, after appearing to consider it carefully. After all, he could not be too eager to accept or Roman would be suspicious and wonder what he was up to.

"Good," Roman twisted in glee, already planning on how to aid Simon without Saul's knowledge.

"Just one thing," Saul said, all friendliness disappearing. His eyes turned dark and his wings unfurled to intimidate the Dark form in front of him, making Roman seem small in comparison. "Should you go back on your word and attempt to hunt Jaxon and Hannah when the fight is over, it will be you and I that will fight next. And this time there will be no calling a draw and walking away. One of us will fall." A smile spread across the Guardians face, but he looked anything but friendly.

"You can't scare me!" Roman shrieked, "And you can't threaten me!"

"I do not threaten." Saul replied, a hint of calm power in his voice. "I only promise. If you doubt me, try me. See you soon." Saul jeered and vanished, leaving Roman smoldering and impotent in his rage.

"Soon!" he spat out, "Soon it will be our turn!" and he too vanished, on his way to join Simon. He would make sure death would be the only thing Jaxon Riley tasted, and it would be his own.

Chapter 69

Jaxon stood in the parking lot long after the car with his friend and his woman had disappeared out of sight. He did not feel the blazing heat of the afternoon sun or the sweat that trickled down his body because of it.

All he felt was rage at having to give up someone he had finally found to love. He had assured Hannah that it would only be for a week or so, but he could admit to himself that he was not so sure.

He did not fear the fight with Simon Small, as there was no question in his mind that he would be the last one standing. So he was not sure why he had the feeling that he would never see Hannah again, but he did.

Jaxon shivered in the heat as an icy breeze touched his skin. His eyes tracked everywhere, but he could not find the source of the chill.

"It's you, Roman. Isn't it?" he growled. It was the only reason Jaxon could come up with, for the freezing blast of air that had swept over and past him. He didn't expect an answer and he didn't get one. But it was enough to get him moving and back in the apartment.

Once inside he moved around Hannah's home, lightly touching the small objects that decorated each room. He wanted to feel her next to him and, by touching her things he thought he might. But they were just things. Nothing could replace the flesh and bone of his lover.

Jaxon's wandering brought him to stand in front of the desk that held her computer and the printer that went with it. He was not interested in them, but he was in the paper that was loaded in the printer.

He took out a few sheets and, grabbing a pen, went to sit at the table that seemed way too big without Hannah sitting across from him. He spread the sheets out in front of him and picked up the pen. He wanted to write Hannah a letter. One that she would find when she got home.

He sat quietly for a few moments before he put the pen to paper and the words began to flow. He had done this every time he had gone on a mission, writing a letter to his men in case he did not return. He had no one else to write to. He had never told them he performed this ritual, always returning to retrieve the letter himself before it was found by another. He hoped that would be the case this time, also.

When he was finished, he read the letter one final time.

Hello my love,

> *If you are reading this, something must have gone horribly wrong. I am sorry for not being able to keep my promise to you. The promise that I*

would come for you so we could spend the rest of our lives together.

I promised someone else that I would keep you safe and I know that I have kept that promise, even if it meant giving up my life for yours.

I love you, Hannah. I never thought I would find a woman that I could love the way I do you. You have found a place in my heart and I am only complete because of you. With you.

From the first moment I saw you, you worked your magic and turned a lonely man into one who could not imagine life without you in it.

Your sweet smile, your wonderful laugh, your soft touch, your warm kisses, all the things that make you special, have become like food to me. I know it sounds overly dramatic, but I don't think I can live without you by my side.

Sending you away today was the hardest thing I have ever had to do. A part of me went with you and will always be with you. If there is a way to keep watch over you and to keep you safe, I will find it.

I hope you have good memories to take out and look at when you feel sad or miss me, because all the goodness and love we have shared will go with me and sustain me until we can meet again.

Please be happy my love! Never forget I love you with all my heart! If there had been any other way to save you, I would have found it.

I'd like to think that I will be able to hear you if you talk to me and, when you sleep, I hope I will be in the dreams that give you peace.

I will remember the way you felt in my arms. The perfect way your body fit so closely to mine. You are my world, Hannah, and I thank you for loving me.

The only regret I take with me will be the regret that we did not have more time together. Time to get married and have a family. Time for more kisses and more touches. Time to grow old together. I consider myself the luckiest of men for having loved you for the time we did have.

I must close now my sweet. I hope I will be tearing up this letter before I come to get you. If not, hold me close in your heart until we can be together again.

I love you!!!

Jaxon

Jaxon sighed as he finished reading his letter. It was the hardest one he had ever written. Keeping to his tradition, he placed the pages in an envelope and licked the flap closed. He wrote Hannah's name on the front, then walked into the bedroom to place it on her pillow. Before he let go of it he lifted it one more time and placed a kiss over Hannah's name. A kiss that she would never know was there, but one that gave him comfort anyway.

Jaxon went to the window, noticing that the sun had set while he had been writing. It was time to change clothes and ready himself for tonight.

He needed to be quiet, to go over what he had planned. The letter did not mean he was giving up. Far from it.

He knew that if he failed, he would never be able to hold Hannah again. Just the thought of that happening built his rage to an all consuming fire. One that he would let loose on Simon Small until he fried.

Fried in hell!

Chapter 70

imon had spent the day hiding across the street in the same alley were Jaxon had threatened him, humiliated him. He was hot and tired and ready to give up on the day when Roman suddenly appeared at his side.

"Hello, Simon," he greeted his killer. "What have you learned today?"

"Nothing, except it's hot and I have wasted yet another day waiting for Jaxon Riley to come out and play with me," the Small man replied.

"No, not a waste," Roman purred, "as he has just sent Hannah away and will be alone tonight. I believe your waiting is over."

Simon's heart jumped, both from fear and anticipation.

"I believe tonight will see your prey finally coming out in the open. You must be ready to strike him dead. He does not know that you are aware of this. He will be vulnerable to your attack. Tell me your plan," Roman demanded.

Simon's hand went to his pants, as he grabbed the handle of his knife to give him courage. "I will wait until he comes out," he began, "then follow him until we are in an area that is deserted. I will come up behind him and swing my knife, cutting him, paralyzing him for a moment. While he is frozen, I will cut him to ribbons. Until he is in shreds. But before he dies, I'm going to tell him in detail what I am going to do to his little girlfriend after I am finished with him. I'm going to watch his eyes go glassy. I'm going to smile in his face so he knows I have won. He will know the last thing he sees will also be the last thing his girlfriend sees, too, as she is dying by my hand. Is that good enough for you?" Simon asked, excitement in his voice.

"I believe it is a good plan" Roman agreed. "I will caution you that I will not be able to help you, though. Jaxon also has a Guardian on his side, but he will not be able to interfere the same as I. This fight will be between you and Jaxon alone."

"I never asked for your help," Simon boasted. "I can do this on my own. I have been doing this for some time now. Remember?" he replied indignantly.

Roman's eyes grew brighter, as he was given attitude by his pawn. "Do not fail me," he warned. "If you do, you can be sure you will be seeing a lot more of me when my followers drag your soul down to hell to join me. I am not a forgiving being to those that fail me."

Simon was not scared of Roman, as he believed he would be successful in his mission. "I need to go home and get ready for tonight," he said, walking out of the alley to get into his car.

"Be back by dark," Roman hissed. "I'll be waiting when this is finished." With that Roman disappeared, leaving Simon to drive home alone with his thoughts.

When he reached his apartment, he showered and dressed all in black. '*Just like in the movies,*' he thought.

He did not hide his friend, but carried it once again in his briefcase. There was no need to hide anymore. Simon knew what he was going to do and he wanted his friend by his side and ready.

He sat in his chair, still and quiet, until the sun set. Before leaving, he took one shot of liquid courage to settle his nerves.

Grabbing the handle of his briefcase as if it were a lover's hand he was taking, he left his home. Taking the elevator to the lobby, he exited, sorry that the doorman was no where to be seen. He might just have taken the time to slit his throat for practice before leaving. He shrugged off his disappointment and climbed into his car.

The traffic was light so he made good time. Soon he was, once again, parking on the street next to the one where Jaxon and Hannah lived. He did not want to alert his opponent that he had arrived before he was ready.

Turning off the car, Simon found himself engulfed in a quiet so deep it made his ears ring. There was no one on the street. The last car he'd seen pass was nothing but a red dot in his rear view mirror when he got out.

'*Strange,*' he thought, '*that there was no one around. No one at all. Maybe they knew. Knew that something was about to happen. So they were all hiding behind their closed doors.*'

'*Fine by me,*' Simon thought. '*Fewer eyes to see what was about to happen. Fewer witnesses to take care of,*' he reasoned. He really had thought of everything, right down to the clean-up of any prying eyes.

Simon crept from shadow to shadow, until he stood in the deep blackness of a doorway across from

The Inner Self. He held the knife loosely in his hand, caressing the handle with his thumb.

'*Come out Jaxon,*' he willed his prey. '*Come out and meet my friend. After all, he's dying to meet you!*'

Simon did not have to wait long. As a bell in the distance pealed out the hour of midnight, Jaxon boldly walked out onto the street. He turned south and began to walk into the darkness.

Simon followed.

Chapter 71

"I know this is hard on you," Brandon said into the quiet of the car. "Why don't you talk to me, just to pass the time."

Hannah pulled herself away from her thoughts and looked at the giant sitting beside her. The sun had set long ago. The only light in the car cast a bluish glow over his face, hiding his expression from her.

"I'm sorry," Hannah said quietly, "I'm not very good company am I?"

"Like I said, I know this is hard on you, but you have to have faith that things will work out. So talk to me. Take your mind off things for a bit."

"How about if I ask you to tell me why Jaxon picked you? I really would like to know," Hannah said, turning her attention to Jaxon's friend.

Brandon knew why Jaxon had picked him, but he was not going to tell Hannah. This time it was Brandon who fell silent as he thought back on the missions Jaxon and he had shared. All the blood and guts they had spilled along with the rest of the unit, as they fought to save and rescue the innocent.

Those thoughts flashed through his mind, but he knew the one that tipped the scales for Jaxon was one he had handled on his own. A personal mission of sorts.

Brandon had been seeing a woman, Crystal, whom he thought was 'the one'. He'd been happy and had shared this happiness with his friends, bragging about what a fine woman he had found to love.

This included his best friend, Michael. They had been friends, best friends, for years. When Brandon had the time, Michael, Crystal and he would hang out together, going to concerts, fishing, riding motor cycles, or just watching TV at home or in a bar.

He never had a clue that Crystal and Michael were two-timing him behind his back. That is until another friend had not been able to stand their treachery any longer and had spilled the beans to Brandon one night.

Brandon had confronted his friend, asking him if it was true that he and Crystal had been sleeping together. Michael, like the bastard he was, denied it until, finally breaking down, he told Brandon the truth. He said they had been seeing each other for months. He had the nerve to laugh in Brandon's face, thinking they had been so clever deceiving his friend.

His ability to keep a secret was not the only thing to break, as Brandon saw red and plowed his fist into his friends face, breaking bones with one punch.

It had taken four more friends to pull Brandon off the two-timing bastard, as he drew back, readying to land a punch that would have most likely put his fist through his deceitful friends head.

Michael had lain on the ground, bleeding like a stuck pig and crying like a girl when Brandon walked away.

Brandon endured the pain of betrayal, laughing when Michael had the balls to ask if they could still be friends. He was astounded and sickened when Crystal attempted to get him back in bed. She had no conscience when she tried to do the same thing to Michael that had been done to Brandon. He wasn't about to get back with her. Who knows how many others there were.

Brandon had severed all ties with them after paying for Michael's medical bills. Even after Michael claimed it was Brandon's fault and he should pay. The way Brandon and his friends saw it, it was Michael that should have had to pay, since he was the cause of the fight. It was his dick that couldn't say no when Crystal wagged her tail in front of him.

But Brandon did the right thing. Eventually he enjoyed having the satisfaction of Michael crawling back to him to tell him he was right when Crystal cheated on him too. "Told you so!" felt good to Brandon, but by then he did not give a flying shit one way or the other about either one of them.

Jaxon had been there for Brandon when he needed to talk and had seen the pain he went through because of their betrayal. Jaxon knew he could trust Brandon to take care of Hannah without worrying about him trying something. Jaxon trusted Brandon's strength and his character and Brandon had the honor of calling Jaxon his friend. That was a rare thing indeed.

The true self of Brandon that Hannah had seen, had been spot on. He was a fierce beast when the situation warranted it, but was not a threat to innocents.

But there was no way he was going to share any of that with Hannah. So he blamed Jaxon's choice on the missions they had participated in and the friendship that had grown from that.

Hannah seemed satisfied and turned her head to look out the window. The only thing she could see was her reflection, as the dark turned the window into a mirror.

Brandon fell silent too, as the long, lonely miles hummed by, with only the whine of the spinning tires to break the silence.

'Be safe!' he thought over and over, as he wondered what was happening in Colorado.

He wasn't ready to give up his friend. But the beast inside that Hannah had seen, was more than willing to go back and finish the job that Jaxon had started if need be. If it came to that, there would be nothing left but scraps of flesh and finally an end to the pain that was unimaginable. But only if Jaxon fell.

'Guns up, Jaxon! Come on buddy!' Brandon thought, as his hands tightened on the steering wheel, staying that way as the miles flew by.

Flew by in the dark.

Chapter 72

J axon waited until midnight before walking out the door and locking it behind him. He left the key in the secret hiding place Hannah had chosen so nothing would tie him to Hannah if things went bad.

He knew Simon was watching from across the street. The little man was nowhere near good enough to fool him, so he felt confident walking out into the street, taking the lead in this game.

He walked for a few blocks before turning down a side street that boasted only one street light. He stopped and waited, his back to the creeper behind him.

He waited until a tell-tale shadow fell in behind him, before turning around and confronting his enemy.

"Hello, Simon," he said, his voice quiet as death. "Finally we meet."

Simon had kept to the shadows while keeping Jaxon in sight as he was led to this street, never wondering where they were going, never caring. Only watching for an opening to strike.

When Jaxon had stopped beneath a lone street light, he had continued on until he too entered the light. He raised his arm to strike at the back of his foe but stopped when Jaxon turned and spoke to him.

"Did you hear him?" Roman whispered into his ear. "Did you hear the tone of disrespect?"

Roman had been unable to trust his monster, so had wiggled his way again into the dark corner of Simon's mind. From there he planned on driving, directing this final death dance.

Simon only twitched as the voice in his head spoke up, telling him to pay attention to the words Jaxon spoke, the way he spoke.

"Don't exchange words with him," Roman said, "Move in now and cut him as planned."

But Simon did not listen. Instead he stopped and lowered his arm. "Hello, Jaxon," he responded, hate in his tone, "Nice night for a stroll isn't it?"

"I will give you one chance to pull back before this goes any farther. One chance to live to see tomorrow. Should you choose to ignore my offer, I will be forced to kill you as slowly as I can. Until **you** will scream for death. Beg for it. This is the one and only chance you have at mercy. Your choice," Jaxon warned the man wielding the knife.

Simon curled his lip as he stood and looked at a man who was everything he was not. Tall, handsome, strong and confident in his abilities to take on anything life threw at him. *'Well he had never dealt with someone like him, someone like Simon Small.'* he boasted to himself.

"I choose to split you from groin to chin," Simon jeered. "I choose to spit on you as you lay dying at my feet. Where's your weapon?" Simon asked, sure no one would show up to a fight such as this unarmed. "Bring it out so I can see."

"I don't need a weapon to beat you," Jaxon said, still quiet and sure. "I only need my fists and my strength to squash a little bug like you. You're nothing!" he said and laughed. "You're less than the weakest woman I have ever met. I see you are hiding behind the knife in your hand, but I will be the one to watch you die. That little blade will not save you. By coming after Hannah you have signed your own death warrant. By not taking my offer of mercy, you will be no more after tonight. And no one, that's right, no one will care when you are dead."

Jaxon taunted Simon until the smaller man fairly shook with anger. He looked at him with contempt in his flat, cold eyes, showing no concern when he crossed his arms over his chest, never giving Simon an ounce of respect.

Jaxon wanted Simon mad, angry, and reckless. He wanted him to act without thinking, and he wanted this over with.

"Come on little man," he coaxed, "Come and show me what you're made of. By the looks of you I would say it was crap, and not even a big pile of crap at that," Jaxon laughed.

"Now!" Roman screamed, "Do it now! And Simon's blade sang . . . .

Jaxon stood looking at the scene before him, Saul at his side.

"Is this the way it was supposed to end?" Jaxon asked the Guardian.

"Unfortunately, yes," Saul answered. "The moment you accepted the task of protecting Hannah, your destiny changed. Would you have agreed to help me if you had known this was to be?"

Jaxon looked at the two bloody bodies at his feet. The first was what was left of Simon Small after Jaxon had bested him in a fight to the death, using nothing more than his fists and his strength to end the life of the Dark's pawn. The other was his own human form, covered with cuts from the blade Simon had wielded and the blood that had flowed from his wounds.

He remembered leaning over Simon, watching his enemy die. His hands wrapped around his throat as his own blood dripped from his face, marking his enemy. He'd made sure his bloody, gloating face was the last thing the bastard saw before cold death took him in its grasp and drug him into the Dark.

Jaxon had fallen to his side, his breath coming in shallow gasps, his strength being sucked from him, carried out with the dark blood that formed rivers as it ran and pooled on the pavement underneath him, around him and ran into the gutter. He remembered the pain that had bit at him until it was all he could think of, all he could feel. Letting it finally have its way, but only after he was certain Simon would not rise up one more time, his task was at an end.

'I need to just lie down until someone calls an ambulance,' he had thought and had fallen to his back. His eyes gazing up into the night sky. He had not noticed the street lights, as they illuminated the grizzly scene he was a part of. All he remembered seeing were the stars that had been covered by the man-made light, only moments before, suddenly becoming so clear. He had marveled at the peace and warmth they had brought to him. Their beauty had seemed to grow in brightness, until their white light had fallen down around him and he remembered no more.

"Yes," Jaxon said, with no doubts in his tone. "Yes I would still have agreed to help you. It was worth it. It was necessary."

Saul nodded his head, having come to know this human and his goodness, and expecting nothing less as an answer from him.

"We need to have a talk before we move on," Saul said to Jaxon, needing a decision from this new Immortal before they could go any further.

"You have earned the right to take your place as a Guardian, if you so choose," Saul began.

"Or?" Jaxon supplied, as Saul paused.

"I would like for you to consider becoming a Hunter," Saul said, already knowing the next question Jaxon would ask.

"I'll bite," Jaxon said, "What's a Hunter?"

"As a Hunter you would be given the full-time duty of tracking down the Dark and dispatching them, even before they can take over a human and cause chaos and death. Or, if that is not possible, to track them down and foil their plans as they use mortals to do their bidding."

"How many other Hunters are there?" Jaxon asked, his curiosity raised. "Why did they let this situation get so far out of hand?" was his next question. Understandably.

"There are very few Hunters in our ranks," Saul explained. "It is a duty that is offered to very few humans when they join us. It takes someone special to do what they are asked to do. It takes special skills and a keen mind to be able to find the Dark where they hide. They are everywhere. There are more of them than there are of us and, sadly, their ranks are growing every day."

Jaxon paused for a few moments to think before giving Saul his answer. The night air was suddenly filled with a chill and a cold laugh was carried on the night breeze.

"Now let's give the boy all his options before we expect him to answer, shall we?" Roman asked, appearing on the other side of the bodies on the ground. "You really didn't think I was going to let you steal this talent for your side without giving him the option of joining me, did you?" he asked Saul with a sarcastic sneer in his voice.

Roman was not in the least bit intimidated when Jaxon crouched down, fists bunched and muscles ready to leap at the first sight and sound of the powerful Dark Master.

"Why would you want to join up with Saul and his do-gooders when we both know that you are much more suited to become a follower of the Dark?" he asked Jaxon. "You love to hunt and you love to kill. You can't hide that from me," Roman continued. "That's why you were so good in Special Forces. You loved what you did and you thrived in the killing of humans. You were made to join me, help me, have fun with me, and kill with me. I could see this inside you when you were alive. I can let all of it loose now that you are dead. Let the power loose inside you, to do what ever you want."

"Be honest with yourself," Roman reasoned, "my offer is much more to your liking, isn't it? If you have to be here an eternity, why not make your time fun? Why would you want to saddle yourself with rules and restrictions? Come join me and mine," Roman offered, holding out a dry, withered, black stick that passed as a hand. "Take my hand and we will have struck a bargain."

Roman's eyes glowed the bright red of fire and his mouth leaked black drool that dripped off his chin and burned the pavement like acid. His worm of a tongue darted in and out of the hole that passed as a mouth, as his confidence grew with each second Jaxon hesitated in joining with Saul.

To have one in his army with Jaxon's mind, will, and strength would be a huge advantage to the Dark. He would almost be unstoppable. No Immortal in Saul's army would be able to stand up to him alone. '*Oh yes,*' Roman thought, '*I want this one!*'

Jaxon had straightened up while Roman had been talking. Eventually his arms had risen to cross in front of him, resting on his chest. When Roman had lapsed into silence Jaxon turned his head and looked at Saul. The mighty Immortal did not look angry, he did not look upset, and he did not look concerned.

"Do I have to wear those stupid robes you were wearing when you first talked to me?" he asked Saul, his eyes usually so cold and serious, now crinkling at the corners.

Saul looked down his form at the jeans and polo shirt that had become his norm. The only hint that he was anything but mortal was revealed when he turned around and the wings that lay folded on his back unfurled and cast the scene in shadow.

"No," Saul said, laughter in his voice, "You can pick whatever look you want. Just close your eyes and concentrate on what you want to look like."

Jaxon shrugged his shoulders and, doing as Saul instructed, closed his eyes. He flipped through images like he was looking through a closet. It didn't take long before he opened them back up and looked down his length to see if it had worked. To his pleasure, it had.

Instead of the torn and bloody clothes he had died in, he now saw a black pair of jeans hugging his thighs, a pair of black high topped tennis shoes, and a black tee shirt gracing his powerful form. Jaxon liked his look. Turning to Saul he nodded his head, letting the Guardian know he had chosen.

"I see you have made your choice," Roman hissed, furious that he had not been picked. "But don't the good guys always wear white?" he sneered, trying one last time to show Jaxon that, even by choosing black for his color, his true nature was showing through.

Jaxon turned his head to eye the powerful Dark creature Roman and, at the same time, he knew what the burning in his back meant. With a twitch of his shoulders, Jaxon unfurled a massive set of black wings that marked him as one of Saul's Immortal Hunters. He turned his head from right to left, looking at the expanse of blackness that was three times his arm span. He liked it.

Jaxon nodded once at Saul to confirm his choice, before turning towards the dead bodies. He focused on the form twisting on the far side. Letting a cold smile curve his lips, Jaxon let the flames in his eyes grow until they burned from the need to hunt.

"You will regret your decision!" Roman wailed. "You will regret joining forces with Saul!"

Jaxon locked gazes with Roman, blazing black eyes clashing with molten red, and uttered, in a voice that made the world shake, only one word to his now foe. "RUN!"

HANNAH

Saul stayed at Hannah's home for the next two days, waiting for her return. He knew he would be needed. He had promised Jaxon that he would take care of her, do whatever he could for her. Only by giving his promise was he able to convince his new Immortal Hunter to leave and begin his training.

Saul did not have long to wait, as he heard a key in the lock and Hannah walked in to the cold, quiet apartment alone. Saul could see the hesitation and expectancy in her step as she scanned the apartment.

Admitting, only to herself, that she still held on to the hope that the news Brandon had been given was just a sick joke. A trick to bring her home. That she would see Jaxon when the door opened. He would be there to gather her in his arms and tell her it was all a mistake. A huge mistake!

But only silence greeted her and the only arms that gathered her close were the ones of grief and despair.

Hannah closed the door and wandered the apartment. She passed the doorway to the bathroom and stopped as she saw his toothbrush still hanging by hers. She saw the towel he had used hanging on the rack and his shampoo sitting on the shower ledge. His cologne shared a space on the counter top.

She walked, as if in a dream, to where it sat, picked it up and breathed deeply. She could smell Jaxon, as if he were standing right beside her. She left the bathroom, still holding the bottle clutched to her chest, and made her way to their bedroom.

She opened the closet doors and there were his clothes, waiting, as if he would be back at any second to pick out a shirt to wear. Hannah reached in and took out a shirt at random, holding it to her nose, breathing in more of Jaxon's scent.

Her legs threatened to collapse, as she stumbled to the bed to sit down. As the bed dipped beneath her weight, something white caught her eye. She reached for the envelope lying on her pillow, her name scrawled in Jaxon's hand writing across the front.

Her hand shook and her heart raced as she held the letter in her hand. She did not want to open it. If she opened it and read his words, all hope would be lost. The hope that she clung to so desperately would come crashing down and she would die. She would want to die!

She sat for awhile, caressing the letter, before she realized she just had to know what Jaxon had written. She opened the letter and read the words of love he had written to her. The same words that he had spoken to her at their last meeting. She could not breathe. Her chest tightened up and her eyes filled with tears, as she clutched the sheets of paper to her face and sobbed. Sobbed until her soul ached.

Outside a light rain began to fall as Saul, feeling her despair, cried with her. He wanted to help her. He wanted to tell her Jaxon was not completely lost to her. That a part of him would always be with her. But he could not.

The most he could do was whisper in her ear, "Be strong, Hannah. Be strong. All is not lost." He gave her what comfort he could, until she curled into a ball on the bed and fell asleep. He let her sleep, for he knew that her destiny may not include Jaxon at her side, but it did include their child, already growing in her belly.

She would never be alone again.